D0658490

A Free-Range Wife

For nineteen years Vermont-born Mercy McCluskey had been a faithful wife to Hector, Scottish chef at an exclusive French château hotel. Then she decided to roam. A private matter and nothing to do with the British police, one would have thought, especially as they order these things differently in France. But when bodies began to turn up as far afield as Portland, Oregon, and Paris, they were of men known to Mercy, and the killer had made his opinion of them puritanically plain. To Chief Inspector Henry Peckover's superiors at the Yard it seemed providential that their nearest approach to a poet should be holidaying with his wife at the château.

Strictly speaking, only Henry was on holiday, while Miriam acted as temporary chef during Hector's absence judging a cookery contest, but that was brushed aside. Would he, English-speaking and on the spot, make a few discreet enquiries? Henry would, and the results of those enquiries put him more than ever on the spot.

They also took him to Lourdes, here viewed from an unusual angle since its crime rate is second only to that of West Berlin, and to Andorra, tax-haven and duty-free Mecca for thousands of motorized French. And they took him into Mercy McCluskey's bed, a point on which Miriam kept discreetly silent, perhaps because it enabled Henry to trap a murderer, perhaps because she had lost her voice.

Michael Kenyon has lived for several years in south-west France, which he portrays with a journalist's sharp eye, a kindly wit, and a gourmet's lyrical pen.

R

MICHAEL KENYON

A Free-Range Wife

A Henry Peckover novel

COLLINS, 8 GRAFTON STREET, LONDON W1

William Collins Sons & Co. Ltd
London · Glasgow · Sydney · Auckland
Toronto · Johannesburg

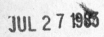
First published 1983
© Michael Kenyon 1983

British Library Cataloguing in Publication Data

Kenyon, Michael
A free-range wife. — (Crime Club).
I. Title
823'.914[F]   PR6061.E675

ISBN 0 00 231364 2

Photoset in Compugraphic Baskerville
Printed in Great Britain by
William Collins Sons & Co. Ltd., Glasgow

CHAPTER 1

'*Chérie*,' he breathed.

In the circumstances he could have done little with *chérie* except breathe it. Blond tresses and an earlobe filled his mouth. He could hardly have proclaimed *chérie* as if he were president. He would have had a job beaming the presidential smile and raising both arms above his head.

'*Chérie*,' he breathed, more raspingly this time, lifting his head. If the woman had looked, the light being on, there would have been the whites of his eyes and the irises wetly swivelling like two peeled Muscat grapes. '*Chérie*,' he rasped like tearing calico. '*Je viens!*'

That, she knew, having heard it before, was French for 'I'm coming,' which she knew he was because she was too, he had not needed to tell her, for with or without explanations he was a lovely lover, Jean-Luc, and she loved him. Dependable, always on time, and above all bilingual, without which their love never could have blossomed. There would have been no advance beyond *Bonjour* and the handshaking.

If he had not been dependable she might still have loved him for his intellect, his soul even, but she doubted it.

'*Oh, mon coeur!*' he said. In moments of passion, Jean-Luc Fontanille, Professor of English, reverted to his native tongue. '*Chérie! Oh, ah, merci! Merci!*'

Yea, yea.

Mercy McCluskey, shuddering agreeably, found that a corner of her mind remained detached in spite of everything. The trouble with the name Mercy, she reflected, not for the first time, was that in this country

she never knew whether people were addressing her or
saying thank-you. Or, still more confusingly, saying no-
thank-you, which was what the French meant, often,
when they said *merci*. If Jean-Luc was telling her no when
he plainly meant yes he was even more confused than she
was.

He was not confused about his body, or more to the
point, hers. The only lover to match him was Heinz, but
Heinz was never around. The other trouble with Heinz
was his name. How could you take seriously anyone
named Heinz? Some Christian names had much to answer
for.

'Mercy!'

Yea.

Mercy McCluskey was at least an advance on her
maiden name. Mercy O'Toole had been a gift for the wits
even at Bennington, where one would have supposed
sights might have been set higher. She still sometimes
wondered whether she had not married simply to change
her name: too abruptly, too young, on the very bank and
shoal of the feminist breakers which had been about to
boom in. Had they boomed in a little earlier they might
well have sent her scampering back up the beach.

Twenty years. Unbelievable.

'Mercy! *Merci!* Mercy!'

Distantly a doorbell was ringing. Mercy tried
pretending that the summons was not from her doorbell
but from the bell to one of the apartments above, or
somewhere a telephone, not hers. Pretending was easy.
There were in those moments so many bells inside her
that her head, the bright bedroom, and all of France
were melodiously tintinnabulating.

With lulls, the ringing persisted. Nine o'clock,
according to the Westclox Big Ben on the bedside table.
Nineteen years old, the clock, eleven dollars' worth,
bought by Hector in Burlington the summer after the

wedding, and dented now, chipped and wobbly, but never once a repair, not even a check-up or an inner dusting, and as reliable as Jean-Luc. He was rigid and listening in his exotic position, above her but askew, one limb here, another improbably there.

Mormons didn't call at nine, did they? Nine in the morning? If it were a functionary to read the meter she would spit.

Could be a telegram. Could even be a telegram bringing good news, though she could not imagine what. Some people succeeded in not answering the door or the telephone but she had never understood how.

Could be Ishbael, the acutest pain in the universe, fifteen and contemptuous of her put-upon Mom who did her best. But Ishbael with a broken leg perhaps, or sudden eczema, or debts. Could even be goddamn Hector.

Except Hector was in Hong Kong. No worry there. Hell, even if it had been Hector . . .

Brrrrr.

Mercy gave Jean-Luc a despairing don't-blame-me-just-our-lousy-luck look which already, with wet Muscat eyes six inches away, he was giving her, and with better justification, the apartment not being his. Grunting expletives, he disentangled himself.

She put on the bathrobe given to her by Hector as an anniversary offering. The robe, almost as old as the Big Ben Westclox, and cherished, like a family dog, was sombrely tartan — the McCluskeys of Inverbrae — and durable, as was everything acquired by Hector, including his wife. Mercy wondered if ever in his life her husband had bought anything which had not been sensible and hard-wearing. She mopped her face with a tissue from the robe's pocket, combed her fingers through her hair, and before leaving the bedroom turned off the light.

Once the living-room light was on, no chink was going to show under the bedroom door, but still . . . Life being

booby-trapped with surprises, one learned to pay attention
to the details. If Jean-Luc continued with his mutterings
and throat-clearings, or chose to tramp out after her,
okay, that was something else.

Barefoot across rugs, Mercy felt her way round the
loom which filled too much room space, and past the
divan bed on which Ishbael occasionally passed a night,
when she was able to bring herself to tolerate sleeping
under the same roof as her Mom, and on which Angus,
seventeen, had once entertained one of his school doxies
under the impression that Mom in the bedroom was stone
deaf. Next, past the hopeless, mountainous, abandoned
drum kit of Fergus, eighteen, which he refused to sell,
and which his father refused to have up at the ale-house.
She switched on the light.

She stooped, the spyhole in the door to the corridor
having been positioned for French midgets. Through the
spyhole she saw nothing. Not even the corridor.

Hector had insisted on the spyhole. He had never
stayed in the apartment, had visited it only once, but a
woman on her own — when she was on her own, he had
added with that throwaway indifference which had
throbbed with meaning; and he had organized and paid a
spyhole carpenter. Probably this was the only spyhole in
Mordan, unless the banks had some. Madame Belot in
the apartment above had thought it was for ventilation.
Always before now Mercy had seen something through it,
if only the corridor.

She blinked, dabbed her eye with tissue, and peered
again. An eye at the other end of the spyhole was drawing
away. The withdrawing eye, together with a second eye, a
nose, and other regular facial features, became when
finally assembled a shaved, male face topped by a brown
hat. Not Dracula, if appearances were a guide, but Jesus,
who knew? He was retreating from the door with pursed
lips and a jigging, shuffling gait.

Mercy was familiar, as was every red-blooded girl, with the figures, roughly.

*Fifty per cent of all rapes took place in the victim's home in daylight. (Okay, if she drew the curtains and opened the shutters it would be daylight.)

*Eighty-seven per cent of rapists carried a weapon or threatened their victim with violence or death.

*Ninety-eight per cent of rapists planned their attacks after marking their victim down some place. That was why women ought to practise assertiveness in public places, walking with head up, shoulders back.

*Forty per cent of rapists were acquaintances, colleagues, or friends of friends of the victim.

*Rapists came from all socio-economic groups, professions, trades, backgrounds.

These, admittedly, were the figures for Los Angeles, Rape Capital of the World, not for Mordan (Pop. 14,000. Priory of Notre Dame, 13th century. Roman sarcophagus. Château de Mordan, 8 km.) All the same.

This was not an acquaintance or colleague, though he might have been a friend of a friend, and he might have marked her down outside in the Rue du 17-Août, or on the boulevard, because although 6ft 1in tall she certainly was not beefy and she did not walk with assertiveness in public places or anywhere else. On the contrary, when you were 6ft 1in and fifteen and the school wits called you High Fidelity, you acquired habits of unassertiveness, whether walking or standing still, and habits clung, even though at forty you had learned not only to live with being tall but to pity the gnomes who people the rest of the globe, France especially. The man on the far side of the dilapidated stone corridor, wagging his head and wiggling his feet, was now fully-frontal in burgundy slacks, tie, and unsuitable lightweight jacket.

The month might be merry May but the weather was not that warm. There had been frosts. Five miles north,

Hector's shebeen was high up, true, a mountain eyrie, but on Monday snow and burst pipes had visited it, or so she had been told by Jean-Luc, who read about such matters in the local paper. From a pocket of the man's linen jacket jutted a plastic bag containing, judging from its rectangularity, books, or a box of candy. He was looking down at his suede feet, which he moved rhythmically, heeling and toeing.

A dancing rapist? A gas-meter reader with verrucas? At least he was not Hector.

' 'Ello? Mrs McCluskey?'

He had seen her. He had seen something through the peephole. Or heard her. Though the door was solid enough and locked, Mercy thought of the Ovarian Yell, which she had never tried, but which was said to instil greater confidence than a squeal or shriek. The Ovarian Yell originated in the abdomen. She imagined a vigorous yodelling sound, like Tarzan, if properly done, which would bring out into the Rue du 17-Août the *pâtissiers, charcutiers, grandmères,* and Alsatian dogs.

What was important was to act positively in the first thirty seconds. The place to go for was not where you would have thought but the knee area because the knee joint bent one way only so a kick from any direction could incapacitate.

The police on the other hand counselled against fighting back. Fighting back, they said, could be fatal.

'Who is it?' Mercy called.

'Police.'

Mercy watched through the peephole. His 'Police' had not sounded very French, and wouldn't a French policeman have said, '*La police*'? *La* or *le*. Not that she would have known. He looked as if he might be whistling, though she heard nothing, and he was repeating his soft-shoe shuffle, pistoning his arms and making fists as if rattling maracas, rehearsing for rumba night at the

Coconut Grove.

Mercy called, 'May I see your badge, please?'

'Badge?' He came to a stop. 'No badges, ma'am. Won a medal once, now you mention it. Runner-up in the Scotland Yard Wellie-Throwing.' He was fishing in an inner pocket of his tourist jacket, bringing out a wallet. 'Just joking. Got a nice snapshot. That do you?'

From the wallet he selected a blue card which he held up to the peephole. He drew the card back, advanced it, and drew it back again. Mercy made out the words Metropolitan, and Pecker or Peck something, but the rest was blurred print and a photograph, advancing and retreating.

'That's me, the good-looking one,' the man called.

There was only one photograph, a passport face which might or might not have been the dancer in the corridor. Rapists did not whistle and jig like this, reasoned Mercy, and she opened the door. If she had misjudged, in the bedroom were reinforcements. She had only to scream.

Would her Jean-Luc, her legionnaire, her bright bilinguist, her Napoleon of the bedchamber, be a man of action out of bed as well as in? The visitor was raising his hat.

'Chief Inspector Peckover, ma'am. Sorry to trouble you—'

'What is it? Is everything all right?'

'Far as I know. If you mean your family, everything's *merveilleux*. That the word? May I come in?'

He was in, closing the door, dropping his hat on the table beside the pile of recent, unread issues of the *New Yorker, Vermont Life,* and *Christian Science Monitor*, and looking about him at the white walls hung with paintings, the leather sofa which had cost a ransom, the salvaged, restored fireplace with tongs and poker, the overpriced bits and pieces culled gradually, guiltily, from antique shops.

'Nice,' he said.

Screw 'nice', Mercy believed she would have said had she said anything. With the drums and the impossible divan the room was not a work of art, but it was not far off.

'Routine inquiry, as we say fairly automatically,' the policeman said as he drew back the woven green curtains. 'Shouldn't take a minute. We say that too. I do anyway. If you find the preliminaries tedious, 'ow d'you suppose we feel?' He was opening the windows, then the shutters. 'What a day! Look at that sky!' He had to lean out of the window and crane his neck to look at the sky. *'Bonjour.'*

His greeting was addressed to a gnarled woman in a black shawl who was passing the windows carrying in each hand a trussed, squawking chicken. She turned her head in alarm and scuttled on.

'Gawd, France! Marvellous!' the policeman said, folding back the shutters. He closed the windows. 'Did I wake you?'

'I was having breakfast.' Mercy drew the lapels of her robe closer together, though he was not staring, he was not even looking at her, he was on his way again, and reaching the half-open door into the kitchen, peering in, 'Thinking about it,' she said.

'Do I smell blueberry griddlecakes with maple syrup?'

Lemon-fresh Ajax, bleach, metal polish, thought Mercy, who yesterday in a fit of energy had scoured the kitchen, but had cooked nothing all week.

'I'm not hinting. I've had breakfast.' He had resumed his saunter. 'What a breakfast! What a palace! I'm staying at your place, the château. Every way you turn, a new perfume. Attar of roses, lily-of-the-valley. They had these bits of paper round the croissants, like you get on the lamb cutlets at the Dorchester, not that I'm a regular there. Breakfast music coming up through the carpet. The music's perfumed too, I wouldn't wonder. Still, no

need to tell you, ma'am. D'you lend a hand there sometimes?'

'Off and on. Up front. I meet and greet in the
restaurant when my husband's away.'

'He's away now. In Hong Kong, I gather, judging a
chop suey competition.'

'We don't meet and greet for breakfast.'

'So you live 'ere, do you?'

'Yes. Could you tell me—'

'And the children?'

'At the château. When they're around.'

'They're not around?'

'Ishbael's still at school. She'll sleep here tonight after
the movie, or the disco, whatever she's got on.'

'Nice. Handy. Gor, still, what an 'otel! Mind you, and I
probably shouldn't say this, but I 'ad to ask for
marmalade.' He was leaning forward, studying a framed
photograph on the bureau: Fergus, Angus and Ishbael in a
paddling pool. He gave an approving nod, then wandered
on. 'Took a while getting them to understand. Took
about seven of them. Not that they were French, I'm not
saying that, not all of 'em. Spaniards, are they?
Bullfighters, I expect. Lithe little fellows. Took 'em
another ten minutes to find it, the marmalade. Those
titchy containers they brought, the ones you get on
airplanes. It wasn't marmalade either, it was *mirabelles*.
'Ave I said that right—*mirabelles*? Tasted of plums. Don't
you get many Brits up at the château?'

'Not many.'

'What's this then?'

'A loom.'

'Right, yes. I meant this. Rug, is it? My word, all that
detail! Gives you an insight into the Bayeux tapestry. Do it
yourself?'

'It's not finished.'

Had the moment been other, and the circumstances,

Mercy might have explained that it was not a rug either. But like the Lady of Shallott he had left the loom, he had made three paces through the room, two anyway, and was approaching the bedroom door. When he reached the door he halted. He regarded the door handle, looked back towards the kitchen, and inhaled, as if comparing loom smells, Ajax, and a possibility of blueberry griddle-cakes, with the Château de Mordan's air-fresheners. Mercy realized that she had stopped breathing. The policeman sauntered past the bedroom door.

Mercy, breathing, said, 'I'm still working on it.'

'And this—fantastic!' He flicked a cymbal, tapped a footdrum with a suede toe, and dragged his fingertips across snares. With the vibrations still in the air, he opened his mouth and went to town, beating a two-handed, inexpert tattoo on a side drum, and singing, 'Ta-ta ti tum-ti TUM!' He smiled delightedly at Mercy. 'You're a drummer!'

'They're my son's.'

'Angus?'

'Fergus. What is it you want?' If Jean-Luc had needed to blow his nose, then, with the drums banging, had been the moment. Her mind alert for sounds from the bed-room, Mercy gestured towards a circular, wickerwork chair behind the policeman. 'I mean, sit down, if you've time.'

He had time. He picked needlework bristling with needles from the chair's cushion, arranged it on the rug beside the chair, and sat. The wickerwork creaked.

He said, 'It's probably nothing. Your French police asked if I'd have a quick word. When I say your, what I'm saying is their. France's French police. Rick, er, Ziegler.' He hesitated over the name. His smile had become uncertain, as if the name Rick Ziegler must so obviously be the invention of a Hollywood scriptwriter that merely to utter it rendered himself, too, unreal, or at best an accessory after the fact. 'I suppose Rick is Richard. Does the name register?'

'He had a restaurant in Portland. He was a friend of my husband.'

'Was?'

'He died last week.' By lifting a leg she could have sat on the edge of the table. She remained standing. 'I guess it was last week.'

Holding the lapels of the plaid robe to her throat, Mercy was aware that more was expected of her. But her concentration was on keeping her eyes from flitting to the bedroom door behind which Jean-Luc was behaving impeccably. His silence was monumental. What was he doing?

'He was murdered,' she said. 'Mr Ziegler. In Portland.'

'Stabbed.'

'Right. Sorry. You obviously know more than I do. What ' I've said is it. All I know. Hector—my husband—he flew over for the funeral.'

'From Hong Kong?'

'From Paris. He went on to Hong Kong after the funeral.'

'In Portland?'

'Buffalo. Rick was from Buffalo. He used to say Vermont snow was frosting, like decoration, compared with Buffalo snow.'

Was her imagination on overdrive or was the cop as alert as she was to the closed door into the bedroom? Jesus, it was too silly! She wished Jean-Luc would breeze out, shake hands, and make coffee. What did it matter? What business was it of this cop whom she was never going to see again anyway? A routine inquiry, like he'd said.

Poor Rick. Horrible.

For the here and now it mattered not a pin if this Inspector Pecker, Peccadillo. Peck-a-dildo, whoever, if he knew she had a hairy swain on the other side of the door or not. He was not going to shout it in the streets. He would not even find space for it in his notebook.

Too late now for introductions. To avoid embarrassment, either you were honest in the first ten seconds or you kept your little peccadillo going and hoped for the best.

She said, 'I really didn't know him, Mr Ziegler, Mr, er, Inspector—'

'Peckover. 'Enry.'

'So what can I tell you?'

'Blessed if I know!'

Hugely smiling, thrusting his head forward, the policeman made the pronouncement with an air of manic wonder. Mercy thought: Is he flying? Is he on speed? From behind the bedroom door sounded a faint scraping noise. Silence followed.

The cop was leaning forward in the wickerwork chair, grinning like one of the gargoyles over the Priory's west door.

'Fact is, ma'am, I'm on my hols. Sort of. A long weekend. Longer the better, I can tell you. France is all right.' His voice dropped as his delight mounted. He was a hushed, thrilled conspirator, a prizewinner, not yet at liberty to divulge the prize to the world at large. 'So what am I doing 'ere inquiring about this Ziegler, you're asking yourself, when I'm on 'oliday—and a Brit to boot?'

Mercy nodded. He was wrong. She had not asked herself.

' 'Ow's your French?'

'My French?'

'The parley-voo.'

'Not hot.' Honey, thought Mercy, you flatter yourself. 'I get by.'

'But not fluently.'

'I'm okay on the weather. *Pluie*. *Soleil*. I can buy bread and gas.'

'If you asked for bread and you got gas, would you be amazed?'

'I'd be ecstatic. A baguette's a couple of francs, gas works out—'

'All right, if you asked for a barometer and they handed you an aubergine.'

'Happens all the time. Look, my French is weak. Not the pits, we've been here three years, seven when you count before Milan, but it's not sensational. Neither's my Italian. I'm ashamed. Now, can I help you?'

'You do, you have. I'm here in what might be described as a translating capacity.'

'You speak French?'

Mercy was astonished. Yet it was possible. His English was so weird, the accent—Cockney, was it?—he might well, as compensation, have flawless French. German, Finnish, Xhosa too.

'*Ils ne passeront pas,*' he said, abominably.

'Hunh?'

'Inquiries are taking place, ma'am, into the murder in Portland, Oregon, of Rick Ziegler, restaurateur. Bit of a puzzler, I understand. They're building up a picture. Trying to. Statements. You and Mr McCluskey were among those who knew 'im.'

'I haven't seen Mr Ziegler for two years.'

'I'd never heard of him until yesterday. I've been asked to 'ave a word because, one, I 'appen to be here, two, I have the Queen's English, and three, they're bone idle.'

'Portland?'

'Mordan. Inspector Pommard. Know 'im?'

'Sounds like a wine.' The way this character pronounced it, the wine had gone off. 'I don't know any policemen.'

'He knows you. Rimless glasses. The only English they can manage, the whole barrel of 'em, is "Do you speak English?" Whereupon guffaws and slapping of thighs.

Inspector Pommard thought your French was about the same level. So, Buggins of the Yard happening to be dropping by with his Michelins, red and green, his Worcestershire Sauce—'

'Rimless glasses?'

Last time she had presented herself to have her identity card renewed, the fat cop who had taken down the details had worn rimless glasses. When she had signed her name left-handedly he had asked if she did everything with her left hand. Yes, she had said. Everything, madame? he had asked with a godalmighty leer. Everything except complaining to the Prefect about adolescent cops, she had told him, which had been a pretty toffee-nosed thing to say, and she'd had to try about four different ways of saying it before he got the gist. But he had got the gist. She could believe he might have been reluctant to see her again, about Rick or anything else.

'Two years,' the cockney copper was saying, 'you say, since you saw 'im, Mr Ziegler. What—April, May?'

'August.' Mercy tightened the robe's belt and put her hands in the pockets. He was taking up her time and her chair but he did not leer. 'Nearly two years. My mother's in Vermont. We go every summer, or I do, with the children.'

'Vermont, eh? That's up at the top. Sounds green. Verdant Vermont. Now, sorry about this one, ma'am, it's going to have a melodramatic ring, but did 'e have any enemies you know of?' Instead of waiting for an answer, the policeman, leaning still further forward in the creaking chair, hurried on. 'Probably not. Matter of motive, you understand. Motive's half the battle. What I'm askin' is, is there anything else at all you can think of?'

'Can't think of anything.'

'Splendid!' The policeman, beaming, sprang from the chair. 'That does it then. Immensely obliged, ma'am. Great assistance. Apologies for troubling you.'

'No trouble.' She watched him scoop up the needle-work and replace it on the chair. 'You don't write it down or anything?'

'Write what down?'

'I guess there wasn't much.'

'It's up 'ere, ma'am,' he said, smiling, tapping his head with a forefinger, and heading for the table.

Mercy picked up the brown hat and offered it.

'*Merci beaucoup*. It's just possible I'll be back for a statement, very short, but between you and me, ma'am, unlikely. 'Ope not anyway. Nothing personal. Speaking for myself, I've a load of ambience to get in before Monday. Meeting my wife at ten if she can get away.' Walking, he looked at his watch. 'She's lost her voice.'

'Hey! She's not the one from London, your Royal Archæological Society or something, the cordon bleu, for three weeks—'

'That's 'er.' His smile spread. 'Miriam.'

From behind the bedroom door sounded a crash and a cry.

Then silence.

At the door to the passage the man and woman looked at each other, Mercy with one hand on the doorknob, the policeman with his smile evaporated, his eyebrows hiked high. He was slightly the taller but he was wearing shoes.

'Mice?' he whispered.

Mercy sought explanations. She believed she was not going to find any.

The policeman said, 'Dropped his tooth-glass, I expect.'

'It was outside. In the courtyard. Kids. They have this game.'

'Don't I know it. Kids and dogs, it's the same every-where.'

She opened the door, and with a bow and a cheerful smile he was gone, padding along the passage towards the outdoors, ambience, and a cordon bleu wife who had lost her voice. Mercy closed the door, bolted it, and sprinted to the bedroom.

Beyond the bed with its enveloping patchwork quilt, on the floor under the window, sat Jean-Luc, pale and naked amid broken glass. He stared across the patchwork towards Mercy, rocking slightly, and nursing a bloody forearm around which he had attempted, was still attempting, to wrap her nightie. The breeze from the courtyard billowed the curtain. One curtain was still drawn across the window; the other, partly drawn, had been slashed in two places. In winter Mercy shut the shutters, but not now, when in the morning she could peel back the curtains and watch the sun over the court-yard, and the swifts wheeling and darting.

'Someone was outside,' Jean-Luc said. 'When I went to look, the window smashed. I saw only the knife when it came through the curtain. I tried to hold his arm.'

He looked down in disbelief at his own nightie-swaddled arm and wrist. Then, in French, he started methodically on a succession of expressions which Mercy did not believe she could have translated word for word, but of which she got the drift.

CHAPTER 2

Detective Chief Inspector Peckover, vibrating with energy and expectation, looked both ways along the Rue du 17-Août, locating his bearings.

The street was of the medieval sort and the town was taking care of it. There were no glass banks or airline offices, or not so far. '*Vive le roi*,' Peckover told the street. '*Crème caramel. Où sont les neiges d'antan?*' In this street jerry-pots were once emptied from high windows by housewives who cried, 'Watch your head!'

Saturday marketeers plodded with loaded baskets and
trussed livestock. A stately woman dressed in layers of
flowery sarong-type garments had her basket on her
head. Normally, Peckover would have looked the other
way, out of politeness, but as he was on holiday and the
woman wore such a lofty get-me look, he looked.
Portuguese, would she be? Senegalese? He had the
impression that the cunning French had quietly clung to
some of their colonies, but where the colonies were and
whether they were of any use he had no idea. 'Hey,
cumbanchero,' he told the woman balancing the basket,
almost loudly enough to be heard. '*Mañana*.' He lowered
his voice an octave. 'Take me to the casbah.'

Beyond one end of the street, in the market square,
rainbow-coloured brollies over fruit and vegetable stalls
presaged either sun or snow. To Peckover the morning
seemed weatherless, a neutral occasion where the weather
would do nothing, though then again it might. The
natives would know. If they had their brollies up, something was going to happen. He trod right and right again
through massive, weathered doors beside which a plaque
on the stone said, *Porte du XVII Siècle*.

A tree ablaze with blossom filled most of the courtyard.
Chestnut? May? Mirabelles perhaps. Against one wall was
propped a motor-cycle with the front wheel missing.
There were piled crates and mysterious rods and pipes
abandoned by a plumber; or vitally precious pipes for all
Peckover knew. Washing adorned a grid which jutted
from an upper window. The lower windows in the left-
hand wall were black and broken. To the right, at the far
corner of the courtyard, a pair of shutters were shutting.
He heard the grate of the lever clamping them closed.

He headed right, beneath the tree, treading through
blossom. Through the first window he dimly saw a loom.
Drums. Furniture not acquired from the friendly neigh-
bourhood hypermarket. The second window revealed the

empty kitchen.

The third, newly shuttered, was the bedroom. It had to be. Peckover looked behind him, around, and up. He looked down at broken glass. The shutters were as shut as prison gates. He tucked two fingers under a slat and pulled, but there was no movement.

There was blood, though, on the stone sill. Specks and splashes. Had he touched the splashes they would have been wet. Tacky anyway. Had he been able to see through the shutters he would have seem more blood, he suspected, and on the curtains, if there were curtains.

These days, hell's teeth, the games kids played! Broken glass and blood! He leaned against the shutters, listening, watching the empty courtyard, searching the ground for toffee-wrappings.

Only the fiery, snowy tree. Blossom, plumber's pipes, a scrunched Gauloises packet. but no toffee-papers. No ice-cream cartons or chalked squares for hopscotch. No kids, no sound.

An accordion?

Peckover hoped so. He walked from the courtyard and along the street. Accordions were France. Accordions, waltzes, smells of frying garlic, fresh coffee, fresh cat in the alleys, urine from drains in the heat of summer. Most of the town's signs pointed up alleys to the Vieux Quartier, where he assumed he already was. Others directed him to restaurants. On the boulevard he followed a sign pointing to the Hôtel de Police, which whatever else was not going to be a hotel for policemen.

In two minutes he found it, a building of orange con-crete behind a Talbot car showroom. The shiny foyer was deserted apart from a concierge who sat with a typewriter and telephone at a desk in a glass cage, bullet-proofed against attack by Corsicans.

Non, the woman regretted, Inspector Pommard was not in. Could she help?

She could tell him, Peckover said, that Monsieur Peckover had dropped by — Peck-over — and would be in touch. Outside the American lady's bedroom window, in the courtyard, was blood. *Sang*. As well get a sample before the rains came. For the file. Just so everyone was covered. He would be at the Café du Centre for the next half-hour or so. *Ça va? Compris?*

The concierge listened with her face contorted in incomprehension, interrupting with frequent nasal '*Nghs?*' and '*Comments?*' But some of it she got down. When finally Peckover raised his hat and left, he did so with exultant heart.

That was it, finished. Acquitted of his responsibilities. Yet he had worked, in theory he was still working, and that meant expenses. Out of the blue the long weekend paid for: the flight, the château, the *foie de veau aux oignons*, as many beakers full of the warm south as he could manage. Pity he could not spin it out for a couple of weeks.

'I loff Paree in ze zpringti-i-me,' Detective Chief Inspector Peckover warbled, tacking through boulevard traffic.

In the market progress was difficult, no one but himself wanting to move. Either they stood shaking hands and kissing, blocking the gaps between the stalls, or they stood at the stalls pressing their thumbs into the vegetables. The waltzing accordion sounded from loudspeakers at a records stall, though the music was no longer accordions but tambourines and castanets, and a wailer wailing. Peckover sat at a table on the pavement outside the Café du Centre, waiting for Miriam.

Those labouring slaves back at the Yard, if they could see him! Grinning, tapping a suede foot in time to the wailer, Peckover had to restrain himself from waving to the mob of marketeers. None of the other tables was occupied, so with luck the café was shut. He wanted neither a drink nor a waiter. He would keep his breath wholesome for Miriam.

When he got round to it he would give consideration to the McCluskey woman, but not yet. From the plastic bag in his pocket he took Michelin guides, a phrase book, a street map of Mordan, and a dozen mint, misty postcards of the local scene; sheep at sunset, toiling peasants, a font, a geezer drinking out of a soup plate. Which was aptest for the Assistant Commissioner? Whichever, the AC would think he was being got at and he would be right. Peckover squared off the books and cards, moved them aside, and took out notebook and pencil.

Miriam was late. She had not been sure she would be able to get away at all. A convoy of Dutch in big cars were expected for lunch. After three weeks filling in for the head chef she was beginning to resemble one of the Amnesty prisoners for whom she demonstrated and wrote letters: someone who for three years or thirty had lost weight, heart, and seen no daylight. She was insisting she was fine but he suspected she would be more than ready to fly home in another week at the end of her stint. For himself, three days to go, it was pathetic, unthinkable.

What had the McCluskey lady said? 'I haven't seen Mr Ziegler for two years . . .' That was a lie but perhaps she simply had not been thinking. She had been so anxious about the beast in the bedroom that he had felt for her: protective, paternal even, or he might have felt paternal had there been more than two years difference in their ages.

Whoever the beast in the bedroom had been, it had not been Mr Ziegler.

Peckover opened the notebook at a clean page. He put a finger in his ear and bit his pencil. He no longer heard the hum and babble of the market. He bent over the notebook and wrote:

★

Dear Auntie Flo, no news
　From Mordan, downtown France,
Except baguettes, they're up 10p,
　Please send a small advance.

Meat's up, and Camembert.
　Petrol's up as well;
Dear Aunt, just as in Merrie,
　Inflation's struck La Belle.

Some bloke's baguette is up
　A Yank, five metres long.
The baguette or the Yank, you ask?
　(Her husband's in Hong Kong.)

Pas mon affaire, the morals
　Of the international set;
Laissez-faire, I always say.
　Affectionately, Chet.

　Chet was a Yankee first name out of the same bag as
Rick. Rick, Chet, Chip, Rip, Skip, Brewster, and
Hancock. But how could he sign himself 'Henry'? What
rhymed with 'Henry'? The closest he had ever come was
'dispensary'.
　'Monsieur?' a voice was saying in one ear. In the other
ear susurrated sea sounds, the rustle of a spring tide.
　A youth in a turtle-neck jersey, not a white jacket, but
holding a tray and a cloth, stood above him, reaching out
to flick the cloth at the table-top. Above Peckover to his
other side Miriam was positioning a chair. As she
descended, he rose, timing the manœuvre to catch her
cheek with a kiss.
　' 'Ello, love. What'll you 'ave? Don't answer if it hurts.'
　She wore her mac from a Burberry's sale of four years

ago, and round her neck a woolly scarf which he did not
think he recognized, though he would not have risked
raising the matter in case she had had it since schooldays,
or worse, he had given it to her. In spite of her new
gauntish look she was still, in Peckover's opinion, the pick
of the market, of Mordan, of this half of France, and the
other half, and the rest of the Continong. She was shaking
her head, pulling her chair up to the table, and pointing
to her mouth.

'Food?' Peckover queried. 'A slice of the local loaf
spread with something regional?'

She reached for his notebook and pencil. *Laryngite de
catarrhe*, she wrote, and as an afterthought, *Catarrhal
laryngitis?*

Peckover took the pencil and wrote, *Stone the crows.*

Miriam wrote, *No talking for two months!*

Peckover wrote, *You or me?*

He had hoped she might at least have smiled but she
opened her mouth and wagged her head, miming Ha-ha-
ha. When he started to write, *Did the doc* — she snatched
the pencil and pointed to his mouth.

'Not hungry,' Peckover said.

She whispered, 'Hulking imbecile.'

'That's not very nice,' he said. 'How many whispers are
you allowed a day?'

She lifted two fingers at him.

'Monsieur?' said the waiter, fascinated.

'*Deux cafés, s'il vous plaît,*' Peckover said, and he took
Miriam's hand. 'I don't believe any of this. Two months?
What's Sam going to say?' For a two-year-old currently
doted on by grandparents and an aunt, Sam had
something to say about everything. 'You sure it's not
painful? Shouldn't you be lying down?'

She shook her head.

'What was the doctor like? Any use?'

Miriam wrote, *Devastating*, and smirked.

'Bleedin' frog. Is he qualified?'

Her answer was a contemptuous skyward gaze.

'Bleedin' quack,' Peckover said. 'What do we know about 'im? He didn't prescribe any of those bombs up the bum, did he? It's all bombs up the bum in France, you know that? Bombs and great cupboardsful of powders and potions. The doctors are in league with the chemists. Here—what is it?'

She was nodding at him, her eyes filled with love and despair. Frightened, Peckover took both her hands, but she withdrew them to grapple with her handbag. She brought out a folded form which she unfolded to disclose more paper, a loose white sheet with doctor's scribble. Prescriptions. A list as long as a marathon.

'Which one's the bomb up the bum then?' growled Peckover, picking up the pencil. 'We'll 'ave that out for a start.'

'Monsieur?'

Glaring at the paper, vainly seeking the bombs prescription, Peckover assumed the interruption was the waiter with coffee. When none landed, and he looked up, looking down through rimless glasses was paunchy Inspector Pommard. At his side stood an eager lad with an inadequate moustache: scrappy, accidental hairs on his upper lip.

'*Monsieur Peckover, qu'est-ce que c'est ce singe? Singe*—monkey, yes? We find no monkey. Zis 'ere Enquêteur Gouzou spik English.'

Enquêteur—inquirer? Detective-constable, Peckover assumed, regarding the cub's wispy lip and trendy leather jacket. He presented Miriam, who moved her lips silently. A waiter arrived with coffee and additional chairs. No reports, Enquêteur Gouzou urgently said, of missing monkey received. Monsieur Peckover will describe monkey details please? Will draw picture.

'Don't be daft, I can't draw,' Peckover said. 'What kind

of monkey? Small and cuddly? One of the mauve kind?'

'Is your monkey. You make draw. We find.'

Though imperfect, like his moustache, Enquêteur Gouzou's English was superior to his senior officer's, towards whom he now glanced, as if to ask, How am I doing? From behind their spectacles the eyes of Inspector Pommard were glintingly on Miriam.

Peckover would have preferred to have practised his French, but now probably was not the time, not if the monkey business were urgent. What was the lad talking about? Somewhere he, Peckover, had missed the point, as if he had turned two pages at once. Miriam could have helped, or before she had lost her voice she could have. Her French was largely culinary, limited to such expressions as *bain-marie* and *videz cinq poissons*, but he believed they complemented each other, as husband and wife should, his French being less exact but perhaps wider-ranging, the scrapings and leavings of songs and films. *Plaisir d'amour* and *La belle et la bête* and such. He was eager to have a go. Whether Miriam's culinary French embraced monkeys he could not have said but he did not exclude the possibility. The French ate some funny things.

Even when the confusion between *sang* and *singe* had been laughingly ironed out, Peckover profoundly resented the mishearing by the woman in the glass cage. His accent might not have been out of whatever the French equivalent of the BBC was, or the BBC before it had started recruiting from bus conductors and left-wing tobacconists, but common sense should have told her. Paunchy, raunchy Pommard had dragged his eyes from Miriam to consult with his flunkey.

'Monsieur,' Peckover heard Gouzou telling him. 'Is information from Paris to you. Confidential. If Madame was perhaps leave — *zut!* — if Madame is off —'

'Madame not off, Madame stay,' Peckover said. 'What information?'

'You telephone please. They ask you go Lourdes.'

'Where?'

'Is more inquiry.'

'Lourdes where they 'ave the miracles?'

'*Les Miracles, oui.* You telephone.'

'Why Lourdes?'

'Is inquiry. More murder. You telephone Paris or your Scotland Yard either maybe. For consolation.'

'Confirmation.'

'Okay.'

Peckover lifted his eyebrows at Miriam. Lourdes. Our Lady of. South, towards Spain, wasn't it? They could go together. Surely she could swing a day or two off. If she were late back for her archæologists someone would stand in for her, they were not going to riot, banging their plates with their spoons and carolling, 'Mi-ri-am! Mi-ri-am!' Half of them had such delicate stomachs they never ate anyway.

The other half ate like goats: those who spent their lives in the field, on their knees in Peru or Carthage, grubbing for shards under a broiling sun and eating and drinking locusts, the stale of horses, the gilded puddle.

Miriam's eyes beckoned to him over the rim of her coffee-cup. She lowered the cup and moved her lips. Peckover, inclining his head away from the gaze of the police pair, sent a discreet kiss in return, whereupon Miriam began to pout and arrange her lips in contortions unattempted since the salad days of their passion. Or was she trying to tell him something and he was to lip-read? He might have been watching a silent movie.

'I love you,' Peckover lip-read. Or it might have been, 'I leave you.'

Another alternative was, 'I'll eat stew.' As a professional cook, Miriam often talked about food. On the other hand, this was early to be thinking of lunch.

'I love you too,' Peckover soundlessly mouthed across the table.

Miriam's mouth clamped shut. Her face was thunder. She gathered her handbag and pushed back her chair.

' 'Old on, I haven't paid the bill yet,' Peckover grumbled.

He gathered up books and hat and went into the café in search of the waiter. When he came out, Inspector Pommard was holding Miriam's hand in what might have been a farewell handshake, if the imagination were stretched. At least she was taking the experience impassively. He told Gouzou he might be along to the Hôtel de Police to telephone shortly, or he might telephone from elsewhere. He nodded at Pommard, extracted Miriam from the lecher's grip, and guided her away through the market.

'Sorry,' he said.

She squeezed his hand. So it was all right, whatever it had been. Peckover's pleasure at being in France surged back, to the exclusion of Miriam, whom he forgot, including her hand in his, while he looked about, inhaled, and rejoiced in the berets and shawls, the alien smells, the hubbub, the loudspeaker's dreadful thumpings, and the unabashed Peugeots and Citroëns honkingly forcing themselves through the crowd on their way to or from the side-streets off the market square. One stallholder, weighing artichokes with handscales, was using gross sawn-off carrots as weights. With whisperings and the finger-tracing of letters, first on a wall at the edge of the market, next on the backs of each other's hands as they threaded along the boulevard, Peckover and Miriam conversed.

She had to get back to the château to look after the saffron soup. Also the pigeons casseroled with asparagus, the trout stuffed with preserved duck—Miriam grimaced and made a clutching gesture at her heart—because that was why she was here, why they both were here, and though the Dutch party might eat gigantically and blindly, one or two might also be aware what they were eating. He was not to come with her unless he intended to chop onions. He must explore old Mordan and profit from every moment. Especially if he were going to have to dash to wherever—Lourdes? She would not be free before around three o'clock, and then only for two hours at most. If he had dinner in the restaurant he must promise her not to touch the foie gras, or the stuffed goose neck which she would be cooking for three hours in goose fat, or the fritters. Whether the Yard were paying or not.

Lunch where what you? she traced on his hand.

'Thought I might ingest a little raw cauliflower, with a glass of mineral water,' Peckover said. 'I'm not going to Lourdes either, or anywhere. I'm staying with you.'

Balls, traced Miriam.

'Balls yourself. You're ill. I'm not leaving you. You'd 'ave no one to talk to.'

He watched her drive away along the boulevard in the loaned château car which had been part of the contract: car, keep, return air fare, two days off a week—in the last two weeks she had apparently managed one half-day—and a salary fifty per cent above what her archæologists brought her. The McCluskey bloke, the boss, the one off judging meat patties in Hong Kong, had not argued, not seriously. With his regular chef in hospital having a nervous breakdown, the assistant chef scarpered overnight to the galley of a tycoon's yacht bound for the Greek Islands, and two replacements in one week having been sacked for drunkenness and theft, McCluskey had not had much choice. He himself did no cooking these days, being too busy writing food columns, exposing himself on the box, and jetting hither and yon judging pastry contests. Word having seeped along the European cooks' grapevine, Miriam had made herself available.

Château de Mordan had two crowns in the Michelin, though admittedly for the birdsong and furnishings rather than the food.

Château Rip-Off, in Peckover's view. What he had seen of it. Crossed carnations on the Châteaubriand, and a welter of Scottish imports—tartans, antlers, busts of Burns and Scott—which lifted the rates still higher on the basis that customers were being treated to not one but two experiences: Gallic and Gaelic, the Auld Alliance. His first night he had spent uncomfortably but gratis in Miriam's cell in the staff annexe. Now that he was on duty, working and laughing, and the Yard would be picking up the tab, he had moved self and Miriam to a double in the château proper. The Rob Roy Room. Peckover had giggled and sobbed when he had seen the price of the Rob Roy Room printed small but clear on a card behind the door. Question was, would a question be asked in the House of Commons?

Grrrr, shuddered Peckover, striding and starting to hum. He would take a speedy turn round the vaunted Priory so that it would be off his conscience. Then a beer or three at one of these boulevard cafés: a pavement table from where, reaching forward, the customer could touch the passing juggernauts. Then the phone call to the Factory.

'Cock?'

'Henry? That you? Took your time. What're you up to? Picking grapes?'

'Sweatin' at it, mate. I envy you lot, feet up, scratching yourselves. It's round-the-clock 'ere. Ought to warn you, the expenses are climbing. I've seen the woman.'

'What woman?'

'Go back to sleep. I've met the local lot too, an Inspector Pommard, he of the raging libido and filmy eyes. I'm at the cop shop now only there doesn't seem to be anyone else 'ere, they'll be having the long lunch. Miriam's lost 'er voice but she's learned how to stuff bat. Stuffed bat's wings, speciality of the region. Weather stunning. Dancing in the streets, goes without saying. It's all go. The woman, McCluskey, she lied about Ziegler. Said she 'adn't seen him for two years.'

'Who's Ziegler?'

'None of your business. We 'ad a monkey on a window-ledge.'

'And an elephant in the bath?'

'I'll send a Telex about five o'clock. The File on Madame McCluskey.'

'Sonnet sequence?'

'Rhyming couplets. What's this about Lourdes?'

'Bad. Bite on the bullet, Henry. Ready? Australia, a hundred and fourteen for no wicket — that's the lunch score.'

'Lourdes, not Lords, you mooncalf, sir. Are you listening?'

'Yes.'

'Lou-u-rdes.'

'Henry?'

'No, you don't pronounce the "s". I think. It's like this. Lou-u-ur-*da*. I'll be honest, I'm not even sure you pronounce the "d". Lou-u-urrrgh!'

'Henry?'

'This part of the world, mate, if you don't get your pronunciation spot on, you're sunk. They take you for a tourist.'

'Henry! Can I speak? I wanted to know if you were all right. Seriously.'

'Seriously, tip-top, old fruit.'

'Exactly the impression that was coming across loud and clear. What's wrong?'

'Whaddyer mean, what's wrong?'

'I mean d'you want to be pulled back tonight, today,

immediately? Personally, I'm ravished you should be so perky, but you know as well as me, if it gets round you're enjoying yourself, if the Guv'nor hears, you're going to be summoned back home on the first bus to Victoria. Got a pencil?'

'Wait. Who's perky? I'm not perky. Listen.' Peckover snarled into the mouthpiece, then he sobbed chokingly. The echoes bounced, fading, off the office walls. ' 'Ow's that? I'll do it again. Can you get it on tape?'

'Susan Spence. She's a widow residing at eighteen, Rue Jacques Brel, Lourdes. If you prefer, Lou-u-urrgh. Got it?'

'Roughly.'

'I'll spell it.'

No sense of theatre, the young 'uns, Peckover decided. Give 'em a snarl and a sob and they turned stone sodding frigid. All right, Superintendent Veal must have been all of a year younger than himself, perhaps two years, but they were calendar years. What about experience years? What about wear-and-tear years? Had Veal suffered obloquy and demotion for writing limericks on lavatory walls at the Yard?

Tasty limericks too, the best of them, those about the Assistant Commissioner.

'The husband, Charles Fordyce Spence, he was a businessman.'

'From Portland, all this, is it?' Peckover said. 'By way of the Factory, and Paris.'

'You're asking boring questions, Henry. Ask why Mrs Spence is a widow.'

'Why is Mrs Spence a widow?'

'That's a good question. New Year's Eve, it says here, that's four months ago, Mr Spence was found stabbed to death in his bed at the Hilton in Paris. Now ask if Mr Spence was mutilated.'

Detective-Superintendent Frank Veal, CID, Scotland

Yard, feet up, scratching himself, listened to several bars of silence along the air waves.

'Sorry if "mutilated" offends but it's the word I've got here, one of them,' he went on. 'Mutilated apart from being stabbed, naturally. No details of the actual stabbing, you'd have to get on to Paris, or Portland. Go on then, ask.'

'That's the link, is it? They both lost their *modus vivendi*? Ziegler and Spence?'

'I'm just a clerk here. I'm not Hercule Poirot.'

'I'm not bloody Hercule Poirot either. The plot sickens.'

'What plot? Don't get fanciful. All you do is talk to the Widow Spence, in English, and send us the sonnet sequence. You're lucky. Think of the kudos. You could be on your way to unmasking a new, international Jack the Ripper, and—who knows?—likely the first gay Jack the Ripper.'

'What if Jack the Ripper is Suzy the Chopper?'

'The Widow Spence is pure lavender and lace. She'll serve you jasmine tea.'

'Let 'er serve it to the Lourdes lot. I'm not ready to lay my manhood on the block.'

'When she comes in with the jasmine, keep one hand in your trousers pocket. Wear your cricket box, that should delay her.'

'What's a cricket box? What you keep crickets in?'

'You know, against the fast bowlers.'

'I don't know. I don't play cricket.'

'If you see her actually picking up a cleaver, phone us sharpish. There's no rush getting there, she's not expected back until tomorrow. She's in Gstaad with a boy-friend, leaving tonight. G-sta-a-ad. How's my accent? Incidentally, the mutilation bit, it's still not public so keep it under your beret. Paris is terrified of copycats and Portland's playing along—for the moment. You haven't asked about the deceased, the Widow Spence's bloke, what business he was in.'

'I didn't like to pry.'

'He was a gun-runner.'

'Wouldn't have minded being a gun-runner myself. All that wrapping the Winchesters in calico and buckskin, nailing the crates, loading 'em in the chuck wagon.'

'Lourdes, chum, not Laramie. He called himself a travel agent.'

' 'Course 'e did. So would I. Wait. Lourdes. We're not talking about the IRA?'

'All we've got is a whisper from Belfast. They're holding a disillusioned Provo. Tomorrow we'll read about it in the papers. I'd say it's totally irrelevant to your inquiries—'

'I'm not inquiring, I'm coming 'ome.'

'—but Charlie-boy was a trading-post for the IRA and the Basques, or trying to be. Possibly.'

'What time's that bus to Victoria?'

'Coward.'

'Dead right, mate. I've nothing against the Basques, all I know is they wear berets, but I'm not messing with the IRA. Come to think of it, the IRA wear berets, don't they? At funerals?'

'Buy yourself a beret. Told you, it's irrelevant, I offer it as background. Don't want to go naked into the Widow Spence's conference chamber, do you?'

'Up yours.'

'You're sounding better already. Our 'Enry, the old grouch, sour as a lemon.'

'And you, cock, are one sour grape. You're stuck in your plate-glass hutch with one thought. Sabotage the bugger's weekend. Listen to this then.' Peckover held the telephone at a distance and sang Caruso-like, 'I loff Paree in ze zpringti-i-ime . . .'

Ere Chief-Inspector Peckover had reached the point of

loving Paree in the fall, Superintendent Veal had hung up, and the office door had opened to admit Messieurs Pommard and Gouzou, who entered but a step before stopping to stare, and to cast anxious glances at each other.

CHAPTER 3

'*Bonsoir, monsieur, madame,*' Mercy McCluskey said, smiling hostessily, carrying matches and menus, and bearing down like a pirate schooner through the aqua-marine ocean of carpet. She wore a sleeveless black gown and her blonde hair was up, held by a forest of combs. '*Une table à deux?*'

They were not going to want a table for fifteen but you had to greet them with something. This pair she identified as Parisians, probably, though they had a forlorn air which she did not associate with Parisians, who considered themselves lords of the universe and expected to be treated accordingly. Possibly Belgians? They might be Dutch, though usually the Dutch arrived in groups. Not English anyway, and certainly not Irish. You could tell. The English were rumpled. The better bred they were, the more heavily rumpled, and they arrived in good humour after a stopover at the bar. The few Irish she had greeted, parties of millionaire cattle-breeders or flushed politicians with a mistress in tow, arrived glassy-eyed and hinge-kneed, either singing or speechless, after a bar session which might have begun in mid-afternoon. The French, Germans, Dutch, all the Continental rich, elbowed the bar and came straight in to eat.

'Why don't we have that table right there, where we had breakfast?' the man said. 'Arthur and Martha Rickett. We have the Gleneagles Suite. *Bonjour.*'

Davenport, Iowa.

Mercy, full-rigged, listing as she rounded the restaurant's Doric columns, led the couple to the empty table in front of the piano. At least she was able to converse with English-speakers, and usually was willing to, her condition as expatriate being that of more or less uninterrupted homesickness, for the English language above all. But today had been wearing. She was disinclined to chat. She was not homesick for Davenport, Iowa.

The table was immaculate but busy: geometric place settings with goblets for red and white, a mysterious folded card like a wedding invitation, fingerbowls with floating rose petals, bulbous candles, a crystal vase sprouting an orchid of breathtakingly sickly nastiness, napkins in coronet shapes, and an imitation Fabergé ashtray which large numbers of guests pocketed. The card recounted highlights from the history of the Château de Mordan. 'In 1631, Gilles, Duc de Mordan, hanged his wife upside down in chains, for the whole of Lent, from the window of the south turret, now the linen room . . .'

The Ricketts arranged themselves: he in grey, she in navy blue. Mercy applied a match to the candles and handed over the calfskin-bound menus embossed with an assemblage of cones like witches' hats, purporting to depict the château's 16th-century towers. At least the pianist was missing. Arthur took spectacles from his pocket.

'So what,' he inquired, 'do you have for us tonight, little lady?'

Little lady? He must have been blind. Martha too was putting on glasses. Attached to hers was a silver chain which fell to her bosom, then abruptly looped up, swept over one shoulder, round the back of her neck, and out of sight. To what, wondered Mercy, was the chain's disappearing end attached? What was certain was that if their French was as suspect as their eyesight she might be able to keep up the pretence that she was French, therefore unable to understand a word they said. That would nip in the bud Davenport small talk. One of the candles went out. 'Shit,' muttered Mercy, and coughed to cover the error. She re-ignited both the candle and her smile. For her meeting and greeting duties she was glad that her teeth were white and plentiful. A smile that's snappy keeps the customer happy, she reminded herself, aware that frequently a smile did no such thing, in fact to the contrary, especially where the customer was a Parisian. Arthur and Martha were frowning into their menus, turning the pages.

Mercy looked round for the waiter who ought by now to have been gliding up and taking over. Though the glow from the candles and electric chandeliers was carefully subfusc, she always felt she should be shielding her eyes from the dazzle of carpet, the polished plaster pillars, the gilded Louis XIV chairs from a factory in Nantes, and the clashing gold-and-heliotrope, Regency-stripe wall-covering. Saturday night and the restaurant was half empty: or half full, as Hector used to insist, encouraging her to think positively in the days of their first puny restaurants in Vermont and New Jersey two decades ago. The pianist, the gigolo Jerome, was sidling into place, back from a swallow of whatever was open and available in the kitchen, and a grope of whoever was open and available among the kitchen maids. Mercy was conscious of him massaging his fingers and cracking his knuckles as if he were goddamn Rubinstein.

She avoided his eyes. He was all of twenty-two, beauti-ful with his flat stomach and curly black hair, and so aware of it that confidence as much as the lounge-lizard looks must have been what felled the girls. These days, if their eyes met, his leered and solicited. Impertinent brat. Knowing that all was not a hundred per cent between the foreign McCluskeys, man and wife, that indeed the wife was having a happening with a local prof, he presumably saw her as ripe for plucking.

Why would he not have known? Everyone knew. Anyone who succeeded in keeping anything dark in pokey, potty, petty, picturesque Mordan deserved a medal. Even had the townsfolk preferred not to know, and gone out of their way to be blind and deaf, what hope was there when Jean-Luc was so thrilled at his luck, like a boy with a new bicycle, that he could not help but boast to everyone of his catch, this cultured, warm mistress, this jewel of womanhood, the American at the Château de Mordan? Rumour was, he, the pianist, who was neither blind nor deaf, whose constant massaging of his fingers rendered them supple, had made Madame Costes. Madame Costes, the housekeeper, was well into her forties: mother of four, ravishing, bright, organized, her own woman, and not a subject of gossip, or not as far as Mercy knew. Against her nobler instincts, such as they were, Mercy did not believe the rumour was mere rumour either, and not believing, she could not for the life of her fathom what a whippersnapper gigolo had to offer a woman such as Madame Costes, apart from the obvious. At her time of life she must have known sufficient of joy, disaster, and men, to have remained indifferent to the sighings of a juvenile, practically a minor, a time-wasting, trainee boulevardier. Wouldn't she have sent him packing with pennies for candy? Told him to go change his diaper? What did they talk about before and after, for God's sake? There had to be a before and after even if lasting only long enough to fill the hot-water bottle. What did he leave her with for her reflective moments? He was hardly in a position to give her the wisdom of the ages or mink, so what had he to offer beyond his flat stomach? Piano lessons?

Flowers, promises, telling her he loved her?

Yes. What more was needed? 'I love you' with feeling

was all that it took. Mercy felt ashamed for her feeble, female sex.

'Whaddya say, honey?' she heard Arthur say to Martha.

They were turning menu pages and mumbling. Had they been French, Mercy might have felt obliged to point out that the truffles in the Périgueux sauce were from Bergerac and that the rolled pig's head with pistachios was a Lyonnais speciality. For Davenport, Iowa, there was little point. They knew what they were going to eat. So did she. Steak and salad. Perhaps with a bottle of nice laxative Evian. Martha, looking marginally the more adventurous with her looping silver chain, just might risk the steak with green peppercorn sauce.

Well, the steak would cost them. Tonight's sirloin out of the freezer was cut in the shape of a Charolais steer's skull with handlebar horns.

Last night's sirloin in fact. The temporary chef, the replacement, the Limey cop's wife with the bust and good bones, had complained in writing. The unwanted scrap of paper, gravy-stained, had been brought to Mercy by the ancient commis who had been slicing vegetables in the kitchen since probably the days of Gilles, Duc de Mordan. Having complained that the sirloin was less than daisy-fresh, the woman had observed in the same breath, or more precisely the same paragraph, that the bull's head shape was idiotic, wasteful, a mockery of a noble beast, and there was too much boring steak on the menu anyway.

She was probably right. But who did she think she was? What did she know about a joint like the Château de Mordan where the exercise was to blind the customers with stage effects? Mercy had been willing to propose to Mrs Peckover that she get on with her cooking and keep her opinions to herself. She had seemed a reasonable enough woman, for a cook, the occasions they had met.

She had presented her observations in writing, for example, not because she was a lawyer or a union official but because she had lost her voice. But the risk in suggesting she zip her lip was too great. What if she downed saucepans and walked out?

They were a touchy breed, top chefs, never mind the smiles they wore for the glossy magazines, photographed with their *filets de sole Prince des Gastronomes*. The heat and panics, the Cognac always to hand, left them taut as a banjo string. A chef flinging the sauce *hollandaise* across the kitchen, then stamping out was common enough to evoke from the staff a shrug. But there might be sympathy, mutiny even, for a chef who had lost her voice stamping out. A woman, moreover, far from home and voiceless. The combination boded ill. Hector was going to be less than ecstatic if he returned to a kitchen on strike, sauce *hollandaise* everywhere, smeared on the walls like in some prison protest.

The day was ending as it began, in vexation and danger.

For all his massaged fingers Jerome was playing not Rachmaninoff but *Falling in Love Again*. Could be his choice might win him a tip too. Could be he was stirring in Arthur and Martha memories of steak and foxtrotting in downtown Davenport circa 1938.

'*Je vais chercher le sommelier,*' Mercy sweetly lied to them, and swinging stern about, she sailed through the aquamarine, by chance walking into the wine waiter as she veered round a pillar.

'Table two,' she told him. 'Say hullo to arrivals if there are any. Be right back.'

She headed out of the restaurant. Lovely Heinz, she thought, and wondered why suddenly she should think of Heinz.

Ah. *Ja. Falling in Love Again.* La Dietrich. Germany. Not that anything about Heinz conformed to the stereotype of a German: lederhosen, a foaming stein, a tuba band oom-pah-pahing. Was there a German play-boy ski-champion stereotype? Even so, Heinz was not flaxen-haired. She would have been hard put to say exactly what he was. In a way she hardly knew him. Three days in his shack in Andorra had scarcely been enough to discover the soul of the guy. He quite likely had the soul of a bastard. Mercy passed through the wide, verbena-scented spaces of the lobby, smiling at memories and lively possibilities.

'Hi,' she said to diminutive Madame Costes, who crossed her path, liftwards, carrying a clipboard and a red rose wrapped in Cellophane.

If it had not been a clipboard and a red rose it would have been a five-kilo carton of Tide. Housekeepers, in Mercy's experience, were always carrying something. Carrying something or carrying on: with a pianist in Madame's case. She envied Madame Costes her ability to get it all together, always, from shoes to ear-rings, with no evident effort, and without looking as if she were being paid to model something. Very French. Shame she could do no better than Jerome.

'Bonsoir, madame,' murmured Madame Costes.

Mercy swung into the passage to the Loch Lomond Bar, and in lieu of absentee Heinz, to the only person, if he had arrived, capable of soothing away the vexation. Later in the evening anyway.

Trouble was, brooded Mercy, stepping out, her hostess smile blown away, trouble was that Jean-Luc's company soothed away the vexation but—unless her imagination was out of control—increased the danger mightily.

Saturday night in the Loch Lomond Bar, Château de Mordan, was different from Saturday night in the Loch Lomond bar, Sauchiehall Street. Such was the opinion of Chief-Inspector Peckover, alone and at ease at the table furthest from the door.

He knew Glasgow hardly at all but supposed that if a Loch Lomond Bar existed there the Saturday-night problem would be forcing a road through the mob to the counter. Here he counted seven customers including himself. Eight humans if you included the sneering barman, which you did only grudgingly. How did such sleek rodents find jobs serving ordinary, agreeable blokes such as himself?

He was slipping: bars such as this seldom served ordinary, agreeable blokes. They served the toffs, or at any rate characters with more money than sense.

To put it another way, the booze was slipping. Slipping too easily down. He might refuse his next round to himself. After a couple of sickly pastis to help the French economy on its way, he had switched to bottled beer, the existence of which plebeian muck in a gilded salon such as this—salon, not saloon, his meandering thoughts stressed—might have surprised him had not the price been three quid a bottle, near enough. He was going to have to recoup somehow, filch some receipts from somewhere.

'To hospitality for Mordan Gendarmerie, taxis, telephones, portable filing cabinet, subscriptions to essential French magazines, oil for handcuffs, repair to truncheon, disguise kit no. 27 comprising beret, goatee, easel and palette . . . £213.35.'

Merry as a lark and ninety per cent sober, in his own opinion, Peckover was also of the opinion that he looked good and smelled good, having bathed and scented himself and changed into the maroon three-piece which he had bought at Selfridge's: or to be exact, which he had bought but Miriam had chosen, since she preferred that he did not enter men's outfitters on his own. Plus tie, of course, tweedy but remorselessly tasteful, a tie being only seemly for evenings at the Château Rip-Off. Tieless, would he have been bounced out into the night?

He continued to wonder at and revel in his presence in France. Perhaps it was the preliminary pastis, perhaps the degraded foreigner behind the bar, but he had not the least sensation of being in Scotland. This was in spite of every endeavour by the management and its interior designers. Top of the bill in the Loch Lomond Bar was a stuffed stag with branched antlers.

Peckover had at first considered the dead beast an unsuitable ornament for a bar, obscuring his view of about one-third of the dim room, unless he leaned sideways. The stag stood on a platform of polished mahogany with a pole like a shooting-stick rising from the platform to the creature's belly as support, or to prevent it from lying down. Now he found himself more tolerant, even with sympathy for the brute, compelled as it was to suffer the presence, day in day out, of the villainous barman. The curtains were tartan, the wallpaper sported a heathery motif. Heather or parsley. Or fleece, might it be? Tufts of Highland sheep fleece caught on the spikey corners of burns and braes? Fleece—to fleece, verb, transitive, meaning to strip, plunder—was after all the motive behind the motif, the music, and every conceivable aspect of this mountain fort.

The hushed gush from hidden orifices he identified as *Annie Laurie*, rendered like goose fat by a thousand violins. He approved of, on the other hand, the blown-up colour photograph of a lake with a steamer and gloomy mauve mountains which covered most of one wall. Loch Lomond, he assumed. He had to lean sideways to see past the stag's backside. The weather over Loch Lomond looked unpromising. He wouldn't much have cared to have been aboard the steamer either, which had an air of immobility, of having been marooned there for weeks, engine kaput, radio operator, skipper and crew blotto from the stocks of Scotch. But he liked big pictures.

He looked down at his table and the card thereon which listed Loch Lomond Bar Cocktails, none of them having anything to do with Loch Lomond. With his ballpoint he crossed out Gin Sling. Gin Fiddle, he wrote in its place. He was making fair progress renaming the cocktails with titles more appropriate to their prices. Already he had a Gyp, a Chiseller, a Rum Ramp, a Swindle Swizzle, an Extortioner, a Twister, and a Bloodsucker.

He looked up. No change in the clientele. At the only other occupied table, three food inspectors, or Common Market administrators on expense accounts, passing through, discussing exchange rates. At the near end of the bar, a svelte young couple with nothing to say to each other. At the far end, the gent with the trimmed beard but no moustache, still reading *Le Monde*. Peckover could see it was *Le Monde* from its tabloid size and unrelievedly grey picturelessness. The gent could go on reading those dense rainswept pages for the next twenty-four hours.

Peckover drew a line through Harvey Wallbanger and inserted Harvey Hornswoggle. When he looked up the bar customers numbered still the same.

No, they didn't.

Yes, they did. The woman who had arrived was not a customer. If she were, she was slumming on her own doorstep. To be precise, in her own doorway, where she stood blonde and sleeveless, peering into the bar. Was she working? 'Off and on, up front, in the restaurant, when my husband's away,' she had told him that morning, betwixt loom and drum kit, clutching her bathrobe to her throat to hide the love-bites.

All right, tonight she was on. Up front. Except she was not up front, she was in the Loch Lomond Bar, or about to be. Looking for himself perhaps to admit her error. Yes, sorry, she had seen Mr Ziegler, in Paris, a few months ago, totally by chance. It had slipped her memory.

Had she spotted him? He was on the point of lifting an arm, rising, hailing her, because at this remote end of the bar, still and umbrageous beyond the stuffed stag, he was not stage centre. She had done peering and was advancing into the bar. If she came over to him and mentioned Ziegler he was going to have to telephone an addendum to the report he had only just sent, dammit.

If she did not mention Ziegler, would that be more significant than mentioning him, or merely a sign of continuing amnesia?

Significant of what?

He could forget it anyway. She was not coming over to him. She was aiming towards the far end of the bar.

The gent with *Le Monde* must have had a sixth sense. His back was to her, and though tall, Mercy McCluskey was not elephantine, her tread across the carpet was muffled, and in any case had to compete with *Coming Through the Rye*, now hogging the sound waves. But he slid from his bar stool and turned with an expression of rejoicing. The buss they gave each other on their cheeks might have been comic, he being a head shorter than she, but Peckover did not find it particularly so. The gent beckoned to the barman, whereupon Mrs McCluskey signalled that this was a false alarm. The barman approached anyway, requiring to be in on anything there might be to be in on, especially anything involving Madame. She shook her head, she was not thirsty, she required nothing. Her friend's glass remained for ever unreplenished, half filled with a red liquid which may have been the Bloodsucker. The barman held his ground on the other side of the counter, looking the other way, smiling the weasel smile, doing things with glasses, and straining to hear what would enable him to blackmail Madame for every sou she was worth, and her capitalist Scotchman husband too, and fetch up owning the château. They turned their backs on him, which brought them approximately profile-on to Peckover, but too distantly in the gloaming for him to lip-read in spite of the practice he had been having. Now he rested his hand on her bare upper arm, which made lip-reading superfluous anyway, because she did not recoil, and in Peckover's view such gestures were not given or received if the topic were farm prices. Their conversation touched on the subject of policemen, however, for both were turning their heads and looking in his direction, then looking away again.

The encounter had lasted some thirty seconds when the gent was hoisting himself back on to his bar stool and she was walking towards the couple at the near end of the bar. The barman watched the separation in dismay, head flicking from him to her and back again like a Wimbledon spectator.

After a smiling word with the svelte couple, Mrs McCluskey walked diagonally through the bar, past the stag, to the three Common Market administrators. If she had remembered to bring menus now she would have been offering them, Peckover thought. Her hostess chat and smile won return smiles from two administrators and a scowl from the third whose punch-line to an anecdote she had killed.

Now, smilingly, she was taxiing towards himself, mouth opening to say, 'Hi, having a nice time?' He stood up.

'Hoots,' he said.

'Hunh?'

'Hello. Have a drink. Love your bar.'

He stepped round the table and slid out a chair for her. If he were going to be given a buss, now was her chance.

No buss. The vaccination mark high on her upper arm reminded him of a pressed, colourless flower.

'What'll you 'ave?' he said.

'Sorry. Got to get back. Your table's ready. Would you

like the menu or will you go straight in?'

'I insist. Two minutes.'

'Is it what you were asking about this morning?'

'What was I asking about?'

'Hope you had a good day anyway, not working non-stop.'

'We could meet back here for a *digestif*. That what they're called? One of those sticky, primary-coloured jobs.'

'Did you meet anyone? Get everything you wanted?'

'Told you, I'm on my hols.'

She was fishing. He tried to keep his eyes off the vaccination mark, which he feared he was about to find moving, being too intimate and private a thing, worn since infancy.

His present beer would be his last, no question.

'Ever know anyone named Spence?'

'No,' she said.

Too quick, Peckover thought. She's lying again. Spence was not such an uncommon name. You'd have needed to think before being certain you had never known a Spence. Spence was not like Spelunker or Knightley-Cadwallader.

'I'm seeing his widow tomorrow. Mrs Spence. In Lourdes.' He fondled an earlobe, frowning and remembering. 'Eighteen, Rue Jacques Brel. He was a singer, did you know? You need a dictionary of national biography to get the best out of France. Tell me, will I do it in a day, there and back—Lourdes?'

'You might. How far is it? Reception will tell you. If you like I can—'

'When did you say you finish?'

'Late. I shall really have to get away. Your wife is truly exceptional in the kitchen, Mr Peckover. We're distressed about her voice.'

'Could be worse. Not as if she were an opera singer.

You're going back to your flat then?'

'Yes. If you'd care for another beer, on the house? I'll have the menu brought to you. I can recommend the *cabillaud* — that's cod. I think. Your wife has baked it in cream.'

'Your friend at the bar, the beaver, p'raps we might share a table? If you'd introduce us?'

'He's not eating.'

'Hurt his arm, has he?'

'What?'

'Got 'is arm bandaged. There's a bandage poking out under his cuff. Or there was.'

Though he had turned his head, and Mercy McCluskey too, to observe the gent with *Le Monde*, the Bloodsucker, and the bandage poking from under his cuff, he had gone.

'What was his name?' Peckover asked.

'He's a regular, kind of, he drops by sometimes. Excuse me. Have an enjoyable evening.'

She was already backing, and now she swivelled and with gathering speed retreated out of the bar. Peckover carried his beer to the counter. The barman ignored him.

'Jack,' Peckover said, 'Pedro?'

No response.

'You, cock. Hey!'

'Monsieur?'

'Good evening. *Encore une bière, s'il vous plaît.*'

'Hng?'

'Don't try that. 'Ow many languages do you 'ave? Six? Sixteen? Either buy yourself a drink or keep the change.' Though it went against the grain, Peckover slid a fifty-franc note towards the barman. The change would just about buy the barman one beer: or anywhere else a crate of it. 'The bloke who just left, what was his name?'

Pedro poured Heineken.

'Smith, p'raps?' Peckover wondered.

'Not know.'

'You know. You know mine too. D'you know Inspector Pommard?'

'Pommard?'

'Mate of mine. In Mordan. A mate of his is the geezer who calls to inspect your measures, check the stock, see 'ow much water you've sloshed into the whisky. *Comprendo?* That bloke who was sitting there. Name?'

'Fontanille.'

'Pierre?'

'Jean-Luc.'

'What's he do with 'imself for a living?'

'*Professeur.*'

'In Mordan?'

'*Si.*'

'He's not staying here?'

'Not know.'

'Is he or isn't he?'

'*Non.*'

'What sort of car's 'e got?'

'Hng?'

'You 'eard. Car. Toot-toot.'

'Simca GLS.'

'Pink?'

'White.'

'White for chastity. *Si.* See—easy, wasn't it? Didn't know how well-informed you were till you tried, did you?'

The barman retired in a sulk towards the less threatening reaches where Jean-Luc Fontanille had read his newspaper. Peckover gulped the beer and trod fast out of the Loch Lomond Bar. At a crossroads in the passage he hesitated, looking to left and right, restraining himself from calling out, 'Coo-e-e-e, Jean-Luc, where are you?'

If he were going to have a word with the prof, better at once than when the effects of the last fizzy beer had taken hold, which would be any moment now. Or after the next

fizzy beer or next of similar. After all, Saturday night,
dinner to come, tomorrow the lie-in, and the Yard
picking up the bill, God bless the British taxpayer.

He was less certain how far any of this was his or the
Yard's business, or whether Portland or Paris were going
to be excited. But she had lied about dead Ziegler. She
may have lied about dead Spence, trading-post for the
Basques and the IRA, possibly. Jean-Luc, wherever he
had got to, was not dead, not anyway up to a couple of
minutes ago, but he was bandaged. About him, Mercy
McCluskey had carefully given away nothing.

If she had chosen to say anything about Jean-Luc, that
probably would have been a lie too, given the consistency
of her batting record.

And if he, Boozy Buggins, Bard of the Yard, being
wiser after the event, had suspected that the night was far
from being over, that before it was over, everything would
be over for ever for one denizen of the Château de
Mordan, he would have taken only black coffee, if that,
from this point on.

CHAPTER 4

Peckover found the Gents in the passage off the passage
from the Loch Lomond Bar. He pushed open the door.

Monsieur Fontanille, bandaged prof with a white
Simca GLS, was not there. Not even an attendant in a
turban and curled shoes was there. There was, as if in
compensation, a gleam of glass and marble, piped music,
and exaggerated smells of sandalwood, cedarwood and
sweet white wine.

Apart from the woman with the gold-filled mouth
behind the reception desk no one was in the foyer either.
Where, even in recession-time, did everyone go, Saturday

night at the poshest hotel for fifty miles?

Peckover wasted no time with the receptionist. Unlike barmen and hall porters, receptionists never knew anything. They had no incentive to know, not being at the receiving end of tips.

No one outside. 'I'm counting twenty then I'll call "Coming",' Peckover announced, descending the feudal steps.

The night was crisp. He walked an exemplarily straight line along the drive. This sweep of driveway and the flaking limestone of the château were gaudy with flood-lighting. Beyond the floodlights and azaleas, to either side of the drive, the woods were dark, as if curtained off by a stage director. Peckover breathed in the scented night. Ahead, in the half-light of the parking area, stood a meagre row of cars.

Eight or nine. Miriam's château car was the one crookedly parked, taking up two spaces. Having long ago decided she was useless at parking, she deliberately, in her husband's view, parked crookedly. He peered in at a window. On all seating except the driver's seat there had accumulated bits and pieces: her shoes, her knitted helmet, new blue unfamiliar knitting, a towel — wherefore a towel? — a box file, an unexplained kettle, and dammit her book, which later in bed she was going to complain she could not find so what had he done with it? Mechanically, a policeman in spite of abroad and alcohol, Peckover tried the doors. To his surprise they were locked. Being surprised, he felt guilty. He walked along the row of cars observing a big flashy number, probably Pedro's, bought out of the profits of watered whisky; then a battered black Mercedes bearing a Château de Mordan sticker; next, and here Peckover paused, a white car with metal letters identifying it as a Simca GLS.

The Simca was impeccably parked, its interior swept

and orderly, but with stickers like a plague obliterating most of the rear window: stickers supporting wild life, careful drivers, various seaside resorts, bicycling, Mordan Rugby Football Club, Mordan Youth Club, and stickers damning hunting, pesticides, nuclear weapons, and war. If he held an opinion of the professor, now it would have slipped, blinding his window with all this paper. Assuming this was his car.

He might have been a family man, of course, as adulterers were inclined to be, and the paper the work of his children.

Peckover tried the doors. Locked. He walked round the car. Tyres in reasonable shape, licence plates and tax dockets in place. Nothing a London bobby would have taken exception to. He looked over the wall of the parking area at France by night. He congratulated the stars and wondered if the clump of yonder low-down lights, below eye-level, might be Mordan. He had mislaid his bump of direction.

Ah, the smells though! Pines? Mushrooms? Whatever they were, they were authentic.

He sat on the wall, took out his notebook and a ball-point and tried to find the words, scratching in and scratching out. The chief problem was the gloom which made it impossible to see what he was writing. *Marriages of Inconvenience, 1,* he thought he would call it. Number one because there were so many different ways in which a marriage could be inconvenient he might fill the note-book before he was finished.

> Yes, I'm incredible, just how
> I get things wrong, and at my touch
> Even a good old family row
> Does not amount to much.
>
> The other day I made a pass
> At a colleague's cousin's wife

But scarpered when she bared her arse.
One more turning of the knife.

My own wife's given up. That's best,
When hubbie makes botch after botch;
But if she upped and skipped the nest
Ten to one I'd hit the Scotch.

Dying's to come. O fateful cup!
O boon! O everlasting night!
A thousand ways to cock death up.
I'm hoping hard to get that right.

That last bit was as gloomy as the light in the château
car park. Wasn't true either, or not entirely true. Still,
best not show it to Miriam, no sense looking for trouble.
Rhyme was the real problem, diverting him from what he
had intended to say, shoving him off course, like fat
women in a bus queue. There were blokes who eschewed
rhyme but he was not one of them and neither, he
defiantly informed the stars, had been Shakespeare. Not
the Shakespeare of the ditties.

Cuckoo, cuckoo! O, word of fear,
Unpleasing to a married ear!

How much, Peckover wondered, did the married ear of
Mr Cuckoo McCluskey hear of the goings-on of Mrs
McCluskey? Presumably he did not care or she would not
have had her own flat in town. Or he might care but there
was nothing he could do about it. Maybe he had his own
goings-on. Peckover strained to hear the cuckoo's call
from the woods. In vain. What he believed he had in fact
heard had been a soft crunchy sound which might have
been a footstep. What he had seen was a movement in the
dark wood beyond the floodlighting.

Lovers? This was the country of lovers. The occasional murder. With mutilation.

Peckover held his breath, listening and watching.

A poacher perhaps, poaching mushrooms.

Nothing.

Bloody DTs, mate, you want to get a hold of yourself, Detective Chief Inspector Peckover advised himself, sliding from the wall and starting back along the drive.

In the restaurant he looked without success for his hostess. Gawd, quarter to ten! If he were the last to eat, keeping the staff on their feet, and Miriam, who had been slaving all evening, all day, over a hot stove . . .

> Fear no more the heat o' the stove,
> Nor the maître d's neuroses . . .

A man in a morning suit led him to a table. A sinewy young bullfighter in a red waistcoat and with greased flat black hair, a sprig, definitely an apprentice bullfighter, presented a menu.

> Thou hast stirred in bay and clove,
> Basted well and prayed to Moses . . .

A piano was playing. Scattered customers were still eating or finishing eating: except for one couple dancing on a patch of parquet beside the piano.

> Gourmets, gourmands, piggies, must
> At some point leave the trough, or bust.

'I'll 'ave the 'ouse wine, a jug of it, and let's see,' Peckover said, opening the menu, fearful of delay. 'To start, snails. D'you have snails?'

'*Les escargots?*' said the bullfighter, bending at the waist to point truly and cleanly at the fine *escargots au vin*

rouge with a finger gored at many a true and fine corrida.
'One snails. *Après?*'

'Chips.' Tell the chef I love her, Peckover considered
adding but decided against it. Every kind of complication
might arise, beginning at the moment the message
reached the wrong chef. 'Wine, no starters, and a nice
plate of snails and chips, okay?'

He did not want snails, he merely wanted to get them
over, because you could not decently spend a long weekend in France without a few snails, never mind you could
get them any day of the week at the fancier dinettes in
Islington. He waited for the red waistcoat and lacquered
hair to perform truly and bravely a couple of veronicas,
but the lad being dead on his feet all he did was gather
the menu and hobble away towards the kitchen. Grease
under pressure.

Peckover dipped his fingers into the fingerbowl,
swashed them about, and trapped a rose petal. Mercy
McCluskey had come into the Loch Lomond Bar to speak
to Jean-Luc Fontanille, for no other reason. Her excuse
for not dallying with himself had been her meeting and
greeting duties elsewhere, which was reasonable. So why
had she not meeted and greeted him?

The pianist pressed on down Memory Lane, sidling
crab-like out of *Deep Purple* and into, with an intro-
ductory hip-wiggle on the piano stool, Peckover did not
doubt, *Begin the Beguine.* Peckover was unable to see the
pianist for pillars but he pictured a man with a wig and
make-up who once had played for the bouillon-drinkers
aboard the *Mauretania.* Or a woman with a chin too
many who once had performed for café society, who had
loved Hutch, or Carroll Gibbons, or their Parisian
equivalents, and filled in for them when they had had
'flu.'

Anyway, there she was, his hostess, beyond pillars, by
the door. Peckover half stood, arm aloft, and held the

position until finally she looked his way.

The wine arrived first. Not a jug but a bottle with a menacing label. Perhaps the house wine, perhaps the last bottle of its kind in France, dug from the deepest recesses of the cellar. The waiter poured a driblet.

Snails arrived with tongs, a spike, and a dish of raw carrot, cucumber, cauliflower, pepper and tomato.

Mrs McCluskey arrived not at all. Having seen him, she had gone again. Out of the restaurant.

Peckover plied spike and tongs. Perhaps, having considered, she had concluded he was no threat, not being one of the local boys in blue, but an interloper, a foreigner of no consequence, whose writ did not run in Mordan, and who could be talked to or not, as she chose. Of course she was right, in a way.

The first snail came out of the shell a treat. Hard to tell it was a snail through all the breadcrumbs. Tasted all right. Garlicky.

The wine, fine. Piano, fine. Dancing couple the hit of the evening, him in his Lyceum Ballroom grey, she in midnight blue, quick-stepping the night away. Between them they must have totted up a hundred and twenty years.

Shouldn't there have been bread?

Second snail, okay. Not much to them, snails. He might already be going off snails. The third snail tasted a little tired. Perhaps it had been jogging.

Peckover lofted an arm, and when his bullfighter arrived, said, 'Bread, please. And I'd like a word with Mrs McCluskey. About finances, tell her.'

If finances did not bring her, nothing would. True, this was not a restaurant where the owner's wife sat by the door like the OGPU, seeing all from behind a desk with a cash register, counting her banknotes, tits resting on the desk. But most people had two obsessions, money being the other one, and he did not see why this Yankee châtelaine should be immune.

The bread, when brought, was brown, stale, and sliced to the thickness of communion wafers. Other customers' bread was straightforward succulent country bread. The level in the bottle had dropped alarmingly. Evaporation, that was the snag to these vintage wines. The snails and raw veg having been polished off, a piece of cod arrived, possibly baked but not in cream or in anything. Peckover lifted the fish with a fork, looking for the folded note which would say, 'That's your lot.' He did not know how she would know he felt the night was young, that he had this urge to lead the remaining customers in a sing-song, but she knew. She would be cross and apprehensive that he might be embarrassing.

No note, though. No chips either and there were not going to be any. Miriam's foot was down. He pointed pointedly at the empty bottle and clinked it with a spoon for good measure. He lowered his head towards the fish, examining it for signs of wheatgerm.

There were signs of something. Perhaps it had been on the floor. With Miriam in the mood he suspected she might be in, could be mouse poison.

'Everything all right?' said Mrs McCluskey.

'Not really.' He rose, then sat. 'It's Miriam. She sent this note saying, "My French peasant soup is made from the finest French peasants, with whom you may sleep tonight, for I have aided and abedded you long enough. Yours sincerely, Miriam." What it is, it's the wine on the breath and the snoring. Can you blame her?'

'Sorry?'

Wine arrived. Mercy McCluskey was smiling professionally. The smile lacked joy. Well, tough, thought Peckover. If she lacked joy because of conscience she could try sitting down and talking about it. She could talk about the cod or even about Ziegler.

'If everything's okay, then,' she said. 'Maybe I'll see you

before you go.'

'Go where?'

'Well, leave. Isn't your reservation for three days?'

'How about the bar in fifteen minutes? A nightcap.'

'I don't know. It's the weekend. There's stocktaking.'

'This time of night? I'll be there. Meanwhile, a favour. Would you take this to the chef?' Peckover poured wine into his second glass. 'Congratulations, tell 'er, on the cuisine, apart from the chips. From an admirer.'

Mercy McCluskey took the glass and departed. I wouldn't have volunteered information about Rick Ziegler either, Peckover ruminated. He speared cod. Rick Ziegler did not exist, never had. How could anyone believe in anyone named Rick Ziegler.

Rick Ziegler knew that the redhead fished out the East River was Lola Pianola, Ace Darrow's moll, because the slug in her heart of gold had been put there by Coco Delmonico, who had fingered Clint "Curry Puff" Alcatraz the day the Battery Boys raided the Bink Bank and Schultz "Born-Again" Scholtz had counted out one thousand gee for his night of romance with Patty Bunratty, companion to Zizi Uffizi, the airline hostess . . .

'Salade, monsieur?' suggested the bullfighter.

'Any chance of seeing your upside-down pudding, the orange-flower-water cream . . . the trolley?'

In sorrow the bullfighter shook his head.

'Thought as much. Cheese? Spot of Camembert? The one that's supposed to smell like the feet of God.'

'*C'est possible.* I ask.' He hobbled away.

Peckover stood with care. He skirted the patch of dancefloor upon which the couple were backing and advancing. 'Jealousy . . .' he heard the pair singing with soft intensity as he passed. He had never mastered the tango. The only Latin capering he had ever managed was the conga. More his meat in long-ago adolescence at the Hammersmith Palais and the Bethnal Green Labour

Club's New Year's hop had been the last waltz, so crucial to the evening and to the heart. Last waltzes, veletas, gentlemen's excuse-me's, military two-steps, spot dances, the palais glide.

' 'Ow about *Underneath the Arches*?' he told the pianist.

'Hng?'

'Doesn't 'ave to be, but if you could finish with the tangos. Tangos, no good. Tangos, *pfffft*. No reflection on your playing, monsieur. No, no. Very artistic. 'Ow about a slowish quickstep?'

This character had never heard of the *Mauretania*. He was post-war. He was practically post-Vietnam. In the epoch of Hutch, the Mitfords, Evelyn Waugh, Thomas Beecham, the storm clouds gathering, this berk never would have been allowed through the doors into the Savoy. From the same class as himself, Peckover would have bet. One of the plebs, except this one was sneery with it. Too much curly black hair, the five o'clock Latin shadow nurtured to display virility.

Thing was, he probably was virile, he'd have women waiting in line, probably only had to flash his teeth, strum an arpeggio, and they were his. Gall was all.

Militarily upright, swaying not so much as a centimetre, yet nonchalant withal, Peckover stepped round the piano and on to the parquet.

'Madam? Sir? *Pardonnez-moi*. Might I be permitted the pleasure?'

The bloke in grey blinked and beamed. The lady looked from the intruder to her man and back to the intruder. The big fellow in the maroon three-piece asking for a dance would be a modest memory, Peckover guessed, so why not? 'Course, if he tripped, toppled on top of her, the two hundred pounds of him, that would be a more enduring memory.

'Son, you have chosen the loveliest lady in the land,' the man said.

Peckover did not sweep off the loveliest lady in the land in a dazzle of dancing pumps and swirl of crinoline as Tyrone Power did to Maureen O'Hara in—was it?—*The Sea Witch*. Neither did he clasp her closely and put his cheek against hers. They stepped decorously, Peckover hoped, although concentrating on his feet without watching them, and simultaneously trying to take in what his partner was saying, took no small effort. He held his head at an angle so that his breath, richly fermenting, would steam past her right ear and over her shoulder, well away from her nostrils.

'We're Martha and Arthur Rickett . . . such a wonderful trip . . . five days at this beautiful château . . . so restful after Paris . . . you're from England?'

'Yes, madam.'

Quick-quick-slow. Wait. Was it slow-slow-slow? What the devil was the pianist playing? Peckover glimpsed Arthur seated at a table, waving to them. When he discovered he was searching the restaurant for a sight of Mercy McCluskey, he admonished himself. Smack botty. One thing at a time.

Quick-slow-quick-quick?

They circled the parquet. At what point might he decently hand Martha back to Arthur? She had probably had enough and they never could continue indefinitely without calamity. Cornering was the dicey part as it always had been. At least she was a dancer. Feathery. Kept her feet out of the way.

If he fell he would release her instantly and try to keel over either sideways or backwards. Afterwards he could explain that he had a war wound which often took him unaware, shattering his equilibrium.

'. . . sidewalk cafés with all those young people at three in the afternoon . . . couldn't figure it, can you? . . .

unemployment . . . Mr Reagan . . . wonderful job . . .'

'Oh yes. Yes.'

A gallant hand on her arm, agreeing and bowing, Peckover conducted Martha back to Arthur.

'Sir, ma'am . . .'

'Son . . .'

Peckover tracked out of the restaurant. Fifteen minutes at least since he had told Mrs McCluskey, 'Fifteen minutes.'

She was not in the Loch Lomond Bar. Only the svelte couple and Pedro were there. After half an hour the svelte couple left. Peckover ordered another Armagnac. Same as Cognac far as his palate could tell but the equivalent of one, not two months' salary, this make anyway. Not that he was paying.

He was not going to go looking for her. Probably she was on her way back to Mordan. He was no longer sure he even wanted to question her again.

She had more or less denied knowing two men. What it came to. Possibly she had not known Spence but her denial had come very smartly and he saw no reason why he should believe her. What Ziegler and Spence had in common was that she had denied them and they were dead.

Had she denied them while they were alive or had she known them, in the Biblical sense, and what if she had? If Jean-Luc were to become dead would she deny having known him?

She had done so already, pretty well. 'He's a regular, kind of, he drops by sometimes.' The description lacked the smack of intimacy.

If Jean-Luc were the jealous kind and had been around for some time, which was to say around Mercy, and she had been seeing Spence, and Ziegler, he might have removed them, or had them removed. How much did a professor of English earn and what was the going rate for a hit man in this corner of France?

Highly unlikely. He'd have had to have been painfully, possessively jealous, Jean-Luc. Had another rival for Madame's favours cut up his arm with window-glass or was that an accident due to too ferocious shutting or opening the window?

Final question: What had any of this to do with him? Answer: Nothing really. He was the temporary English-language interviewer in these parts, and while he thought of it, how about another of these Armagnacs?

Half past eleven. He would not have minded a dance with Miriam but he knew better than to seek her out and ask. Miriam was *contre* fermenting breath. In any case, the pianist would have packed it in by now.

'What car does Mrs McCluskey drive?' he asked.

'Citroën Diane, grey,' said Pedro. He had thawed somewhat. 'Sometimes black Mercedes if Diane *foutue* — busted.'

Peckover left the bar, and the hotel, and weaved in good heart along the drive. Finding himself kneeling among azaleas, he assumed he had weaved off the drive. The ground was soily and dewy and his nose was in an azalea.

'My good man, pull yourself together,' he told the azalea.

Crunch, sounded twigs and leafmould somewhere in the dark.

On all fours Peckover listened to the silence. The noise, he eventually decided, had been one of nature's insoluble noises: a woodland mole, a nightjar — wasn't there a bird named a nightjar? He levered himself to his feet. In his absence the parking area had been moved.

He sought the car park on the drive and among the pines. When he emerged from the trees and came upon the cars he knew they were the same cars as before because there aslant stood Miriam's château car.

There too Jean-Luc's Simca; also a Diane which might well have been Mrs McCluskey's, and a Mercedes. By now, close on midnight, surely the pair should have been moving on, either separately or together.

'*Vive l'amour*,' Peckover said, looking up at the floodlit castle walls. Some windows were shuttered, some not. Even as he looked a light came on in one high window.

Perish the thought that Mrs M herself had had a finger in the demise of two boy-friends, if boy-friends they had been. All the same, thought Peckover, he might have worried had he been Jean-Luc.

CHAPTER 5

Long live love was not for the moment a sentiment with a hold on Miriam's heart. She stood in front of the bath-room mirror with her mouth open, striving to see her throat. Past midnight, probably coming up to one o'clock, and where was Henry.

When he drank too much he was so stupid, he snored, he smelled. Disgusting.

Not violent though, she realized with a jolt, astonished that after so many years here was a phenomenon she had never given thought to. His non-violence when boozed she had always taken for granted. Yet half the violence he had to cope with as a policeman arose from drunkenness. More than half to hear Henry tell it.

Curious, because sober he could be violent. Not with her of course. She'd like to see him try! But twice at least, provoked by ne'er-do-wells he had particularly not cared for, he had gone over the top and got himself into trouble. When he broke that gangster's arm, Willie some-body, and was demoted from sergeant to constable, the family income had dropped with a bump.

Standing in her nightie in front of the mirror in the terrifying bathroom, peering into the reflection of her open mouth to see if she could see what catarrhal laryngitis looked like, and seeing nothing untoward, Miriam wondered if in his occasional cups a little painless violence might not be preferable to soppiness and silliness.

The Rob Roy Room's bathroom was mostly mirrors. What was not mirrors was streaky, granity stuff, purplish and black, including the sunken bath which was also streamlined, as if about to rev up and go somewhere. Did it sink into the rooms below, creating a streamlined bulge in the ceiling? Probably not. The floors in a fort like this, walls too, must have been five feet thick.

She was unable to make up her mind whether the bathroom, and even more the bedroom, was exquisite or vulgar. Whichever they were, they missed being the other by a whisker.

She went into the bedroom, which Henry referred to as 'Versailles', and hunted again through drawers and possessions, and under and in the canopied, curtained four-poster bed. Henry merry and missing was the least of it. She was worn out, unable to speak, and now had lost not only her voice but her Boswell, a virgin volume eleven of his journals left by an archæologist in the dining-room and unclaimed for two months. If she had lost it and the owner came looking for it, would she own up? Some was slow going but by and large it was smashing.

Funny though, Henry's reaction to the bit about self-castration she had read to him in bed last night: the German jeweller with the unrequited love for his landlady. In the end the jeweller had told her, 'You bitch, you shall have it one way or the other,' and cut it off and thrown it at her. Henry had hardly reacted at all, just a grimace and a thoughtful look. Obviously not a yarn to tickle the male ego.

Bookless and frustrated, Miriam climbed with maga-

zines into the four-poster, being careful first to remove
the foil-wrapped chocolate mint placed dead centre of
the pillow by the chambermaid after turning back the
cover, and assuring herself that she did not care where
Henry was so long as he stayed there and did not come to
bed. But he would come to bed. He always did. When she
was fast asleep he would arrive singing, turning the light
on, then off, bumping into things in the dark, and
shushing himself with the stifled agony of a pressure
cooker so as not to wake her. Amazed to find that she was
awake, he would ask solicitously why she was not asleep,
sit on the edge of the bed, and tell her about his evening.
Then he would make a great clatter in the bathroom,
dropping the toothpaste and singing. Then he would get
into bed and announce, 'I demand my marital rights
though I'm not saying they have to be this minute.' He
would open his book, close it, turn on his left side, and go
to sleep with the light on, leaving her to switch it off.

Miriam giggled. She started to read the ingredients for
Caribbean callaloo soup, progressing as far as 'one pound
of callaloo leaves available at Caribbean markets', which
was not very far, before switching off the light and falling
instantly asleep. Whether the light went on after ten
minutes or an hour or longer she could not have said, but
it dazzled. Henry was tiptoeing towards her across the
carpet carrying a bunch of azaleas and halting, smiling
uncertainly, when she opened her eyes. His hands were
dirty, the knees of his trousers were smudged and damp.

'Can't you sleep?' he whispered.

Miriam pulled the blankets over her head. After what
seemed a long enough delay for him to have snipped the
stems, stripped away the lower leaves, and arranged the
flowers in vases, she felt her shoulder persistently tapped,
anxious not to awaken her. When she did not awake a
hand drew the covers back from her head.

'I brought you these,' he whispered. A soily drip

dropped from the flowers on to her cheek and lay there like a beauty-spot. 'Begonias.'

Miriam sat up and mouthed voicelessly.

'They're fresh,' Peckover said. 'Do I put them in water? Don't say anything. You must save your voice. Nod once.'

She did not nod but neither did she remain monumentally still. While her mouth worked, telling him something, she leaned far sideways, and yet further sideways, away from the gusts of vinous breath.

'Can't 'ear a word,' he said.

He walked round the bed, through pile carpet towards the bathroom, singing, 'I loff Paree in ze zpringti-i-ime . . .' When there came a rush of air and a fluttering sound, and a magazine hit the carpet near his feet, he turned and watched her again telling him something. His lip-reading prowess having advanced of late, he decoded a message to the following effect: 'Stop singing that horrible song! You've been singing it all horrible day!'

Poor love, she's collapsed, it's the long hours, she'll be all right, Peckover thought. He said, 'That's not my entire French repertoire. Don't think I'm limited. 'Ow about this?' He drew breath, then began to bray: a jarring, vibrating sound on roughly one note.

'*No-o-óng, riang de riang, no-o-ong, je ne regrette ria-a-ang . . .*'

Braying and vibrating, he pivoted and disappeared into the bathroom, whence sounded a bang and a cry.

'Aaaagh! Fallen in the bath!'

Peckover's grinning head appeared round the bathroom door. 'Gave you a fright, dinnit? I 'aven't really.' The grin slipped. 'Probably will though. They ought to 'ave railings round it. Red lamps. It's like a bleedin' building site in 'ere.'

She was not laughing. Normally she might have. He was not discouraged.

' 'Old on a minute. Got something for you. Don't go away.'

He loped from the Rob Roy Room, closing the door behind him, and leaving the light on.

This time Miriam did not fall instantly asleep. Assuming he would be back any minute, half an hour at most, there seemed little point trying. She turned the light out to discourage him when he did come back. Some hope.

Apart from awaiting his return, she smouldered with too steady a heat to sleep. How dare he! Keeping her awake all night with his schoolboy antics, and which of them was slaving all day? She was tempted to find a sofa in a lounge to sleep on, or even the car, but he would find her and wake her up again. In any case why should she? He was the one should be sleeping in the car.

The one move she must on no account make was to turn the key in the door and lock him out. He would start by tapping as softly as an elf. When there was no response he would gather steam and soon be rapping like a bailiff, calling to her probably in his boozy French and awakening the whole château.

Apart from all that, Miriam failed to sleep because of noises which were faint, unextraordinary, hotel-by-night noises, interspersed with silences, but sufficient to keep her listening, awaiting the next noise. Doors closing along the passage. Doors opening. Voices. Padding feet. Half the château seemed to be awake even without rapping and singing from Henry.

Yet she was on the rim of sleep, perhaps had slept, when she heard the door open and felt light on her eyelids: not dazzling light but a diffused milkiness as if from an advance party of glow-worms. As she turned her head towards the door, the thought occurred that her visitor did not necessarily have to be Henry.

After opening her eyes, Miriam opened her mouth to

scream. She might have done so had she had a voice to
scream with. A shapeless silhouette of God knew what
filled the doorway. Light percolated from the corridor.

Martians, Blobs, Things from the Deep, all such super-
natural horrors had never exercised Miriam's imagination, not anyway since the common nightmares of
childhood. But here was an apparition so shocking in its
suddenness that she believed she would have been unable
to scream even had she had a voice. In those instants, the
closest she came to forming an idea of what it was she
gazed at, if it existed, if this were not her first nightmare
since childhood, was of a black, dead, phantom Henry on
horseback.

Henry had never been on a horse in his life. Was it a
horse? It was more mule-sized and with jagged horns. Her
eyes coping better with the half-dark, Miriam saw that
part of the shape was moving.

'It's a stag party!' called the shape. 'Watch. We've got
wheels! 'Ere we come!'

The moving parts were his knees, which bent as he dug
his toes into the carpet. His legs straightened, and the
shape, increasingly three-dimensional, launched into the
room, moving briskly for two or three metres but equally
abruptly coming to a stop, bogged down in shagpile.

'Sod. It's like bicycling across the Sahara.' He was
wearing his hat but no jacket. 'We're on wheels, did you
know? Wheels or castors. Watch. Gee up, Rudolph!'

He pushed with his feet. Beast and rider ploughed
through the carpet. Another double-footed thrust kept
up the momentum. Miriam, unamused, sat upright in
the four-poster, her knees raised beneath the covers,
thumping them with her fists. Rudolph, travelling well,
struck his nose against the south-east bedpost. The bed
shuddered, the rider jolted forward, an antler tilted his
hat.

'Whoa, boy!'

Miriam failed to utter a cry of fury but she threw the bedcovers aside.

'It's tomorrow's menu, save you a trip to the market,' Peckover said. 'Venison *farci*.'

Miriam stormed round the end of the bed. Unable to voice her opinion, she started thumping Peckover. His hat fell off. He dismounted on Rudolph's further side, out of range. His folded jacket which had served as a saddle slid to the floor. Miriam, in pursuit, thumped Rudolph's rump.

'Whoa, girl! Cruelty to animals!' Peckover backed, out-stretched arms warding off her tiny blows. 'Moose-n't be cruel to dumb animals. Comprenny? Moose-n't — wait, no, not that!'

At the second attempt, Miriam succeeded in goal-kicking his fallen hat high and far. They watched it soar across the Rob Roy Room. In the doorway, looking in, stood a petite, pretty woman in a filmy peignoir with lace at the neck and shoulders. Her eyes were wide, her mouth slightly open, and she carried a fat, rolled-up eiderdown as if in search of a place to bed down. The room and its inhabitants on which she gazed did not appeal. Observed, she scurried away, leaving the doorway empty.

Miriam seemed unnecessarily upset. All his lip-reading achieved was, improbably, 'Housekeeper.'

'Housekeeper? What about it?'

Miriam ran and slammed the door.

'Can't see,' Peckover said, groping in search of lights and walking into Miriam.

She flailed at him. Retreating, protesting, gasping, laughing, Peckover backed into a door, found a handle, and made an exit. Someone had turned the lights out and left behind a smell of soap and cologne. He was in the bathroom.

He turned on the light, then the bathtaps. Now, Peckover reluctantly supposed, was probably bedtime.

Just when he was enjoying himself.

Odd creatures, women. You never could tell whether they were going to see a joke or not. Water gushed into the streamlined, sunken bath. After watching and considering for some minutes he experimentally pressed a lever. The plug plunged into place.

He soaped and sang, but softly. Once she had told him he had a nice singing voice. A light baritone, had she said? *Bel canto? Largo al factotum rallentando?* She must have said it during an affectionate phase. Not like tonight.

'Girls were made to loff and kee-e-ees,' Peckover sang with bravura, soaping and giggling.

He had brought her begonias too. And Rudolph. Hurt, he pouted into the face flannel. Ah well.

Towelled, pinkly steaming, bare-bottomed, mouth aglow with viridian Close-Up, or Très-Près as this version insisted on having it, he felt his way through cossetting shagpile, round Rudolph—'G'night, boy'—and up and into the four-poster. Miriam turned away.

'Gawd, what's that?' Peckover turned on the bedside light. He groped beneath him. 'Bugger. Sat on my mint.'

He drew forth and held to his eyes a flattened disc of foil out of which had squelched, was squelching still, chololate and white mint filling. Stickiness was on his fingers and under him. A glistening white glob decorated with a brown flake fell into the hair on his chest.

He was wondering what he was expected to do about all this, whether for a start he was going to need a second bath, when someone screamed in the passage.

CHAPTER 6

Whether the scream sounded outside their room, in which case it was half-hearted, or further along the passage, or in a different passage altogether, or on a stair or in a remote room, in which case it must have been full-throated for them to have heard it at all, neither Peckover nor Miriam could have said.

Neither would either have sworn under oath that scream was the word. Cry they might have accepted. A protracted yelp? A squeal? But high-pitched and there-fore, unless falsetto, probably female.

Peckover and Miriam, sitting up, looked at each other, and towards the door. They were aware that while they sat and looked, time was wasting. No built-in policeman's trigger mechanism impelled Peckover like a bullet out of bed. Damn, damn, damn, he brooded. Had he been a quantity surveyor or an archivist on holiday from the British Museum he might fairly reasonably have stayed where he was. No one would have thought much the worse of him.

He lost a further five seconds putting on one of the bathroom's pair of bathrobes: a too-small, satiny garment with the château's logo of inverted ice-cream cones on the back. He felt like a professional wrestler. He was tempted to rinse chocolate mint from his hand which would have lost five more seconds. He hastened through the bedroom and into the passage.

The passage was dimly-lit and deserted. Not a sound. Anyone sleeping, as most guests presumably were, might well have slept through the scream. Equally, they might have been archivists or similar and good luck to them.

Peckover was reasonably sure the scream had been to

his left, northwards, roughly. The more he considered, the stronger his impression that what he had heard had been full-blooded and distant rather than half-hearted and to hand; though it might have been nearby if muffled by—what? Cupboard doors? A mattress? As he set off along the corridor the next door along opened and an elderly white head in a hairnet appeared. On seeing him bearing down, the eyes closed tightly, the head withdrew, the door shut. As Peckover passed, the door was alive with metallic sliding of bolts and turning of keys.

On the landing he hesitated. The passage continued on the far side of the landing. The lift in which he had ridden with Rudolph was in the passage which led off at a right-angle. Here were stairs up and down. On the hand-rail of the polished banister he observed an unacceptable cerise smear of paint. There were tubs of flowers, pedestals bearing busts of Romans or Scotsmen, a chandelier, and the Ricketts, if he remembered the name rightly, standing in night attire in the doorway of the Gleneagles Suite.

'Hi,' Mr Rickett said.

'Hullo there,' said Mrs Rickett. The bodice of Peckover's dancing partner's nightgown was cut startlingly low. 'You heard it?'

'An owl.' Peckover bestowed a reassuring smile. 'One of the Mordan owls. The rutting season, you know?'

'Rutting season?'

'Fledglings. Throstlings. Please, back to bed. Everything's all right.'

He trod barefoot across the landing and into the passage opposite: past a door which said Burns as if awaiting casualties from a fire, but too tardily to pass the next door before it opened to reveal, above striped pyjamas buttoned to the neck, a bald head and blinking eyes. On the nose were purplish pinch-marks of spectacles but no spectacles.

'*Qu'est-ce que c'est, alors?*'

'We think it's owls. *Hiboux.*' Peckover was delighted with *hiboux*, recollected from fourth-form French as one of a handful of words taking 'x' in the plural along with *bijou, genou,* probably *frou-frou,* and others he had forgotten. 'Back to bed, sir, please. *Au lit. Dormez.* Everything *ça va.*'

'Everything *ça va* okay along there?' Mr Rickett called. He stood in the mouth of the passage holding the hand of Mrs Rickett.

The other way, deeper along the passage, Peckover heard a door open. Jean-Luc with a flustered expression, one hand tying his tie, looked out. He saw Peckover and shut the door.

I'll fluster you, thought Peckover. He reached the door as the bolt slid home. At least the bugger was alive. He knocked.

'Hello? *Allo?* Monsieur?'

Silence. Peckover knocked again. '*Momento, s'il vous plaît.* Monsieur Fontanille? Open up, please.'

More silence.

Isle of Skye, read the plaque on the door.

I'll sky you, I'll kick your arse across the sky if you don't open, Peckover fumed, Who did he, everyone, think he was? He kept up the knocking. If the whole château was not awake already it soon would be. He was aware of white at the far end of the passage. The white was the petite one. Was it? The looker with the lacy peignoir and eiderdown who had watched Miriam's hat-kicking. She had rid herself of the eiderdown but she was too slow if she wanted to be rid of foreign coppers. Though she stepped back round the end of the passage he reached her in five strides.

'Evenin'. Name's Peckover. 'Usband of your cook, Miriam, if that 'elps. Bit of a circus going on here, wouldn't you say? You'll be Madame . . . ?'

'*Comment?*'

'The housekeeper, right? *Gardien de la maison*. Speak English?'

'*Non.*'

'Yes you do, some, 'ousekeeper in a pub like this. There was a scream. *Un cri*. Where? Don't say "*comment?*".'

'A scream. Is possible. Not know where.'

Possibly she did not. She was as white as her peignoir and trembling.

'You all right?'

'All right.'

'Who's in your Isle of Skye Room?'

'Not know.'

'Mrs McCluskey, where does she sleep?'

'Not here. In Mordan.'

'She must stay sometimes. Which is Mr McCluskey's room?'

'He in Hong Kong.'

'I didn't ask that. Where's he sleep when he's here?'

'East wing. Other side château.'

'Here it's all guests, is it?'

'*Oui.*'

' 'Ow many at the moment?'

'Twelve, fifteen. Is early. Season starts next—'

'So you've plenty of spare rooms?'

'*Oui.*'

'What's through there?'

'Staff.'

'Show me.'

'Through there' was a green baize door like an up-ended billiards table, barring further access along the passage.

'*Qu'est-ce qu'il se passe, alors?*'

Peckover turned. He might have tweaked the ear of the bald busybody in pyjamas had it not been for the reinforcements: the Ricketts, the svelte pair from the bar now in svelte dressing-gowns, a woman with a black plait which hung over a bosom and down to her hip like a mamba. About half the guest complement, Peckover judged. Arms spread, he herded the delegation back along the passage, round the corner, and still further back, reliving crowd-control days in the Mall and Trafalgar Square.

'To your rooms, please, ladies and gentlemen. Nothing to see, promise you. Messieurs, mesdames. A little co-operation.'

'*Qu'est-ce qu'il dit?*'

'*Alors . . .*'

'*Qui est-ce, ce type?*'

'We most surely heard . . .'

Over the tops of the guests' heads Peckover glimpsed Jean-Luc scooting across the landing and disappearing down the stairs. He continued herding, advancing, and ignoring questions. With difficulty he refrained from hurrying the bald man backwards by placing a hand on his stripey chest and pushing. At the door to the Isle of Skye Room he reached out and turned the handle.

Locked.

'Goodnight, mesdames, messieurs. *Merci.*'

Peckover hastened back along the passage and round the corner. No housekeeper. He continued on and opened the green baize door.

'Madame?'

She halted, turned, waited.

'You were about to show me,' Peckover said.

'Is nothing.'

She was almost certainly right. If there were something and it was concealed, the chances of his ferreting it out were probably zero. He would have needed a dozen reliables from the flying squad and half the dog section to have turned this warren over. While neither recognizing nor remembering these passages, Peckover believed that it might have been here somewhere, in the staff annexe, that he had spent his first night. He wished he were back in bed. Couple of minutes, he would be.

But you went through the motions. Someone had screamed.

Of course, could have been entirely innocent. Horseplay. Foreplay, Saturday night at the Château de Mordan, springtime, there'd be a fair amount of both. A fellow and his bird getting experimental, exaggerating a bit. Late-night jinks and some character trapping his toe in a light socket.

Yes, yes, quite, or how about, envisaged Peckover, guiding Madame forward, rehearsals for the Mordan Thespians? One of the Greek tragedies. There was a fair amount of screaming in some of the classical stuff.

'No need to introduce me,' he told the housekeeper. 'Just ask 'em what they heard. Where. What they know about it.'

Eight or nine staff had assembled on a landing in a haze of cigarette smoke and a variety of night attire. The only face Peckover recognized was his greased bullfighter from the restaurant wearing boxer shorts and a T-shirt. Peckover nodded and was rewarded with a wide smile. There were no flowers, statuary, or chandeliers. In place of carpet was dung-coloured linoleum; the flaking brown paint on the walls dated from the era of Gilles, Duc de Mordan. Peckover, patient, listened to the interrogation. He had the impression the housekeeper was making little headway with her questions. Among the staff was much honest head-shaking, a degree of nudging.

She told him, yes, they had heard it, but not know where or who, nothing. Certain not here in staff wing. In guest wing.

Peckover was inclined to agree. He doubted whether from the Rob Roy Room he would have heard a scream in this staff annexe. Presumably quite a few staff were not here, he suggested, aware that he should be getting the names of those who were here, just in case, and equally aware he was going to do no such thing.

Madame Costes told him, yes, many staff not here, sleeping maybe, or go Mordan after work. *Les boîtes, discos.* Saturday night.

'Could you find out what that's all about?' he said, nodding in the direction of a group of nudgers and whisperers.

They were mainly girl-staff, one of whose number, subject of the nudging and pushing forward, was a nervous teenager in flowery pyjamas and woolly slippers. Beckoned by Madame Costes, she advanced a reluctant step, then retreated into the refuge of the group. She answered in hushed monosyllables, and quite inadequately in the opinion of her fellows, who began cueing her, then finishing her sentences, then starting them, and finally taking over from her entirely, narrating on her behalf, with or without embellishment, what she had seen. Peckover watched and strained his ears. The word which seemed to keep recurring sounded like *fantôme*, which he would have guessed, had he been challenged, meant phantom.

Madame Costes informed Peckover that what the girl said she had seen was a ghost. She was Sylvie Delpech, a chambermaid who had been availing herself of leftovers in the kitchen when she had heard the scream. Her second unlawful act had been to avail herself of the guest stairs because they were quicker than the staff stairs and at that hour nobody would be about. Apart from ghosts. She had been turning the corner into the passage to the green baize door when she had heard a door close, looked back, and seen it. For an instant only, vanishing round the corner towards the stairs up which she had come. The white flapping, evidently, of a traditional ghost.

'An Arab?' Peckover suggested.

'We have not Arabs,' Madame Costes told him very stiffly.

Peckover looked at Madame more closely. She might have been a Jew. She might, come to that, have been an Arab. If she were a Jew she had every right to be anti-Arab even apart from the price of petrol. And vice-versa. How did one recognize, by looking, an Arab, unless there were a burnous and a falcon, or a Jew unless there were the nose and shaggy beard as in the colour picture of Shylock in his Shakespeare? She was bloody toothsome whatever she was. Had he not been spoken for, he would have raised no objection to sharing her eiderdown.

'Ask her,' he said, 'how long between the screams and when she saw the ghost.'

Madame Costes and Sylvia Delpech parlayed.

'Quick,' the housekeeper told him. 'Few minutes. More quick maybe. Is in fright like shock, *la jeune fille*. She not with us long in Château de Mordan.'

Peckover was unclear whether this meant *la jeune fille* had not been a chambermaid at the Château de Mordan long enough to be precise about times and distances up and down stairs, or if she were about to be sacked for infringing château by-laws, or if she suffered from a mortal ailment and was not long for either the château or the world.

'Grateful,' he told the gathering. '*Merci*. Just thought I'd ask. Why don't we all get some sleep?' He placed his hands together as if for prayer and rested his cheek on them. '*Au revoir*. I'll see you to your room, madam.'

'Is not necessary.'

'I insist.'

Gallant, a half-step behind, he accompanied the housekeeper back along the corridor. She stopped at the last door before the green baize.

'This one?' Peckover asked, opening the door.

He found the light and took a step inside. The room

was not to be compared with the Rob Roy Room, or doubtless with any guest room, but personally he preferred this bachelor-girl bedsit with its bookcases, family photos, lived-in chairs, and spruce kitchenette. Obligatory cushions and a rag doll decorated a divan bed for one. Where, though, the eiderdown she had carried earlier?

Had she been bringing the eiderdown or taking it away? Why patrol the guest corridors with an eiderdown at one o'clock in the morning?

Bloody 'ell, why not? Someone had been cold. Bedding was a housekeeper's job.

'Through there,' he said, nodding towards a door beyond the baby cooker and curtained kitchenette area. 'That the bedroom?'

'Bathroom.'

So the divan was her bed and lately she had not slept in it. Alternatively, hearing the scream, and leaping from between the sheets, she had immediately made the bed.

'I'd be obliged if you'd lend me your keys to the guest rooms. One of 'em. Won't take a tick.'

'You will 'ave to ask—'

'I'm asking you. I'm a policeman, ma'am. Someone screamed. Someone could be suffering. They could be dying.' Come to that, he refrained from adding, you don't look too chirpy yourself. 'Accompany me by all means. You're being of great assistance. Might I 'ave your name?'

'Costes.'

'Mademoiselle?'

'Madame.'

Perhaps a divorced Madame, divorced or separated like everyone else, nowadays even the family-minded French, reflected Peckover, waiting while she went first to a drawer for keys, then through the door into the bathroom: a shivering, diminutive, fetching wraith of a woman.

On telly, cops-and-robbers hours, now we'd hear a bang, Peckover mused, or nothing at all for so long that I'd rush in and there'd she be lying in a lake of blood. He took a fast step through the room. Madame Costes came from the bathroom having changed out of the peignoir into a mainly black kimono with a chrysanthemum motif.

Why? wondered Peckover. 'What's 'appened,' he inquired, holding open the green baize door for her, 'to the eiderdown?'

'Someone is cold.' She headed along the passage. 'Telephoning reception saying so cold, is guest, 'usband wife customers, *chauffage* heating not always work perfect, *c'est normale*. Needing more you say blanket but *l'armoire à linge* is on floor under so I 'ave come up from lift pass your room . . .'

Peckover had stopped listening. She had it all written out in her head. If he had not asked she still would have told him.

'. . . *le cerf* also come up in lift pressing button with nose, yes?'

'What?'

'*Le cerf*. The stag?'

Touché. A sidelong glance showed him a hint of a smug smile. When he looked ahead again along the passage, towards the landing, there in the stairwell looking at him were the head and shoulders of Mercy McCluskey in fur collar and peaked Lenin cap. They disappeared down the stairs.

Peckover was in no mood for chasing Yankee six-footers down stairways. The whole rollick was a nonsense, a bedroom farce, people appearing and disappearing, doors opening and closing. You either fell about or you left after the first act, and personally he intended to leave, first opportunity, which would be tomorrow, daybreak.

Probably the French invented bedroom farce, and there must have been memorable ones, but a little went a long way.

In any event, they had reached the Isle of Skye Room.

'This one,' he told Madame Costes. 'Mrs McCluskey, she usually works this late?'

'Not know.' The housekeeper unlocked and opened the door. She switched on a light.

'Ta.' He sauntered into and around another too exquisite guest room. Only a plashing fountain was lacking. A gamboge telephone echoed topaz, saffron and daffodil shades of walls, carpet and furnishings. The effect was less the Isle of Skye than the Yellow Peril.

He eyed the carpet for dropped hairpins or a bandage but saw none. At an admiral's inspection the tumbled, unmade four-poster would have required someone to have been tied to the yardarm. Damp soap and towels in the bathroom called for a further twenty lashes.

'Fine, thanks, grateful,' he said. 'Good night.'

In the passage outside his and Miriam's room stood Rudolph, dry-nosed, expectant, as if about to suggest, 'Walkies?'

' 'Ello, sweetheart.' Peckover had to roll him backwards before he could open the door.

Semi-supine with a magazine, propped on pillows, Miriam failed to rush to greet him. Instead she gave him a look and pointed, presumably over his shoulder, towards Rudolph. Her fingers made a flicking get-rid-of-it gesture.

'All's well,' he said with a smile. She had wheeled Rudolph out of their Rob Roy Room but she had not, he noticed, picked up his hat. Still, at this hour he was on the side of peace and love. 'All quiet. Touch of fornication 'ere and there. Not everywhere, I'm not saying that. Some of 'em are having midnight feasts. Cocoa and sardines.'

Miriam, deep in her magazine, pretended not to hear. Peckover sighed, shut the door, and with one hand on an antler, the other on what he believed might be a haunch, steered Rudolph along the passage. Finally the Château de Mordan seemed to be sleeping. On the landing at the head of the stairs he paused, reaching out to touch the cerise smear on the banister.

Wet. Smelly. He wiped his fingertips on an adjacent patch of banister. It was going to need a go with turps anyway.

Abandoning Rudolph, he searched the carpet for similar smears but saw none. None outside or on or near the door which had been opened an inch by the little old lady in the hairnet. Opposite, outside the Gleneagles Suite, was similar spotlessness. Peckover tiptoed sprightly from the Gleneagles door before it should be opened by his dancing partner and her spouse, hand in hand declaring, 'Hi.'

He reached the further side of the landing. The Burns Room. Was this where the bald man was lodged? Peckover believed not, the baldy had been in the next room down, though the coming and going had been a mite confused, he would not have cared to have sworn to anything. If not the baldy, who had the Burns Room? A cerise smudge decorated the porcelain door handle.

Peckover put his ear to the door. Nothing. Positioning thumb and forefinger as far as possible where the porcelain was unsmudged, he turned the handle and opened the door.

More nothing. No snores, protests. An outline of the compulsory four-poster and a reek of paint. The light switch was where it ought to have been.

Peckover closed the door behind him and surveyed ladders and a trestle-table piled with buckets, brushes and rolls of wallpaper. Most of the furniture had been piled into a corner and covered with a dustsheet. No dustsheet was in evidence for the four-poster, and no curtains, canopy or bedding either, though on the mattress lay the eiderdown which Madame Costes had carried, or if not the same eiderdown, a similar. The colour-scheme ordained by the interior decorator, so far as could be judged from one partly-papered wall and glimpses of unprotected carpet and furnishings, was rubescent variations on cyclamen, coral, and carbuncle. No paint pots were visible, no flush-blush start on doors or skirting had been made, yet the paint smell was powerful.

The footprint splodges, Peckover observed, led from not to the bathroom. Their gaudiness at the closed bathroom door faded with each step across the dustsheet. Where he stood they no longer existed, which was fortunate for the unprotected carpet in the passage outside. He stepped alongside the prints, listened at the bathroom door, and entered.

Here anyway was the paint: stinking, streaking the granity floor, splashed across mirrored walls. On the floor lay a cerise-sodden towel which may have served for wiping feet on, though not thoroughly if the wiped feet were those which had crossed the dustsheet. Peckover's bare feet stepped with care over and round sploshed paint.

Most of the paint had gone into the sunken bath. At the taps end, on the oily, red-flecked surface of substantial bathwater, floated an empty five-litre paint drum from which, Peckover guessed, the paint had not involuntarily leaked, but deliberately been poured. The paint had sunk like syrup through the water, coating the bottom of the bath from end to end, and the naked body which lay there.

The eyes and mouth were open and paint-filled. On the neck, chest and belly the cerise had mingled with a darker red from stab wounds. Peckover swallowed and stared. At least the bloke's cock was intact, if it mattered. He believed the body was the pianist from the restaurant. Paint was thick over the face.

He walked out of the bathroom, past ladders and the trestle-table, and opened the door into the passage, where he stepped into Madame Costes in her black kimono.

'Good, just comin' to see you,' he said. 'Phone the police, you'll do it better than me. No, sorry—not in there. Your eiderdown's safe, it'll wait.'

'*Qu'est-ce que—?*'

'Just phone, please, and come straight back. The police will ask the questions. Tell 'em we've got a murder. Quick!'

Hercule bleedin' Poirot, where are you? Peckover, sentinel in the passage outside the Burns Room, saw what remained of the night reaching ahead in whorls of tobacco smoke, end-to-end coffee-cups, and questions and statements in gibberish French.

Tomorrow too, except he was not going to be here tomorrow. He had his instructions. There were gun-runners' widows to be talked to. His own statement would take fifteen minutes. Well, thirty.

'Stuff you, mate,' he told Rudolph, watching him from beside the stairs.

He had never felt more sober.

CHAPTER 7

Susan Spence, widow, being weary and in a vile temper, having twenty-four hours earlier and five hundred miles away been sorrowfully told by her lover that they were incompatible, or to put it another way, though he had not, being diplomatic and cowardly, that she was

ditched, cried out when the doorbell rang, 'Piss off, whoever you are!'

Whoever it was, it was no one she wanted to see. She
had no friends in this dump nor wanted any. Couple of
days, soon as she had sorted out the packing and the
removals men, she was going to be able to lift two fingers
and never see the place again.

If the ringing was not sneery, unintelligible house-
hunters who would spend the next hour poking in cup-
boards, prodding the walls, probably it was the house
agent come to tell her again that for a quick sale she
should drop the price twenty thousand.

She walked across the landing to the oriel window and
looked down on jungle contained by a redbrick wall and a
fancy white gate fashioned with knobs and curlicues.
Beyond the wall, leafy, blossom-bright Rue Jacques Brel
was filling up with the cars of chemists, lawyers and
accountants returning home after a hard day's lunching
and counting their money. God, the garden was a mess!
The big question was, would it pay to have a gardener to
hack and trim? Would there be garden-lovers among the
house-hunters who would write a cheque on the spot if the
garden looked like Kew?

Charlie would have known. He might have been wrong
but he'd have known. One thing about herself she had
discovered, a woman on her own, was that she had never
cared whether decisions were right or wrong so long as
Charlie had taken them. Some decisions anyway. The
boring ones. If he decided right, fine. If wrong, too bad,
at least she hadn't been to blame.

Below, besieged by pampas grass and nettles, the big
fellow in the beret was having another bash at the doorbell. Persistent. Susan Spence blew cigarette smoke from
the corner of her mouth, away from the glass. He was not
the house agent, though he might have been a prospective
buyer. He might have been a gardener who thought he

had found himself work. She dropped her cigarette into a vase, one of a clustered dozen awaiting crating, recrossed the landing, and in the bathroom mirror gave herself a once-over. To hell with it, she thought. She trod downstairs and opened the door.

'Mrs Spence?'

'That's right.'

'Name's Peckover. Scotland Yard. Won't keep you a tick, ma'am. Purely a formality. May I come in?'

She almost succeeded in not grimacing. She stood back while he came in, looking about him at the crates and piled junk, taking off the beret which, she would not have been surprised, probably still had the price inside. She led the way into a sitting-room in disarray, motioned him towards a tan leather armchair, seated herself in a second such, crossed her trousered legs, and lit a cigarette.

A hard case, possibly, Peckover thought, tightening his jaws against a yawn. She intends making me work. Where, he wondered, was the lavender and lace? She was all right on looks: on the tough side but stunning bones and body. She was also nicotine-fingered and had wrecked the curve of her left tit by stuffing the cigarette packet into her shirt pocket. Her eyes were watery and jaded as if she had been up all night studying calculus.

We're all jaded, darling, you're not the only one been up all night, Peckover was inclined to inform her. Including rewrites, his statement for Inspector Pommard, with copies in triplicate to the Commissioner of Police of the Metropolis, New Scotland Yard, had in the end taken him the best part of three hours. The stag had been tricky, wording the riding of a stuffed stag along château corridors at one in the morning so that nothing could have seemed more natural. Conjecture had occupied a two-page addendum. The person or persons of whom he had been aware while taking the air outside the château, for example, might have been the pianist's murderer, or murderers, engaging in surveillance, watching bedroom lights going on, or off. The ghost sighted by Mlle Delpech might have been the murderer in a dustsheet worn either to conceal his, or her, identity, or paint stains, or as a protection against paint stains.

He had also added as conjecture that Madame Costes might have been having it off, or had been so intending, with the deceased. This conjecture he had expunged as conjecture and inserted in the body of the statement when in the chilly small hours Madame Costes had admitted this was the case to Inspector Pommard.

He had escaped at dawn, surprising Pommard by his departure, leaving him muttering and refusing to believe either in the usefulness of the Lourdes expedition or that the irresponsible, stag-fixated husband of the château's cook would be back tomorrow or ever. The muttering would doubtless have been even more vehement had the thought probably not come to him that, with the husband gone, there might be opportunities for waylaying the cook and pinning her against a wall. The best Pommard had managed in revenge for being deserted by the non-help from perfidious Albion was to fail to come up with the loan of a car.

So, in a rented car with a radio on which he had succeeded in tuning out the foreign claptrap and tuning in, albeit with atmospherics, to the good sense of the BBC, he had arrived: travel-stained, yawning in spite of three hours' sleep along a farm track unvisited since the epoch of Pepin the Fat, and cheerful.

Murder he did not find cheerful. He could not have said he was immune, hardened; that murder was his stock-in-trade. In more than twenty years a copper, murder had seldom come his way. But he had managed to keep passably detached, and when, in spite of his refusal to look, a stabbed cerise pianist had slotted in front of his eyes like a perverse joke in a lantern slide

lecture, he had looked, accepting it, and eventually it had
gone away.

But the compensations! The sun had shone. Driving on
the right had been easy-peasy. The countryside, true, had
been a mite flat, the outskirts of the small towns a little
dreary with their concrete bungalows and petrol stations,
but none the less it had been France and a knockout. And
lunch . . . ah, the lunch.

For months he would be able to bore anyone in hearing
with details of the little undiscovered country restaurant
where he had eaten seven courses for thirty-five bloomin'
francs. Four quid, call it, including the tip. Forty quid it
would have cost in Islington, if you could have got it,
which you couldn't. Not that there had been what you
would call elegance. It was the sort of caff you would
never find if you were looking for it, a dingy house
decorated with a dingier scrap of bunting between petrol
stations, scruffy without, fly-infested within: flies, paper
tablecloths, smells, darkness, lorry-drivers mopping their
plates with bread, others playing cards, a silent waitress
aged nine, and through a door a glimpse of flying chicken
feathers and a whiskery woman aged ninety. He had gone
for the cheapest of the three set menus without studying it
beyond an unsuccessful search for chips. No matter, a
snack had been all that was required for a long-distance
copper en route for English-language chat with a gun-
runner's widow.

The soup had been tepid, filled with soggy bread, and
so tasty that he had eaten his way through most of the
contents of the tureen. A mistake but how was he to have
known? The hiatus before the main course he had filled
by testing several glasses of the plonk, but instead of the
main course there had arrived a platter of cold sliced
sausage, ham, pâté, blood pudding, butter, more bread,
and beetroot, tomatoes and radishes which should have
been the main course but wasn't. The main course was an

aromatic beef stew with a bowl of sloppy haricot beans cooked in duck fat, he judged, and hopping with garlic cloves, enough for four dockers, which had left him panting, unbuttoning buttons, and mightily relieved when he had swallowed the last mouthful because if you were paying for it you did your best to eat it. Then appeared main course number two: half a roast chicken and sufficient crunchy, salted chips to have fed the dockers' wives and children.

He had supposed there had been an error, that somewhere sat a customer waiting, starving; but the nine-year-old who should have been either giggling or vomiting never batted an eye. Salad, cheeses, apple tart . . . Queasy with the memory, Peckover regarded the crate beside his armchair. Framed pictures half filled it but they were stacked upright, preventing him from seeing whether they were Rembrandts or charging elephants. The absence of pale rectangles on the walls indicated they had not hung there long whatever they were. The Widow Spence got up, gathered an ashtray, and sat with it.

Silent Suzy, there's steel in her, or experience, or, thought Peckover, perhaps she simply has a clear conscience and doesn't like visitors. Coppers did not panic her, obviously, and she had resolved that this one made the running. Should he mention Ziegler? If she knew nothing, no. Play it by ear.

He said, 'You're moving out?'

'I'm not bleedin' moving in.'

'So where are you off? The Bahamas?'

'That your idea of somewhere exotic? You haven't seen much. I've been in Nassau.'

'Brighton then?'

'This what you're here for? Guessin' games?'

Peckover was not wholly clear why he was here. Veal, the Yard, they had thought it a good idea.

One, there was what Charlie Spence had in common

with the American, Ziegler, apart from having been stabbed to death. What, more exactly, they had lost in common.

Two, both victims might have been known to Mrs McCluskey. She had known Ziegler. She might have known Spence.

' 'Ow long have you lived here, ma'am?'

'Too long.'

'If you could be more precise.'

'Last June, nearly a year. Off and on.'

'Skipping out when you could?'

'Dead right. Mind my asking what's the point of all this? I had questions for ever after Charlie was killed. Questions, questions. You've had it all. Cross-indexed.'

'Was he queer?'

'What?'

'Did we have that?'

'You mean a poofter?'

'Was he?'

'You rubbishy copper!'

'What've I said?'

'Swannin' in here! Suggestions! I'd like to have seen you ask Charlie that. He'd have done you over, big as you are. Here, mind if I see your warrant card?'

Peckover brought out his wallet. He reached forward, presenting the blue card, keeping hold of it.

'Detective chief bleedin' inspector,' Susan Spence said, blowing smoke at the card. 'I've news for you, copper. I know a superintendent with your lot. Johnny Davis. Okay? He was a chum of Charlie's.'

'When were you last inside?'

'Eh?'

'Holloway, was it? Expect you knew the warden too, Carmichael, or was that before your time? Aiding and abetting, my guess. Taking care of Charlie's tearaway mates in your back bedroom.'

'What're you talking about?'

'Took care of 'em a treat, I bet. How often you change the sheets?'

'Pig!'

'On the game, were you?'

'Shut your hole!' She was on her feet. 'Get out!'

'Get out,' mimicked Peckover, not moving. 'You're from down my way, right? Poplar?'

'Out!'

'Know the Duke of Devonshire in Thornley Street?'

' 'Course I do. What of it? Bleedin' slum, they ought to tear the place down. You'd know it. Just your style.'

'Horse and Groom'll be more your style.'

'What's wrong with the Horse and Groom?'

'Toffs.'

'What're you on about, toffs?'

'Bookies, hairdressers. East End toffs.'

'More flamin' class than your Duke of Devonshire.'

'Nice pint of Whitbread at the Duke of Devonshire. Horse and Groom's all lager and fizz and cabaret night.'

'What I said. Meet your friends.'

'Get your hair permed while you listen to the reggae.'

'All you get at the Duke of Devonshire's a dose.'

'You can get that from the telephone, did you know?'

'Get it at the Duke of Devonshire soon as you go in. Only pub in London you catch the clap just by breathin'.'

'No problem. There's the clinic in the Commercial Road, round the corner.'

'Go there often, do you?'

'Used to. Mondays nine o'clock for the check-up. I'm in Islington now. Gentrified, my bit of it. Different class of clap.'

He was grinning at her. Suddenly she smiled. Equally abruptly she glared.

'You said some nasty things. They're not true.'

'Didn't mean 'em, dear. You got very excited by a

question about Charlie. It was only a question. Anyway, you've probably answered it.'

'Good. It was a stupid question.'

'From a stupid copper?'

'I never said that.'

'I never knew your 'usband. I'm not a psychiatrist either. But speaking out of long inexperience I'd have thought what was done to him might've been, just possibly, sort of an act of sadism by a feller. Not inconceivable. I wouldn't have thought it something a woman would do.'

'Shows how much you know about women.'

'You don't mean that. I mean, you're right, I don't. But you're not saying a woman might do it?'

'Hell, how do I know? Look, I've been asked all this—well, not that. But what are you anyway, a fresh mind?'

'Buttercup-fresh, love. Fresher than your friend, Johnny Davis. You're right, he outranks me, but then we're not on the same floor. Know what he's in?'

'I don't know anything. He was Charlie's friend.'

'Dogs.'

'What dogs?'

'Dog section. He shares out the Bow-Wow Bikkies. Sees their ears are clean.'

Susan Spence giggled. 'That's Charlie. Typical. Just the sort of high-powered contact he'd have. Me, I'm having a gin. Want one?'

'Wouldn't say no to a cup of tea. Philanderer, was he? Sorry, love—don't scratch my eyes out.'

She did not. Whatever philanderer meant, she said, if it meant putting your hand up every skirt in sight, that was Charlie, and any copper on the case who didn't know it must have just arrived from the moon. In the kitchen she put on the kettle, poured gin and lime, and swore when every ice-tray proved empty. Peckover sat at a table manipulating his beret: folding it, rolling it up.

'Didn't it bother you, Charlie's shenanigans?'

' 'Course it bleedin' bothered me. Tell you, I scratched his eyes out a thousand times. But what do you do? See, Charlie had magnetism. They all fell for him. Charlie made you laugh. The bastard.' She stood by the sink, forgotten gin and lime in her hand, looking through the window at back jungle. 'He wasn't witty or anything. He never said anything you'd remember. It wasn't making faces either, falling about on banana skins. It was kind of how he said things. He was just bleedin' funny.'

Peckover, allowing her time to remember, watched her remembering and swallowing gin.

'Funny,' she said, 'but he'd have made people laugh even about what was done to 'im. I know he would. I've thought about it.'

'Can't be much consolation to you but at least it doesn't 'appen every day, to others, what was done to Charlie. After he was dead.'

'No.'

'Ever heard of someone named Ziegler? Rick Ziegler?'

'Don't think so. There was a singer, Ziegler, wasn't there? A woman. My Mum had her records.'

'Left you all right, did he, Charlie—financially?'

'You're joking. He didn't leave a penny. This house is it. The lot.'

'Where did it go?'

'Where does it ever go? Gear, grub, this and that.' She filled a teapot. 'We travelled, mind. Always first class, champagne and stuff. Nothing but the best for Charlie. I've been on Concorde.'

Bully for you, Peckover thought, and for all the birds Charlie was forever making laugh, who had probably cost him a quid, because if there was something some ladies might be more susceptible to than laughing their heads off it could be laughing their heads off over a bottle of

Krug while the big, side-splitting spender tucked a sparkly gewgaw from Asprey's down their stocking-top.

He let it go. 'Still, in his business, you'd have thought he'd have put by a sovereign or two.'

'A travel agent? Don't make me laugh. He wasn't bleedin' Thomas Cook.'

'I was thinking of the guns.'

'What guns?' she said, too quickly, too astonished.

'We know what he was doing, love. Question is, is what was done to him the IRA's latest line in some spooky, sick sort of symbolism?'

For all Peckover knew, that might be the question, being unlikely enough.

'Start of a new glamorous tradition,' he went on, 'like knee-capping and tarring and feathering, you know?'

'No, I bleedin' don't know. You're off your nut.'

'No milk or sugar, love. Ta. You're not suggesting it was the Basques?'

'What Basques? I wouldn't know a Basque from my backside.'

'Because your 'usband was running guns for both the Basques and the IRA. The Lourdes connection, you might say. It's happened before, using the pilgrims as a cover. You'll not remember but there was a charter plane for pilgrims from Cork to Lourdes and back, only it was intercepted. Stuffed with Czech guns. Summer, 'seventy-two—'

' 'Seventy-one. Charlie was hardly out of school so you're not sticking him with that one. Wasn't Cork either, it was Dublin.' Confused, she poured more gin. 'I dunno. Dunno anything. Must have read about it.'

Peckover let that go too. No reason why the Widow Spence should not have been deeply political. She might have scrapbooks on the Irish question. Others on Cambodia, Latin-America.

'How long have you known Mercy McCluskey?'

'Who?'

'Come on, love. The woman's angle. It sometimes helps. What's your impression of 'er?'

'Dim. I don't know who you're talking about.'

'Really. Here's something I'd say you genuinely don't know. Ready? I consider I'm being very patient.'

'What d'yer think I'm being? Told yer—'

'When were you last at the Château de Mordan?'

'Spell it.'

He spelled it.

'Charlie stayed there a few times, if it's the same place. On business.'

'We know. He didn't take you with him?'

'If you knew Charlie stayed there you should know I never did. Right? Never mind.' She was sipping with gathering momentum. 'Look, I wasn't enraptured about Charlie's birds but I wasn't one for cramping his style either. What good would it have done me?' Sip, swallow. 'All right, he took me once. I suppose you could check that if you wanted. Can't see what it's got to do with anything. Plenty of times he'd say, "Come along, gorgeous," and I'd say no, because Charlie needed his freedom. I knew that better than he did. Paris, Majorca, Gibraltar. "You go on your own," I'd tell him. And he always came back.' Sip, sip. Except the last time, she thought. 'Business conferences, he called them. Mind, I'm not saying there wasn't business too.'

'Travel agency business?'

'Straight up, he didn't talk to me about business and I didn't ask. He was a very professional working man. Compartalized, everything in boxes. Compartmentalized.'

He sounds it, Peckover thought, and said, 'Why Mordan? It's not particularly handy for Lourdes?'

'Fancy though, innit? Got class.'

'That what counted?'

'That's what counted. If it had the stars and crossed

cutlery and someone who spoke English, it was for
Charlie.'

'Mercy McCluskey speaks English. She's the owner's
wife. Still saying you never heard of her?'

'Never said I hadn't heard of her, though I hadn't, not
till now. Said I didn't know her.' The Widow Spence,
replenishing her glass from the Gordon's, giggled. 'Name
like that, IRA is she? Ho, Begorrah! Does your mother
come from Oireland?'

'Her mother's American and McCluskey's Scottish.'
Peckover supposed it was Scottish. 'Older than you,
fortyish, blonde, six feet tall. Taller. A Yank.'

'Miriam.'

'Who?'

'Can't be that many six-foot blonde Yanks in Lourdes.
She had on this grey gabardine jacket, red cords,
smashin' necklace. Ivory. Couldn't stop fiddling with it.
She was in a fair old state, my opinion. Edgy. Said she was
Miriam Burns, or Barns. Didn't catch it. She wanted to
know if I knew Mercy McCluskey.'

Peckover thought he might not say no to a gin after all,
if pressed. Mercy McCluskey looking for Mercy
McCluskey but calling herself Miriam. Cheeky baggage.
He blew on his tea and said, 'When?'

'Hour or two ago. Four o'clock. I hadn't hardly got in.
Open house here today, I can tell you.'

'You told her you didn't know Mercy McCluskey?'

'First I'd heard of her. Who is bleedin' Mercy
McCluskey anyway? This Yankee woman, Miriam, or
whoever she is, she seemed to think I should know her.
When I didn't she lost interest. Chewed her necklace and
said goodbye.'

'What else did she say? Before saying goodbye.'

'That's all. She sat where you're sitting. Said she was a
friend of Mercy McCluskey, hadn't seen her for years, but
she'd met Charlie at that château place, and they found

they both knew her, knew Mercy McCluskey, and she was sincerely grieved to hear about Charlie passing on but perhaps did I know had he left behind any clue to where she might find her friend Mercy McCluskey, him being a friend? A likely bleedin' story.'

'You told her you didn't believe her?'

'I should of, p'raps. No point though. Like I said, she lost interest and went.'

'Why'd she lose interest?'

' 'Cause I didn't know bleedin' Mercy McCluskey. Obvious.'

'What kind of clue about her did this woman think Charlie might have left behind? Scent on a silk hand-kerchief? A lock of hair? Letters tied in blue? She say?'

'She said he might have had her phone number or an address or an old photo.'

'And did he?'

'No.'

'You looked?'

' 'Course I looked. We both did. Best way to get rid of her. I brought his address book. You coppers went through it a hundred times.'

'No Mercy McCluskey?'

'Want to see it?'

'That was the point she lost interest, was it?'

'You're good. You should be on quiz programmes.'

'And no old photos, letters?'

'Wouldn't think so. Charlie wasn't one for souvenirs and he never wrote a letter in his life. Nobody wrote to Charlie either. There were some snaps and picture-postcards somewhere. "Wish you were here." Truth is, I haven't hardly looked. Charlie's stuff. I kept out of it when the coppers were here, told them to help themselves. Suppose I'll have to go through it now, packing. Oh God.'

Peckover put down his cup. He started to rise. He

thought she was about to cry out or start weeping. She did neither, but exhaled breathily, almost a moan, and tossed her cigarette-end into the sink. When she spoke again her tone was determinedly bright.

'Any case, I wasn't scrabblin' about in Charlie's things for her, Yankee slag, no better 'n she should be, my opinion.'

'Why d'you say that?'

'One of Charlie's tarts. Obvious. Wetting her knickers in case her husband or boy-friend finds out. Wanted to get her hands on anything that might tie her in with Charlie and flush it round the S-bend.'

'Think so? She waited long enough. Four months.' Alternatively, if what had spurred her had been a stabbed pianist coming on top of stabbed Ziegler she had waited barely five minutes. He watched the easy efficiency with which a widow lit up her fortieth cigarette. 'Still, you'll scrabble round for me, dear, won't you? Quick peek at the postcards perhaps, then I'll be off.'

'Dunno I'll ever find them.'

'I'm supposed to be trained. Did he have a study?'

'Study? That's a laugh.' *Glug* went the gin bottle. 'Mother's bleedin' ruin. Fat lot of packin' I'll get done tonight. C'mon then.'

Twirling the beret on his forefinger, blinking in the slipstream of cigarette smoke, Peckover followed the Widow Spence out of the kitchen, between crates in the hall, and up the stairs. At liberty at last to yawn, he did so capaciously. Ahead, moving with less than alacrity, the widow held her glass in one hand, the banister with the other. Peckover averted his eyes from the eye-level bum, tight-trousered and mobile. Balls, he decided, and defying Puritanism observed with enjoyment. They reached the landing and the bum descended to knee-level or thereabouts. In a corner were piled shoes, some with buckles, most high-heeled. What about Charlie's shoes?

In a bedroom with a musty smell, grandiose bed, and bathroom en suite, Susan Spence opened the drawer of a dresser, and said, 'Socks. That's a comb he found on the pavement in Jermyn Street. Couldn't resist a free gift, Charlie, for all his spending. Yours if you want it. Big deal. And the shirts. What's your collar size? You could wear them open neck. I haven't hardly been in here since — since it happened. Know what I mean?'

At her shoulder, Peckover burped, put the beret to his lips, and murmured, 'Pardon.'

'Charming,' said the widow. She was rummaging among trays of male jewellery: cufflinks, rings, a gold chain and crucifix. 'Pooh! What've you been eating?'

Peckover backed. The bedroom which, widowed, she had fled, was luxurious and probably vulgar, though on the latter count he would have preferred the opinion of Miriam. Miriam-Miriam the only Miriam, not counterfeit McCluskey-Miriam, though she too had taste, he recalled, seeing in his mind's eye a restored fireplace, woven green curtains, a loom, and unwanted drum kit. Here on each side of the bed stood a veneered console, his and hers, as if in a stateroom on an ocean liner, with buttons for room service and added power for the stabilizers. The flock wallpaper was unadorned by flying china geese, or a turquoise oriental girl from Boots, or even gilt-edged Picassos, but there were fitted, flock-wall-papered wardrobes, a reproduction cabinet with silver knobs, and everywhere considerable shine and velvety purple stuff. The lampshades had fringes and there was concealed lighting which you could spot if you looked hard enough, though Peckover would have bet that with all the lights on there would not have been enough light to read by. In an alcove in the wall opposite the bed, aimed at the bed, was the colour television and video-scope.

'You could have had that cheap except it's a selling-point,' said the Widow Spence. 'We never watched, not the telly, it's all in bleedin' French. Charlie had his own tapes.'

Peckover was able to imagine. He slid wardrobe doors open and surveyed a hanging score of suits, jackets, blazers, tailored fatigues.

'Make me an offer,' Susan Spence said, arriving at the wardrobe. 'I'm not givin' them to Oxfam.'

On the floor were three or four pairs of shoes. Peckover wondered whether that might not have been a mark of class, or rather lack of it: twenty suits and loss of interest when you reached your feet. He stowed his beret into his pocket and started dipping into Charlie's pockets.

'Smart of you,' the woman said, dipping. 'The coppers did say they'd try to keep everything as it was. Only it was winter. Either the tweed or the cashmere.'

It was the cashmere, from an inside pocket of which she drew out an assortment of papers and a packet of Peter Stuyvesant. 'Have that for starters,' she said, and passed Peckover the return, first-class portion of a Lourdes-Paris train ticket, which he did not want.

The next gem she handed him was a brochure for the new Peugeot, which he did not want even more. Susan Spence hesitated, speculating on a picture-postcard, turning it over.

'Just like Blackpool Tower, innit? From Janice, whoever she is. "Six goals to our side, Big Boy." Bleedin' slag. Here, take it.'

She was already looking at the next postcard, an ethereal, chiffony bridechild on a bed with one leg up, examining her toenails, very arty and fond of herself. As far as Peckover could see, there were only two postcards. Little else remained. Some photos.

' "From D"—D for dirt cheap,' said the Widow Spence, and gave the chiffony girl to the policeman. 'No letters, see? His Visa card, I'll hang on to that.' She slid the Visa card back into the cashmere, finished her gin in a gulp, and regarded a colour photograph. 'His nibs himself by flashbulb in some nightclub, very sweaty, don't ask me who the company is. Here, it's yours. Passport photo of more company—hey!'

'What?' Peckover regarded a passport photograph of Mercy McCluskey, startled and wild-eyed enough to have given any immigration officer pause.

'That's her!'

'Who?'

'Miriam Thing. The one who was here.'

'Honest?' He took the photograph. 'The police see all this?'

'See it? They carted it off, kept it for months. Weeks anyway. Some of it came back in plastic bags.'

'I'll give you a receipt.'

'I don't want a receipt. Here, have the lot.' What remained was a football pools coupon which she thrust at him. 'Something you could do, though.'

Peckover waited to hear what he could do. He waited so long while she gazed in the direction of her husband's suits, seeing probably nothing, that he thought she had changed her mind, there was nothing he could do after all. Finally she said, 'Can't stand this room,' swung round, and stalked out.

Unsteadily she descended the stairs, Peckover in her wake. From a bureau in the living-room she produced the Motorist's Diary.

'I haven't said a thing,' she said. 'Fair enough?'

'Fair enough.'

'His name's Becker. He was a business mate of Charlie's. That's his address.'

'Travel agent, is he?'

'Those are his addresses too, there. But that's the one he's at. Andorra. From today.'

'I don't know, love. Obliged, but quite honestly I 'adn't

thought of going to Andorra.'

'Suit yourself. Thought you'd got that woman on your mind. You wouldn't be the first. If you did have, Andorra's where you might find her, not that I'd know. Becker was the one Charlie used to meet at the château.'

'And the one time you were there you met Becker too.'

'Who said I did? Mind your own beeswax.'

'So what you're saying is Mercy McCluskey might have served 'em both, Charlie and this Becker geezer. With the Scotch eggs and champers. That it?'

'Told you, I'm saying nothing.'

'Sensible girl.' Peckover brought out his notebook and peered at the page in the Motorist's Diary. 'No phone number for Andorra?'

'Maybe he was cut off, couldn't pay his bills.'

'Maybe he's all alone on a mountain top. Villa Azul. What's that mean? Villa up in the Blue?'

'Wouldn't be surprised. What language is it?'

'You've never been there?'

'Never bleedin' will now either.'

'When she left here, Mercy, or Miriam, she say where she was going?'

'No. Asked if I knew a reasonable hotel. I told her the Impérial, four stars, first that came into my head. If she gets a room over the road she'll be able to listen to the traffic all night.' Susan Spence fumbled so cack-handedly with her cigarette packet that the cigarette she produced had broken in two. 'Off to hold her hand, are you?'

'Not particularly.' He pocketed the notebook, unfurled the beret. 'Take care, love.'

'You could stay here if you want. I've got some lamb chops in the freezer.'

'Thanks all the same.'

He was relieved to hear himself say it. She had drunk too much, whether he stayed or left she was pretty certainly going to be doing some weeping, and if he stayed he could see himself packing her crates for her. None of which was the point, because he liked her and was tempted. But he did not trust her and the game was not worth, etcetera. One day six months hence over gin and giggles in the Horse and Groom she would entertain the company with the tale of her little happening in Lourdes with a Chief Inspector Peckover from Scotland Yard. Though it would not be the Horse and Groom. On the proceeds from this pad she would buy something Tudor in Weybridge or Sunningdale. For a year. Then, bored dizzy, back to the East End.

'Piss off then,' said the Widow Spence.

Suzy the Floosie, she thought, crumbling the cigarette, watching his nod and smile, his gesture with the beret, then the big back retreating past crates and into the hall.

Oh, Charlie.

With or without the wedding-ring she would have taken him back, done it all again. Why couldn't they have had more time? Waste, waste. No one knew like Charlie how to please a woman. So he knew how to please a thousand women, so all right. She did not care.

'Get that snotrag Becker!' she shouted.

In the moments of silence which followed, she thought: He's coming back, the copper, he's going to stay. But she heard the front door close, then continuing silence.

'Oh, Charlie,' she sobbed. 'Oh, Charlie.'

CHAPTER 8

'Cock? Mr Veal, sir? That you?'

'Henry?'

'*C'est moi. Bonjour.* Sunshine here, matey. Bet that's more than you've got.'

'Before you go any further, we're up to our eyes.'

'Ho, liverish this morning, are we? Phoned you last night but there was no one except a duty sergeant. Is he new?'

'Who?'

'Sounded like an Indian — a Red Indian. His French was rubbish. You'd have been at Evensong, I expect.'

'Henry —'

'It's Evensong morning, noon and night 'ere. Listen — hear it? They've got loudspeakers everywhere. I'm going to sing-along. Ready? *Pom-pom-pom* . . . Here it comes. *Laud-a-arr-tay, laud-a-arr-tay, laud-a-arr-tay dom-ee-nay* . . .'

'Henry!'

'There's not a lot of variety. When they've done it forty times they start over again. Same thing.'

'Look, you won't know this but we had bonfires in Brixton last night. They've started rehearsing for the summer. And I've got the gaffer's conference in fifteen minutes. Can you hurry it?'

'Yessir. You have my message there, sir?'

'What message?'

'The message I gave the Cherokee, Big Moose Feather.'

'He's a Commanche and he's Big Stag Droppings.'

'Oh-ho. Who've you been talking to?'

'I estimate, old chum, your clowning at that château is going to be number four or five on the gaffer's agenda. Is this what you're talking about — twenty-two fifteen, Sunday? You're in Lourdes, Hotel Galilée-Windsor. You've talked to the Widow Spence . . . Mrs McCluskey's in town . . . "*Lapin aux pruneaux* is one of the more succulent specialities of the region, a gourmet's gorge, serve it with a piping hot *pipérade* as do the Basques, and to follow, why not the local ewe's milk cheese washed down with a heady Jurançon, the golden sweet dessert wine with the herbal tang?" Am I supposed to show this to the gaffer?'

'Read the poem.'

'Listen, you gruesome—'

'For Geronimo. He took it down in real joined-up writing.'

'Jesus! Here then.

      He eyed the *garçon*, gave a cough:
        "A gourmet and a gambler, I.
      "The soup was cold, the fish was off,
        "And now the steaks are high—" '

'Gettit, the stakes are high? Go on then. What've you stopped for?'

      ' "I gambled on the *Guide Kléber*."
      (The little *garçon* winced.)
      "If this is your *cuisine minceur*,
        "Bring me some that's minced." '

'Beautifully read, sir. Needs polishing, of course. Might 'ave to cut it. The proof of the padding is in the deleting.'

'I give up. Who needs Tennyson? Incidentally, who's Ann Dora?'

'Andorra, tosh, is a semi-feudal, practically invisible state in the Pyrenees under the joint suzerainty since the thirteenth century of the President of France, currently Monsieur Mitterand, and the Bishop of Urgel, in Spain, whose name escapes me. The official language is Catalan and the inhabitants are by and large a handful of Spaniards, plenty of sheep, ski-freaks, a ton of smugglers and tax-dodgers, and possibly an arms dealer named Becker, acquainted with the late Charles Spence and his lady, and perhaps with Mrs McCluskey. If he's not an arms dealer he could still be worth a look at because what we seem to have, speaking as an innocent, is a widening network of blokes, some dead and mutilated, one dead and unmutilated, though painted, others alive, between whom the link—'ow's my grammar so far?—the link between whom, for what it's worth, might be Mercy McCluskey.'

'Fascinating.'

'Knew you'd think so. Andorra's not that far. I can see the Pyrenees from here, if that's what they are. Probably do it in 'alf a day. Up to you, darling. I'm happy where I am. Haven't seen the town yet. Haven't even seen a miracle.'

'Go, for God's sake.'

'Really?'

'Henry?'

'*Oui?*'

'You got any days off owing?'

'I've got months off owing.'

'Take them. Take Miriam—'

'I just phoned 'er. There was a terrible amount of silence. Not sure whether I was talking to anyone or not.'

'Andorra's the place, Henry. Go skiing. Smuggle a sheep. Henry?'

'Sir?'

'Don't phone us, we'll phone you.'

'Ah, no you don't. Changed my mind. I'm coming back today. You're trying to exclude me, that's what. When I get back there'll have been a putsch. My trenchcoat will have been confiscated. I'll have lost my desk by the radiator.'

'You've already lost it. The redskin's taken it. 'Bye Henry.'

'Toodle-oo. I've got a poem coming on anyway, I can feel it. My word, if the muse is hopping in Lourdes, what's she going to get up to in snowy Andorra? And oral hygiene's sure to please the fleas that tease in the High—forget it. Catalan story short, nothing your end I ought to know?'

'Yes. I've got a screaming headache. Five minutes ago I was fine. Also, hate to tell you this, the weather's marvellous. And if it's any use, someone named Hector McCluskey isn't in Hong Kong. Never was, according to what I've got here. Never arrived.'

'What 'appened to the cookery competition?'

'Who cares what happened to the—'

'The cooks care, that's who. Blimey, you're insensitive. All those meat patties growing cold. So where is he?'

'Missing.'

'Try Buffalo. He went to the funeral of Ziegler, his mate, another chef, one of the amputated ones.'

'He didn't. He wasn't there. Far as Buffalo knows he was never in Buffalo. Last seen on the sixth when he left Mordan for Charles de Gaulle Airport.'

'You're not by any chance telling me we're going to turn up another dead and mutilated cook?'

'There's only been one. Charles Spence wasn't a cook.'

'All you know. His freezer's full of lamb chops.'

'All I'm saying is Hector McCluskey's missing. You say Mrs McCluskey's in Lourdes, why don't you ask her?'

'I've gone off 'er. She's a fibber and she's too tall. Gives me vertigo. She'll have left anyway, if she didn't oversleep, like some of us.'

Mercy McCluskey had not overslept but she had not yet left Lourdes, though she had been about to. She was on her way to her car, standing at a pedestrian crossing waiting for the lights to change, when she saw him.

He had not seen her. He was reading, alone and sunlit at a table on the sidewalk outside the Café du Terrasse.

At least he was reading, and chewing, not looking for her. Maybe he was looking for her at that. He was weird enough to look for people by sitting in cafés.

Weird, not stupid. She would have liked to have known what he knew, to have seen anything he had written about the night before last, about Jerome, everything.

When the pedestrian light turned green she did not

cross but backed towards the refuge of the shops, watching him.

Arva-a-ay, Arva-a-ay, Arva-a-ay Mare-e-e-yaaa . . .

The greeting chorused boomingly through loudspeakers atop hotels, banks, boutiques, restaurants, and blossoming chestnut trees. Sunshine sparkled on the circular tables, warmed the top of Peckover's head, and toasted his very late breakfast croissant.

This was his third croissant, and out of a blue Pyrenean empyrean he had realized that he preferred a baguette loaded with butter and marmalade. Croissants were on the sweet side and had a gluey texture.

Beside his coffee cup lay, pristine, a guide to Andorra. Squared-off on the guide were Lourdes brochures from the Syndicat d'Initiative, because he had not yet seen the Grotto of the Apparitions. He had also not seen the Panorama of the Life of St Bernadette, the Miraculous Medal, the Basilica, the fort, or the several museums. He had not visited the caves, ridden round the lake on horseback, or up the Pic du Jer on the funicular.

Squared-off on the brochures was his notebook, open at a blank page, awaiting the muse.

Arva-a-ay, Arva-a-ay . . .

The must was plainly the Grotto. After that he would see, but he needed to be on his way fairly soon if he were to reach Andorra by evening. Easier to say what he would skip. The Piscine Miraculeuse for one. On peak August days pilgrims immersed themselves in the miraculous baths, or were immersed, at the rate of one a minute. Over two thousand a day.

Three million pilgrims a year to Lourdes, almost all of them in the summer.

All right, May was not August. Today there might be only a thousand immersions. He still believed he would not feel deprived if he kept away from the miraculous baths. Best not get too involved.

Unless you watched it you got involved, ruminated Peckover, involved against his will, this after all being his long weekend off, or having started out that way. Last night had been a solid achievement, not involving himself socially with the Widow Spence or professionally with Mercy McCluskey.

But what did he imagine he was doing in barmy Lourdes and now off to batty Andorra? Unless you stood your ground, said a firm no-thank-you, you were sucked in. You started off saying yes to giving a half-hour to a simple English-language interview, there being all those jolly figures on the expenses sheet to consider, and before you could blink you were immersed, the liquid closing over your head, more *merdeuse* than *miraculeuse*. Right, a copper was at a disadvantage saying no, someone had to sort out the knaves and ruffians, that was the job, and he was all for it. Just the same. Not every day, after all, did he find a body in a bath.

He should, he knew, have been looking for Mercy McCluskey, but he looked first at his watch, next at the waiter, who having nothing better to do came sauntering. That final mouthful of croissant number three required additional coffee if it were to be floated off the back of his breastbone where it had lodged.

She watched him with some difficulty. The view through the traffic—stop-start, stop-start—was leading to eye-strain. Not that there was much to watch. All he did was eat croissants. He looked like someone aiming at a slot in the *Guinness Book of Records* by eating every croissant in the town.

She would have liked to have known where he was going from here. Back to Mordan? Could be he was staying in Lourdes. How long did she stand here among this ghastly religious kitsch, watching? When he walked away, did she follow? Follow a cop, for Chrissake?

Mercy McCluskey stood inside the souvenir shop watching through what would have been the window had there been a window. These numberless, windowless boutiques, one after the other, a thousand of them displaying the identical conveyor-belt souvenirs, were open to the street: here in shadow, on the other side of the street glistering in the sun, dazzling and tinkling as from ten thousand crystal fragments, Macy's, Saks, Gimbels, Bloomingdale's, where are you?

To the pious who bought it, rubbish it was not; and if people had not bought it, it would not have been here.

Just the same, come the day of reckoning, the last trumpet sounding, and the hordes flooding into Main Street, Lourdes, for string, sealing-wax, toothpaste, bread, what were they going to find? Fifty thousand plastic Virgin-shaped bottles for holy water and fifty million devotional medals, carvings, candles, chaplets and picture-postcards.

Starting to watch her, waiting for her to buy or get out, stood the proprietress, a death-camp doorkeeper with black hair in a bun and eyes like glass splinters.

Peckover watched the traffic, Stop-start, stop-start. He liked best the lurching mastodon tankers filled with yoghurt and truffles. How café society coped when they wanted to hear themselves speak he could not imagine.

She was a fibber and what had he to gain from more fibs? Last night he had gone out of his way to avoid her: past the recommended Hotel Impérial where she might have been, on to the Galilée-Windsor. But last night was last night. She might not be co-habiting with her spouse but did she know he was missing?

She might not care, of course. She might be delighted.

If she did know Hector McCluskey was missing, just what did she know? If she did not know, how would she react when told?

She was not an expert liar. Mrs McCluskey was up to her fine white teeth in the little drama. Stage centre. She could hardly cast herself in the role of innocent spectator when two walk-on players whom she had known had been murdered; a third had gone the same way just along the corridor from where she had been having it off in the Isle of Skye Room, if that was where she had been, what she had been doing; and now her husband might be a body awaiting discovery.

She was immersed. Guilty or innocent, she should have stuck to her loom. She had beaten him to the Widow Spence in pursuit of anything which might link her with Charles Spence, then made a hash of it by actually listening to the widow and leaving believing there was nothing. She could hardly have made it more obvious she had been acquainted with Charlie if she had announced it over the loudspeakers.

Why should she not lie? If she had been having affairs with them, whose business was it but hers? What was wrong with lies in the cause of peace and harmony?

Assuming she had left her hotel, here was as good a place as anywhere to look for her. The world and his wife were passing by. Assuming she had not yet left Lourdes.

Arva-a-ay, Mare-e-e-yaaa . . .

Through the loudspeakers the decibel count was high, gamely competing with the spurt and grind of the traffic. His square metre of pavement space was at a hilly, lively intersection, downtown, if such a commercial term were acceptable for so revered a place of pilgrimage. Peckover thought it might be. Looking for Mercy McCluskey he could look four ways, and whichever way, uphill or downhill, the view was of shoppers and an identical dance and glitter of sunlit holy junk in the shopfronts. Would the croissants cost extra because of the loudspeakers' inescapable hymning?

He remembered how as a young man on his first trip abroad, low on spending money but forewarned, he had chosen for his Champs-Elysées café one without music. No flies on the Young Peckover, Acting Detective-Constable on leave. When the bill for one beer had requested roughly the equivalent of two days' pay, and courageously he had queried it, raising moveover — O green and headstrong youth! — the question of the café's music, which was to say its absence, the waiter had informed him that he could hear the music from the adjacent café.

Not until several years later had the maturer Peckover learned from an article in the *Guardian* the infallible tactic for surly waiters. You accidentally nudged your empty glass over the edge of the table. Were the waiter exceptionally surly you nudged the table's entire contents overboard. With or without an apology, but guarding at all cost your sang-froid, you then put down the money for whatever you had had and walked away. Peckover had never tried this but he had stored the information. Seldom did the public prints come up with advice of such practical value. Whether from dented machismo, docked wages because of breakages, or the public humiliation of being left to sweep up the debris, even the surliest waiter, marooned amid broken glass, was apparently left whimpering.

Peckover watched the shoppers and strollers along the boulevard. North, south, east, west. To see south he had to lean sideways in his chair and twist his head through a hundred and eighty degrees. He knew he was looking south because beyond the rooftops and tops of pines and palms stretched a horizon of sugar-coated peaks.

No leaning and neck-craning were required to observe the high proportion of the halt and lame: groups with sticks and crutches, people in bathchairs. A small boy with red hair sat rug-wrapped in a wheelchair pushed by

an older boy in a yachting cap. Almost as numerous were
hale, grey nuns, and priests in black carrying books and
parcels, and in some instances the handbag obligatory for
French males. Peckover guessed the priests with handbags
were French, or at any rate Continentals, rather than
Irish. Fumes belched from the cars stopping at the lights.

How many in this rubber-necking throng, Peckover
tried to guess, were criminals? One in fifty? One in
twenty? Pickpockets mainly. Pickpockets, petty pilferers,
con men. The summer pilgrimages must have brought
them to Lourdes like locusts. The brochures he had collected were silent on the matter but he knew. The town
seethed with them.

Pickpockets, priests, pilgrims in wheelchairs. The sick
and crippled confused him by failing to look miserable.
They might not have looked radiant but all the same they
were physically ill, not daft, so they should at least have
had an air of being cowed. People you saw walking about
looking radiant in London were usually soft in the head.
Not being soft in the head, this lot came to Lourdes not
for a miracle, he judged, or even for a cure, but for something else. What? Reassurance? Joy?

No Mercy McCluskey.

Becker was a new name out of the hat and an unlyrical
one. Peckover preferred McCluskey. He even preferred
Peckover. He wrote on a white page:

The widow, keeping up her pecker —

Something unconvincing about that line for a start but
he could work on it later.

Rode the Poplar double-decker
Crying, in her role as wrecker,
'Copper, get that snotrag Becker!'

Around the quatrain he drew careful squiggles, then
squiggled densely through and over it, achieving a rhodo-
dendron bush. He did not want to disappoint Susan
Spence but he failed to see himself getting Becker, who-

ever he might be, apart perhaps from an upstanding
citizen and charmer who had told her adieu.

Who he might be was an arms dealer pal of Spence,
which could be fruitful if he were willing to talk, unlikely
as that seemed, even if he were in Andorra and discover-
able. The more honest reason for driving to Andorra was
that he had never been. When all was said he was on his
hols, dammit, and it was there, Andorra, with its sheep,
skiers, and smugglers, somewhere among the icing-
topped peaks.

How many of the blatherers propping up the bar back
at the Factory had seen Andorra, mountain-girt land of
romance? Once he had them cornered he'd blather them
into the floor.

She bought a television set. When she held it out and
opened her purse the death-camp doorkeeper did not
weep and embrace her, but neither did she snarl.

The television set was plastic and fitted in the palm of
her hand and in her handbag. It would also fit in any
trashcan. The battery was extra. When you fitted the
battery and pressed the button the screen lit up, illuminating the Virgin Mary. If she gave it to Heinz would he
roll about laughing or cringe? She had to admit she did
not know him well enough to be sure.

She decided on two more minutes. Okay, five. The
cop might be on duty, looking for Mercy McCluskey,
cerebrating about stabbed Jerome, or he might not. He
looked as if he had settled in for the season. Personally she
had a journey ahead of her and her life to live.

Diagonally across the intersection, deluged in sunshine,
the waiter was unloading coffee.

The coffee was black as Beelzebub and gritty as if the
filter had split. Peckover would have liked to have
returned it to the waiter and told him, 'I'll have grounds

more relative than this,' but in English it would have been wasted and he could not have managed the French. The gun-running, an equally black business, he was sceptical about.

Guns were profitable or they were nothing, surely. Whether Charlie had been trying to flog the IRA Exocet missiles or blowpipes, all he had left his widow was a house in Lourdes of all places. Even taking into account the champagne and girls he should have done better than that, though as in every profession there would be those at the top, coining it, and the also-rans with holes in their socks, scrabbling for the crumbs. Peckover realized he was beginning to muddle gun-running and arms dealing. He had no experience of either but he was ready to accept Frank Veal's guess that gun-running at any rate was irrelevant. Gin-running was the business the Widow Spence would have preferred.

In any case, guns were by definition a dangerous business. Not as dangerous as casino politics on the Côte d'Azur or riding a bike round Hammersmith Broadway but even the gigglers and blatherers at the Factory would hardly have loosed him abroad into a demi-world of gun-runners without at least a small file on the subject, and possibly a gun

If gun-running were irrelevant, what was relevant? Peckover, eyeing the morning crowds, tried visualizing Mrs McCluskey as a gun-runner, or a gun person of some sort, a Ma Barker or an Annie Oakley transplanted to provincial France and requiring that Mr McCluskey, a man of probity, her husband, breathing down her neck, be expunged so that she could run guns in a free and liberated fashion.

No good. Throughout the whole succession of killings and cuttings, knives not guns had been the instrument. More plausibly, she might want her husband out of the way so that she could run her boy-friend, Jean-Luc, in a free and liberated fashion.

France had precedents for ladies with knives. Charlotte Corday and that geezer in the bath, the one who had caught a disease by hiding in the sewers. Murat or Marat. Not Monet or Manet who were also confusable. Ironic if his first name, Marat or Murat, stabbed in his bath, had been Jerome.

Not that France had a tradition of imported American lady assassins, as far as he knew. Charlotte Corday had been French and her motive, if he rightly remembered, political, not an affair of the heart. Today she would have made brief headlines as another fanatic, darling of one of the fashionable terrorist groups.

How about Jean-Luc as cleaverman? The provincial prof, avid for possession of Mercy, the exotic American, the prize from across the ocean, someone to brag about in the staff room, boast about to acquaintances on the boulevard, but himself possessed by a jealousy, a Gallic dignity, which required her to be unattached, widowed even, shorn of husband and lovers, past or present, even though this meant killing them off and cutting their member off, that vile appendage which had presumed to pollute and defile the fairest . . . oh, poppycock. In a manner of speaking.

'*Monsieur? Tenez. Vous me permettez?*'

Peckover turned his head. He was being offered a tract or something by a cigar-smoking pilgrim in a bathchair.

Time to go, decided Mercy McCluskey, suddenly cold on the shady side of the street and suspecting that all hell might be about to break loose.

CHAPTER 9

'*Oui,* thanks—ah, *merci beaucoup,*' Peckover told the man in the bathchair, taking and glancing at the leaflet. He dug in his pocket.

Would five francs be too little, an insult, if he had five francs? If the pilgrim were not seeking money, any money at all might be a worse insult. Impossible to know; and at my time of life, thought Peckover, hard to care. Purveyors of unsolicited anything put the public in a false position. The leaflet was something about La Vierge Immaculée and an Association Catholique.

'British?' the man in the wheelchair said.

'Yes.'

'Pleased to meet you.' The man beamed as if in gratitude for unmerited blessings, placed the wad of leaflets in his lap, transferred the cigar to his left hand, and extended his right. 'My name's Balderstone. This is my fourth pilgrimage. I'm from Birmingham. Hockley Hill, if you know it?'

The only bit of Birmingham Peckover knew was Winson Green Prison, whither he had travelled at one time on a series of escort duties. He shook the man's hand a trifle perfunctorily, not for want of sympathy but in case he was frail. He did not look especially frail, and his grip was firm, but from the waist down he was swathed in a rug so perhaps the trouble was his legs. His complexion was pinkish and the delicate features might have been more suitable for a girl. His hair and beard were clipped so uniformly short that the colour remained in doubt, but might also have been a sort of pink. Fair anyway. The cigar was not excessive, it was more a cigarillo or cheroot, but in the policeman's view the man should not have been smoking at all, not if he were in a wheelchair. Perhaps he came to Lourdes for a miracle to stop him smoking. Peckover brought from his pocket not money but a tissue and dabbed his nose.

'Lovely day,' said the Brummagen in the bathchair.

'Certainly is,' said Peckover, looking around at the day. There she was.

' 'Scuse me,' Peckover said, pushing back his chair.

She was inexpert at everything. She had not wanted him to notice her or she would not have been in such a rush, colliding with fellow pedestrians as she crossed the crossing. Another half-dozen paces and she would have been on the southbound boulevard and out of sight, unless he went into his neck-craning act. But she looked directly at him as she strode. She as well might have carried a banner proclaiming I Am Mercy McCluskey. Had she looked ahead and walked normally he quite possibly would not have noticed her in spite of her height. She wore red trousers and a billowing grey jacket and over her head a knotted silk square, as if on her way to horse-trials. They stared at each other. When he pushed his chair back she started to run.

He had not paid. Leaving his beret, brochures and Andorra guide as a sign of good faith, he ran after her. He could not cross the road because the lights had changed and the traffic was gathering speed, bumper to bumper. He ran along his side of the boulevard, past souvenir shops, side-stepping priests and pilgrims, looking for a gap in the traffic. He had lost sight of her but she was there somewhere, beyond the accelerating roofs and roof-racks, on the other side of the boulevard. When a dozey saloon car left a gap between itself and the van in front he darted through and became marooned in the middle of the road, awaiting a similar gap in the traffic seething from the south and honking at him with the satisfaction of the morally justified. When he reached

Mrs McCluskey's side of the boulevard she was not there.

He ran along the pavement, looking and cursing. People stepped aside and stared. He looked into shops. He ran back and down a side-street she might have entered but failed to spot her. He came back to the boulevard and tried the next turning, twenty yards from the crossing where they had eyed each other.

She was less hopeless than he had supposed. His pits were damp and he had lost her.

He stood for another minute or two in case she should canter up to him and say, 'Hi,' breathless as if late for a date. Then he tramped back to the Café du Terrasse. The waiter hovered with an air of menace. An outsize woman in a shawl, neither nun nor pilgrim, was lowering herself into his chair and her shopping-bags to the ground. At least Mr Balderstone, tract-distributor, had departed.

Peckover sorted change for his breakfast, unfurled and put on his beret, then looked once, twice, through his brochures. He looked on the ground, at the shawled hippopotamus who had taken his seat, round about him at oblivious customers, and at the waiter's pockets. He felt in his own pockets but failed to find his notebook.

The missing notebook was a run-of-the-mill Woolworth's notebook with a wire spiral, without lines, about ten inches by six. That was to say, it was not a run-of-the-mill policeman's notebook, being too large to slip easily into the pocket. Peckover preferred his notebooks unlined because lines imposed limitations. Sometimes he liked to write small and sometimes big. He did not know why this should be: that was something for psychoanalysts. He preferred a largish notebook because he liked to see the stanzas of his verse complete on one page rather than on page after page, jostled by tedious names and addresses, train times, time of the break-in, and so forth. This the Woolworth's notebook allowed because normally he was not writing *Paradise Lost*.

In the notebook was nothing of interest to anyone apart from possibly generations of poetry-lovers to come, and off-hand he was unable to recall whether he had lately composed anything deathless. Neither was there a single entry, he believed, he could not do without. The sole item of moment was the address of Becker and that he was able to remember. He would not have remembered the telephone number but there had been no telephone number.

The cheek of it was what. The impertinence.

He stepped to the waiter. '*Le monsieur dans la chaise*, wheelchair, *chaise avec les roues—où? Quelle direction? S'il vous plaît?*'

'*Comment?*'

Peckover sat on air, mimed wheelchair wheel-turning. When the waiter started to snigger and look about for customers to share the joke against the idiot Brit, Peckover thrust his face close to the waiter's, grinned and hissed. The waiter blanched. His lips wobbled and he pointed west.

Dodging tourists and pickpockets, dazzled by sunlight bouncing off the souvenirs stalls, Peckover trotted west. He passed clerics, pilgrims in wheelchairs, and one supine, smiling pilgrim on a trolley pushed by a man in shirtsleeves. Ahead, briskly trundling along the downhill boulevard, there came into sight a wheelchair's padded back and above it shoulders and a head of fair, close-cropped hair. Peckover trotted faster. Catching up, he caught hold of the wheelchair and dragged it to a stop. It weighed a ton. Mr Balderstone looked up and round with startled, pale eyes.

Peckover presented him with a smile because who knew? As well at least to start amiably. Discovering whether Mr Balderstone had nicked his notebook might take the rest of the day. He could hardly hold a Lourdes pilgrim upside down and shake him in the full public gaze. What if under the rug there were no legs?

'Mr Balderstone? Hello again.'

Peckover stood with his back to an acre of shimmering mementoes. He leaned forward from the waist, watching Mr Balderstone's delicate physiognomy for signs of embarrassment, an apology, perhaps even production of the notebook. Mr Balderstone flipped the rug off his legs. There lay the notebook in his lap. Simultaneously he rose, bringing the top of his bristly skull with vigour and impeccable aim into Peckover's belly.

'Oooumph!' gasped Peckover.

Folded double, he went backwards into the boutique, sat on a loaded counter with a crash which engulfed the loudspeakers' hymning and, still sitting, continued travelling backwards for another metre or two to an accompaniment of further explosive crashings of souvenirs counters. The din and airborne glitter amazed. Holy water bottles and medallions flew. Glass and plastic crunched beneath the policeman's two hundred pounds. He covered his face with his arms because at last he was at rest, grievously winded, the air was filled with colourful little missiles, and hurtling towards him, shoved and released by a blurry Mr Balderstone, came the empty ton of wheelchair: jolting steel and a whirr of monstrous wheels.

Had the wheelchair's aim been as true as that of Mr Balderstone's skull, firemen, in Peckover's opinion, would have been needed to cut him free from its frame and the trellis of shattered planks and joists from the counter now fastening his limbs. The wheelchair missed by the breadth of a breviary and smashed into a hitherto undemolished section of counter. Peckover's beret sat awry. Some fool, sex unknown, was screaming in his ear. He would have screamed back had he had the breath, though he believed it was starting to return, and that he was winded rather than wounded. In front, assembling

on the pavement, he observed the confused inactivity of the
public when granted a spectacle which was free, dramatic,
and unintelligible. Mr Balderstone had departed on
uncrippled legs, leaving behind his wheelchair and rug,
but not, as far as Peckover could see, a Woolworth's notebook.

'*Un miracle!*' shouted someone, watching the fleeing
pilgrim.

Peckover flung timber from off his legs, plucked a
Marian water-bottle out of his lap, and achieved a squat-
ting position. Heaven knew what he had been sitting in
but his rump was beginning to prickle and tingle, suggesting glass as an answer. The shrilling in one ear, perhaps from an aggrieved shopkeeper, was now counter-
pointed by bass barkings in the other ear. A bony hand
gripped the back of his jacket collar and was tugging as if
intent on throttling him. Sick of the entire shower,
persecuted Peckover lashed out, punching upwards and
behind him with both fists. He was rewarded with a yelp
to his left, a stifled bleating to his right, and impressed
diminuendo all round. He found a wrist at the back of his
neck, twisted it, and heard a shriek. Then he was on his
feet, though lurching somewhat.

The assembly on the pavement appeared to be divided
between two main groups: those goggling at him, and
those turned to their right, goggling after the decamping
Mr Balderstone.

'*Un miracle, c'est un miracle!*' chorused some of those
who were turned to their right, though not all.

Peckover barged through. Shedding glitter and wood
splinters, he started off at a run down the avenue. Ahead
was the flitting figure of Mr Balderstone, travelling well,
and now left-turning, vanishing round the end of the
avenue.

Peckover ran harder. His wind had more or less
returned, his size eleven shoes pounded. He felt in

passably good shape in spite of everything, such as the croissants and possibly a wounded bottom. Most people on the pavement scattered but some stood there, whether from surprise or defiance, forcing him to tack.

Someone blew a whistle. Some copper. Typical. Chain-smoking his head off in a back street while the yeggs and cutpurses of this thieves' kitchen were out there snaffling notebooks, and now that it was too late blowing his bloody whistle.

Later Peckover was to learn what he had already guessed: that the crime rate for Lourdes was more than double the French national average for small towns. Even priests and pilgrims—genuine unwell pilgrims, not masqueraders like fit Mr Balderstone—had been known to join in the commonest crime, which was nicking. Notebooks were fair game.

Sprinting round the end of the avenue, Peckover was less concerned about crime statistics than about one rat-bag criminal and a notebook. Why anyone would want to pinch his notebook defeated him. Why the Brummagen who had done so had made such a performance of it, playing the chairbound pilgrim, becoming violent and bolting, was another enigma. Bugger enigmas—where was he?

Peckover ran through open spaces, though they would have been more open without the trees. He did not see Mr Balderstone. At the same time, judging which way he had probably gone was no problem. An elderly man who sat on the concrete esplanade sat with an air of having landed there unexpectedly. Most people were staring in roughly the same direction. One or two were calling out to no purpose.

The sky was a blue bowl. A hundred yards distant rose a rocky hill fringed with green. The immediate land-scape, now he had dashed past the trees, was a wilderness of concrete like a parade ground. The people who dappled the parade ground appeared unhurried, unlike himself, and Mr Balderstone, now eminently visible again, turning his head to look back as he raced in the direction of a monster church. In spite of the sunshine, a majority of the parade-ground military were bundled in rugs in their wheelchairs and on stretcher-trolleys, and though Peckover knew they were not the military he fancied that any stranger parachuted in, in ignorance of St Bernadette and the Grotto, might have taken them for ex-military: soldier casualties of war enjoying their daily dose of sun. The mainly male nurses and porters, some in shirtsleeves, some beefy, others scrawny, trundled the chairs and trolleys, or stood talking with each other, and now gazing after the brace of sprinters who had disrupted the calm. One, crouched beside his charge, was reciting the rosary. A mixed group sang in competition with the loudspeakers.

All this Peckover fleetingly took in as he adjusted his angle of pursuit and lengthened his stride. He was gaining, had already considerably gained. Twenty yards? One Olympic gold-medal burst would do it. Or might if the bugger would trip, twist an ankle.

Laud-a-arr-tay, laud-a-arr-tay . . .

Peckover hoped he was still gaining because his breathing had become like sandpaper, his legs were watery, and he had a stitch. Mr Balderstone, plainly aware of being pursued, was running harder too, or trying to, but Mr Balderstone was losing ground.

Having changed his mind about the church as sanctuary, if that were what he had had in mind, the Birmingham ratbag had veered north, thus running along two sides of a triangle to Peckover's one. A policeman's whistle, perhaps the same chain-smoking policeman's, pierced the May morning. Peckover knew he was in the heart of Lourdes, the point of the place. The parade ground was the processional esplanade; the towering, off-white church was the basilica; those on stretchers were pilgrims; and somewhere was the Grotto. He ran on fading legs. Mr Balderstone was rushing past people on benches, and next hurdling over astonished pilgrims on stretchers parked in a line facing the cliff. At a rocky concavity in the cliff, thronged with pilgrims who kneeled, sang, or simply stood and stared, were candles, a glass screen, and high up in a niche a statue of the Virgin in listless blue and white, none of which Peckover saw, nor was he to, though this was the Grotto. He was intent only on skirting rather than hurdling the stretchers because a boot on an inert pilgrim was something he preferred not to risk, principally for the pilgrim's sake but also for the explaining that would be called for later.

Here between basilica and Grotto, pilgrims and tourists were more numerous than on the parade ground, and to weaving, charging Peckover they seemed to be growing yet denser. Where quarry and copper barreled through, the crowd was also resentful, if too surprised to raise a clamour, or not before the circus had passed. The squash told in his favour, Peckover realized, though with no sense of consolation. When once or twice he lost sight of Mr Balderstone's bobbing head he was able to follow with reasonable confidence the swathe cut by the ratbag through the press of bodies.

'Police!' Peckover shouted.

He believed that Mr Balderstone, barely a dozen paces ahead, had no better idea of his surroundings or where he was going than he had himself, and no goal other than escape. Why for God's sake did none of this idle lot tackle him, infirm or not!

'Police! *Assassin!*' Peckover pantingly cried, particularly pleased with '*assassin*', which was a slander on Mr Balderstone but more colourful than whatever was French for 'robber'. He charged along the channel carved by the ratbag through the mêlée which stood, sat and lay outside a low, functional-looking stone building, and into an iron railing.

'Blast!'

He vaulted over the railing and into a youth on crutches. The crowd was singing a hymn under the leadership of an amplified divine. Mr Balderstone was shouldering through the scrummage, then through a door.

Peckover shouldered after him into a building which was not a basilica, he believed, though it was proximate, and there was a Madonna, signifying very little because Madonnas were everywhere, including possibly a portion of a minature one embedded in his backside. Humanity lined more benches. The subdued babble may have been praying, or grumbling about the greater clamour of song and grievance in the queue outside. The smell, a rich damp, he failed to identify. Mushrooms? Sweat? His own sweat, doubtless, much of it in his eyes. He charged after Mr Balderstone, who had disappeared behind a shower curtain of striped Marian blue and white. He could have reached for and collared him, almost, had he been capable of charging even a grain, a whisker, harder. Had he been able to see through the sweat.

Impeded by striped curtains, flesh, and cubicle walls, Peckover reached fruitlessly for Mr Balderstone. Mr Balderstone had gone. Blinking through sweat, Peckover found himself reaching for a hairy, nippled chest. Not Mr Balderstone's. The outside clamour seemed to be moving inside, augmented by an echoing effect, new shouts, and the whistle of the imbecile, chain-smoking gendarme blowing virtually in his ear.

'Balderstone, you bugger!' someone shouted.

Himself.

At least he was in the men's domain, he believed. Blokes. Stone and tiles, unrefreshing smells, steps leading down to a tub of soupy water. The bath was sunken, as

was the bath in his little Versailles, his Rob Roy
Room—O Miriam!—at which point all resemblance
ceased. Towelled porters, or they might have been lifeguards, were lowering into the liquid murk a pilgrim,
naked apart from the blue cloth round his waist. Mr
Balderstone, sprinter and hurdler, was on present
evidence a non-swimmer. He had turned left round
the edge of the bath. One of the miraculous baths, for
blokes.

Your mistake, mate, Peckover silently informed Mr
Balderstone, sidestepping a lifeguard. He had only to
follow a straight line through the water to cut the ratbag
off on the opposite side of the bath. Then, joy, the
kicking of him from one end of the bath to the other! Feet
first, Peckover plunged in.

The water was no more than knee-deep. He had waded
one step when a hand grabbed his arm. Gawd, what next!
Next, other hands arrived on other parts of him including
the hair on his head. Probably a foot hooked his feet from
under him. There were hands, feet and abuse enough—
the gabble was French but he assumed it was abuse—for a
regiment of lifeguards.

Your mistake, old matey, Peckover reproached himself
as the water closed over him and too late he shut his
mouth and eyes against the miraculous water and
microbes. He would have pinched his nose and plugged
his ears had he been able, but the lifeguard regiment held
him. Already he had swallowed sufficient streptococcus
and staphylococcus to leave him with typhoid for the rest
of his days, which would be few.

He was waiting for the kaleidoscope of his former days
to flash through his mind when the hands jerked him to
his feet with a sucking *shwooosh*. Peckover retched and
opened his eyes. What concerned him still was Mr
Balderstone. No sign of him, of course.

A familiar beret floated on the soup. The hands refused to let him go, and in his head persisted outraged gibbering.

'Oh, sod off, all of you,' was the best Peckover could manage.

Seven hours, much aggravation, one new suit, and the final breezy handshaking with a squad of Lourdes police later, at dusk, Detective Chief-Inspector Peckover drove past unconcerned Customs and immigration buildings into Pas de la Case, Andorra.

The suit was a superlatively stylish needlecord of a beaten-gold hue in which he believed he looked like a god. The beaten gold was polished as well as beaten, so the effect was perhaps just a little glittery, but even Miriam was going to have to admit he had chosen well. The BBC World Service had further lifted his spirits. He had enjoyed Play of the Week, which had been *Uncle Vanya,* the Merchant Navy Programme, Nature Notebook, Business Matters, Sports Report, Classical Record Review, The Farming World, and numberless current affairs discussions. The foothills of the Pyrenees, then quite suddenly the Pyrenees proper, had been *magnifique.* Escaped Balderstone he had erased from his mind, as good as. If ever they met again he would know the ratbag. What principally taxed Peckover was whether typhoid was what he was going to catch, or cholera. Which would be worse? Was it possible to have both at once.

Seen through the car windows, Pas de la Case was a disappointment. Peckover hesitated between finding a room here for the night, as he had intended, and flogging on. He had never seen Guatemala or El Salvador, and in the light of what he read in the newspapers, he doubted he ever would, but Pas de la Case was much as he imagined a Guatemalan frontier town, without the gunfire: flyblown concrete supermarkets besieged by rubble and abandoned bulldozers.

If Pas de la Case meant Not the Case, it had a point. At the same time, here could be a place to get shut of microbes. Out of dismay at where he had brought them they would roll over on their back and give up.

CHAPTER 10

'*Liebling*,' he breathed.

When he went into his mother tongue, things, she knew, were hotting up. Not that she needed to hear words to know when things were hotting up.

'Darling,' she heard herself murmur.

'*Oh, meine Süsse!*'

'Oh,' whispered Mercy, on guard, on exactly the occasion when what she least needed was to be on guard.

But the next endearment was likely to be the one which made her want to laugh, or at least to wonder. She had intended asking him for a translation and always she forgot until now, now being hardly the time or place. She supposed she should try the dictionary. Again, not now. She closed her mouth round a piece of him so that if he said it, and if she giggled, at least it would be a muffled giggle. Maybe he might interpret it as ecstacy

'*Oh, mein Schatz!*'

Mercy bit and moaned. A funny kind of a moan, she would have been the first to admit: staccato, more of a sequence of stifled hiccups, a muffled guffaw. She guessed it was fine though, it would come across as ecstasy. He would construe it as such, being a male pig, and a disappointment.

Mercy, honey, when will you learn?

Hell's fangs, nothing had changed, what was she

beefing about? He was the same charmer who had loved
her and left her in a lather of anticipation apropos this
next, this now. She the same optimist who adored and
opened herself wide, wide, to let the sunshine in. An
understandable condition when you were twenty, Mercy
reflected, though no less painful when the occasional
thunderbolt arrived through the sunshine and hit you
where it hurt. But when you were wise and—um, fortyish.

She was prepared to allow, just, fortyish. She could not
believe she was fortyish though, or that she thought it
mattered, as clearly she did. She lay, more precisely she
huddled, balletically, with her mind unstarrily compos
mentis and his bony elbow, or shoulder, something, in
her tit, God knew how, but if that was what he wanted.

Yea, yea.

All this distance for one night of romance! Okay, it was
to have been several nights until his unexpected business
commitment somewhere the other side of Europe. A
likely story. Yet she believed it, more or less. Even if he
had not had to leave tomorrow—or today was it?—she
would have made her own excuses. She had business com-
mitments too: up front, meeting and greeting.

All these damn languages were to blame. How could
you be two hearts beating as one with someone who called
you his Schatz?

She loved him in spite of it, she assured herself, as she
might love a selfish, vulnerable little boy. She would love
him still more if he would get rid of his elbow. Would she
be here if she did not love him, driving God knew how
many miles to him, still bushed in spite of a night's sleep
which he had not interrupted more than sixty or seventy
times?

French was different and okay, she knew enough
French to cope. Even so. First time Jean-Luc had started
singing out his 'Oh, mon cœur!' they had been almost
there on the tippy-top of the crest of the wave and he had

loused it up with his crazy '*Oh, mon cœur!*' She had
thought he was having a coronary. Loused it for her, of
course. Mercy checked herself from brooding on her
grimmest anxiety-fantasy, second only to the death of her
children in car wrecks or by drowning: namely, the lover
you were in the sheets with snuffing it from a heart
attack. Did you polish away the fingerprints and light out
fast? Put on a funny accent and call the hospital? Slink
into another room and pretend it wasn't you, you were
never there?

No chance of wave-crests for her now, the Schatz had
seen to that, but Heinz was on his way and she could
mime and moan a little. For Heinz. Not his fault he
reverted to German. Kind of a compliment. What was so
side-splitting about being his Schatz anyway?

What wasn't? Mercy heard muffled hiccuping and guf-
fawing. To halt it before it passed beyond control she
gasped and moaned a little.

'Heinz, oh!' Mercy moaned. '*Chéri!*'

Damn! *Chéri?* Had he noticed? Who would he think she
thought she was talking to?

He was oblivious. Another male with his brains in his
dong. He had made no mention of Jean-Luc's love-bites.
How oblivious could you be? Unless he was being discreet,
or postponing the query, or indifferent.

Go, Heinzy, go!

The drawn-out grumbling sound she had been listening
to she now identified as a car outside. She had assumed
the noise to be Heinz's rapture, then for a moment
thought it might have been her stomach, though he had
fed her adequately last night: the obligatory smoked
salmon, partridge he had shot himself, so he had
said—she had cleared away its frozen package with
cooking instructions when he had allowed her to wash the
dishes—champagne with everything, a semi-unfrozen
gâteau. He might be a fairly lovely lover, she supposed,

though dwindlingly, but he was pretty pittsville in the kitchen. Anyway that had been last night. Now was mid-morning, if not noon, judging from the glare through the slats in the shutters, and her stomach would be starting up with blitzkrieg noises if she did not get at least some coffee into it.

Whether or not Heinz had heard the car he was doing nothing about it, not for the moment.

Go, Heinzy, you old Schatzy!

The engine-noise had ceased. Postman? Garbage man come for the partridge carton and empties? Hardly, in this mountain eyrie, twenty times higher and remoter than Hector's shebeen. Still, nothing to do with her, for once. Mercy believed she might be maliciously amused if a doorbell started ringing.

No doorbell, not an electric one, now she remembered. Electric doorbells were *verboten* along with telephones, television, and anything else which might get in the way of the Shangri-la illusion. A nonsense when you thought of it, considering his central heating, freezer, electric can-opener, all that. You made known your presence at the door either by jangling the authentic donkey-bell done up with primary-coloured wool handle and tassels, or by knocking with the carved ram's horn knocker. Which was the more hideous, Mercy had not decided.

Da-da di dum-di DUM.

The visitor had opted for the ram's horn. The tattoo sounded distantly but with spirit. After a pause it was repeated.

Heinz disregarded it.

There followed a longer pause. Then the visitor went to work on the donkey-bell. *Jangle-clangle.* Pause. *Clingle-clangle-jangle.* Pause. *Jingle-jangle-clangle-clingle.*

Heinz seemed to have finished. He was removing himself. Mercy assumed the interruption must have infuriated him but she found it hard to be sure. He had terrific control. All the same, she would not have cared to have been the donkey-bell jangler.

He said, 'Here is a fine kettle of fish.'

His English was not up to Jean-Luc's but it was excellent, and would have been even better if he had not drenched it with idioms. He rarely got the idioms wholly wrong but he seldom got them quite right. Last night after the exploding of the cork from the third or fourth bottle and champagne spurting over both of them, he had said, 'That's put the cats into the pigeons.' When seducing her, so he had thought, and comparing her favourably with Helen of Troy and people, he had called her a horse of a different colour.

He was stepping into exiguous briefs which made him look like an ad for a deodorant, which by now, Mercy considered, he was beginning to need. Next into one of his thousand-dollar robes spun from the silk of the finest Pyrenean silkworms. He closed the door behind him.

Mercy tripped to the nearest shuttered window. She could not have said whether these would give her a view of the postman, not yet having mastered the geography of the Villa Azul, which she thought possibly L-shaped, certainly stairless, though with steps galore for coping with split levels, and with roofs angled every which way, mostly precipitously, like a contemporary church. She opened the windows. Agonizingly slowly, trying to avoid creakings, she lifted the bar which held the shutters. She opened the right-hand shutter an inch. Two inches.

A blue sky dazzled. Mercy breathed chilly mountain air. There he was. Jesus, wouldn't you know it!

Clangle-jangle-jingle.

What in hell was he wearing? He looked like a canary. He was tugging the tasselled donkey-bell and hopping from one foot to the other. Whether because he was cold or because he had rhythm, Mercy did not want to know.

★

'Name's Peckover. Scotland Yard. Mr Becker?'

'Yes.'

'Routine inquiry, sir. On behalf of the French police. And Andorran, goes without saying. Won't take a minute. Not interrupting anything, I 'ope?'

'Absolutely.'

'Good. May I come in?'

'You will perhaps return later. At the moment—'

'Routine but urgent, reasonably,' Peckover said, smiling and stepping past the suntanned weapons' merchant into Hernando's Hideaway, cha-cha-cha. 'I'll keep it short as possible. No need to put on a tie, sir, but if you wanted a shave, make a cup of tea—' organize your love-life—'I'll be right here. Like me to lay the fire?'

In the fireplace were the paltry ashes of a fire which had been lit but not refuelled. There was a stack of logs and kindling. Longer logs made up at least one wall of the vast living-room. The hearth's brick surrounds occupied another wall. The brick was terraced, the terraces were strewn with cushions. He was in a rich man's log cabin.

The owner offered a perfunctory bow from the waist with rigid arms and clicking heels—tricky, clicking bare heels, Peckover was ready to acknowledge—then about-turned and disappeared into the cabin's depths. The policeman heard doors open and close, and later, running water.

Mainly he heard silence. He gazed for a while through a picture window at the Pyrenees, an ennobling panorama for a calendar, empty of roads, aerials, even as far as he could see of sheep. He sauntered, opening heavy shutters and closing again the windows. The books in the pine bookcase appeared to be recent best-sellers and mysteries in paperback and a variety of languages. No Goethe. No Wagner in the record collection which seemed to be mainly classical jazz. Not even *Lili Marlene*. Peckover opened a cabinet gingerly, not expecting nuclear warheads, but you never knew. Boring booze, glasses.

'Eine, Kleine, Na-ha-ha-achtmusik,' he was singing when his host returned with combed wet hair and coffee. Heinz Becker was casually dressed for the European slalom championships, which definitely he would win. Only a knotted silk scarf could have heightened the casualness. His feet were still bare, his skis had gone on ahead with the staff.

'Shall we be mother?' Becker said, gesturing to the policeman to sit. 'Milk and sugar?'

'Drop of milk. I've finished with sugar.' Supposed to have, along with salt, white bread, butter, cheese, eggs, jam, chocolate, ice-cream, chips, anything fried, every-thing tinned, and pretty well anything that was not coloured green. A sensible plate of raw broccoli, that was the stuff. Jerry here in his jogger's clobber and bare feet, Peckover divined, had chosen to be amiable. 'Might I ask 'ow long you've known Susan Spence, sir?'

'Ah. I cotton on. You have been talking with Suzy.'

'Good friends, are you?'

'Were. Simple past tense, is it not so? After her hus-band, you understand, one was sympathetic. One is not saying we have drawn daggers. But it is over.'

'When did you first meet?'

'One would have to think. November?' Becker presented a milky cup of coffee. 'Charles brought her to the Château de Mordan. About a month after he hit the bucket, poor fellow, she telephoned. We met a half-dozen times.'

Take it gently, it'll be all right, Peckover urged himself. He said, 'You met here?'

'Good Scott, no. Here is particular, old chappie. Munich, Athens, where one had business. London, the Carlton Tower, where one is known. Once in Lourdes. A disaster. There is that about Lourdes which is not for gaudy nights. Our adieus we have just said in Gstaad. Is she still upset?'

'Yes.'

'She will survive. Are we to discuss Suzy? One has been questioned about Charles. Suzy is fresh fields and new pastures.'

'Who questioned you about Charles?'

'A commissaire from Paris. He kept harping on a string about Charles offering weapons to the Basques.'

'What weapons?'

'Dear chappie—none. You must know Charlie was a debutant. He wanted slices of the action but what backing had he? Whom did he know? Finally one had to refuse to see him. We in weapons are shall we say a *Brüderschaft*? We are a service for peace within the law. Is one to say the same of the Charleses of the world? Even had he lived and persevered . . .' The downhill racer closed his mouth and frowned at his guest. 'Might I see identification just for the records, old scout?'

Peckover presented his warrant card. This Fancy Dan with the charm of a kidney stone, what did Mercy McCluskey see in him?

He said, 'If we accept, sir, that Mr Spence was not sufficiently involved in guns to have had enemies there, then where? Your personal opinion could be of the greatest help.'

'Charles was from the stews of London, old man. That, one imagines, is where one would look for enemies.'

'Quite.' Stews of London? Impudent bugger. 'What made you choose Andorra, sir?'

Change tack. Charlie and gun-running were a non-starter. As likely this joker and his *Brüderschaft* had killed Charlie to keep themselves exclusive as that the Basques or Provos had killed him for trying to chisel them. Which was to say, unlikely. Plug on, Parnassian Peckover, you with your head in the clouds. The coffee was hot but thin. Peckover suspected he might not be wasting his time on this mountain top.

'Mean to say, sir, Andorra, bit remote for a cosmopolitan chappie like yourself.'

'You have hammered the nail on its head. Tax and sex, my dear fellow.'

Bloody 'ell. Tax and sex. No shame, Germans. All he could hope was they would lose the next World Cup.

'There'll be profits in the weapons business,' he said lamely.

'I work hard, old top. Tomorrow Zürich. I had hoped for three days here but that's how the cookies crumble.'

'Cash before bash.'

'Pardon?'

'Something come up, 'as it, in Zürich?'

'One has a weapons contract.'

'Defensive weapons.'

'*Natürlich.*'

'Still, all work and no play, I'm with you there, sir.' The death-dealer's casually-crossed, ski-clad, skin-tight legs sprouted at their extremities hairless feet and toes, unnaturally tanned, which Peckover would have preferred to have been shod. 'Plenty of 'ealthy copulating with the smugglers and sheep up 'ere, and the particular ones, eh? Not the Suzies.'

'Please? Oh ha-ha, yes, the particular ones. Sheep?' Heinz Becker wagged an admonitory finger. '*Nein.*'

'Mercy McCluskey though, she'd be a particular one if anyone would.'

'Ah?' The toes lifted fractionally. 'You have talked with her too?'

'Might talk to 'er again when I've finished my coffee if no one's any objection.'

Policeman and businessman held each other's gaze from opposite ends of a curling, six-seater sofa which was so low and enveloping that leaping up from it, Peckover judged, would have been impossible for anyone but an

Eastern bloc girl gymnast. Not that he anticipated a set-
to but you needed to be on your guard. He was hazy
about what he might be involving himself in up here in
the ionosphere. When all was said, one expression for
arms salesmen was merchants of death. Had he been
asked to describe for the jury the German's gaze in those
instants he would have said it was glittery. Rather than
trying to leap up he could start, if Becker started
anything, by throwing his coffee over the toes. Drinking it
was no pleasure.

Becker leaned back, looked up at the precipitous log
ceiling, and uttered a resonant laugh.

'You recognized the Mercedes with the château label,'
he said. 'You are a policeman, you snooped and found
her car. When one heard your car, old fellow, one was in
a delicate situation. You catch my drift? But when you
were only the police one was superlatively relieved.
Husbands can be tiresome.' Becker looked hard at his
downhill racer's toes as if for signs of athlete's foot.
'Though not in this case. Hector McCluskey is most
civilized and accepting. You will be amused by something
he told me. To be precise, what he told me he told his
wife. "You have made your bed, go and lie in somebody
else's." '

'When did he tell you that?'

'When? My good chappie, do you not grab the idiom?
"You have made your bed—" '

'Bit of a comedian, is 'e, the 'usband?' Is or was? 'Fellow
of infinite jest?'

'Absolutely. A philosopher. Most tolerant, one would
say. Of course, he needs to be. He asked me, "Does man
have to strive for indifference or is it a gift from God?" '

'Were you able to tell 'im?'

'One considered the question rhetorical.'

'That what he's striving for—indifference?'

'One really has no notion. One hardly knows the chap.'

'He knows about you and his wife?'

'Naturally.'

'And the others?'

'You mean Charles? Charles was nobody. Here today and gone tomorrow.'

'Ziegler?'

'That name plucks no chords.'

'Does Mr McCluskey know about his wife's affairs because she tells him or is he paying an enquiry agency?'

'Certainly not. She tells him, one assumes. Mercy is an honest, sensitive woman. She is incapable of deception.'

'Who says that?' Peckover was confused. 'Her 'usband?'

'One agrees utterly. But he is in a position to specify the unexplained telephone calls, for instance, which a deceitful woman would take pains to explain. Or she would go out exquisitely made-up, he said to me, dressed in her nines, and when she returned — no lipstick. Where had it gone? Perhaps grass on her hair. Immediately she takes shower behind locked doors. Small things. But have they the smackings of deceit? A deceitful woman takes many pains. If you were to understand woman, my old fellow, you will understand she repairs herself.'

Peckover was now thoroughly baffled. As he had feared, the death-merchant's toes had begun to wiggle. Furthermore the bloke's English had deteriorated. Were these indications of strain, a bad conscience, or simply lack of sleep? Pity's sake, a dishonest woman might take many pains but be simply sodding incompetent. Come to that, she might have been being honest.

More than baffled, Peckover was cross. Why was everyone so positive he knew nothing about women? What was it he was supposed to know? He didn't know anything about men either, come to that. If he knew nothing about women, his ignorance had never troubled him. He preferred liking them to knowing about them, whatever knowing about them meant. If this geezer were so hot on feminine psychology, what was he doing jiggling his toes and talking to a copper in this failed hidey-hole while his Yankee passion-flower held her breath in the inner depths? He should have been working on getting shut of the copper and dreaming up explanations and treats for Passion-flower who hadn't driven from Mordan to this mountain via Lourdes to be shut up in the boxroom with the skis and Pyrenean blowflies while her lover entertained the long arm of the law in the front parlour.

'When did Mr McCluskey tell you all this?'

'Yesterday.'

'Thought you didn't 'ave a phone?'

'One has not.'

'Where did you see him?'

'He was here.'

Bloody wasn't, he's missing, don't mess me about, you fornicating, barefoot Hun, you pickled herring.

'You've met Mr McCluskey before, sir?'

'Never.'

'Seen pictures of him, though. In the papers. Cookery columns. Television.'

'No.'

'How're you so sure it was Hector McCluskey?'

'My good chappie,' Heinz Becker said with a dismissive gesture and a shrug so sumptuous that even a Frenchman would have been impressed.

Peckover was satisfied. Not that the intelligence was going to mean instant promotion. He had missed the bloke, now probably missing for ever.

'Where did 'e go when 'e went?'

'One did not pry.'

'Where'd 'e arrive from then?'

'He did not explain.'

'Looking for his wife, was he?'

'Not in the least. He did not know she was here. In fact she was not, they missed each other by an hour, one is happy to say.'

'So what did he want?'

'To warn me about her, one supposes. Warn me off. Circuitously.'

'Thought you said he was tolerant.'

'Absolutely. And anxious on my behalf. He reminded me his wife's lover, Charles, had been murdered. Lover—poof! Another lover, he said, a pianist, had been murdered also. His wife was unbalanced. One refrained from informing him that it was him—excuse me, he—in one's private opinion, who was unbalanced.'

'McCluskey said his wife had murdered Charles Spence and the pianist?'

'Implied it. One was of the opinion he loves his wife a little over-possessively. He accepts. What choice does he have? But he is bitter.'

'How did he know you were here?'

'Fair question. He said that Mercy told him, which was plainly a lie.'

'She denies it?'

'Absolutely, if I were to ask her.'

'You haven't told her he was here?'

'Good Scott, old scout, you are an innocent! Do you not think such news at such a time—*l'amour*, old boy—might not have had an inhibiting effect?'

Peckover had no idea. He supposed it might. The double negatives, like double whiskies, did nothing to help. They might even have been triple.

'You going to tell 'er?' Peckover said.

'One doubts it. Are you?'

'I'm still not too clear how he knew to find you here.'

'My whereabouts are not top secret.' Again a shrug more Gallic than German. 'He may have telephoned Zürich. One tries to guard one's privacy but always there is a clerk perhaps, an unalerted friend. My Zürich office slipped over.'

'Up.'

'Pardon?'

'Slipped up. Heads may roll.'

'Sorry?'

'In Zürich.'

'Ah yes, heads may roll.'

'Say anything else, did 'e, Mr McCluskey?'

'He rambled. One offered him Southern Comfort from which he grew three sails in the wind. It crossed one's mind, when he was leaving, he might drive over the edge of the mountain. But one could hardly encourage him to stay when his wife was, ah, imminent.'

'Would you say, sir, bloke of your insight, 'e was more bitter than tolerant or vice versa?'

'More incoherent than either after half the bottle. He compared unhappiness with the eagle pecking at the liver—Prometheus, was it?'

'That's right, it's what the French all have. *Crise de foie*. Only they put it down to the cakes and goose fat.'

'I am sorry?'

'Go on, then what did 'e say?'

'Unhappiness like the eagle and the liver went on unremittingly, on and on, like an extravagant present—he specified prunes in Armagnac—presented to one's hostess, which she would pass to her uncle for Christmas, and later he gives to a brother, who leaves it in his desk until he needs a gift for a friend's birthday. And so on.'

'I see,' Peckover lied.

'When he left he was weeping. He held my hand and said he was one who loved not wisely but too well.'

'Bit green-eyed, was he?'

'Pardon?'

'Something about rather being a toad than keeping a corner in the thing you loved for other's uses. That it?' Fat use asking this lover-boy. Peckover stood up. 'Most 'elpful you've been, sir. I'll be on my way.'

'You do not wish to beard the lion when she is in the den?'

'Hardly necessary, sir. Give 'er my regards. True, I 'ad thought of striking an iron while I'm hot but I've enough in the fire as it is.'

Watched by Becker from the door and by Mercy McCluskey, he guessed, from behind eentsily-weentsily opened shutters, Peckover climbed into his car. He did not look back. He drove down the stony, serpentine track which eventually joined the main road. For the little he had learned he had come a longish way. But he saw nothing further to be won by waiting around or saying hello to Mercy McCluskey. He pressed the radio's button.

'. . . bottomed out while coffee held firm though sugar was dull . . .'

The question exercising him was less whodunit than whom it might be done to next and where? Unless Mrs McCluskey was as promiscuous as a mountain goat— looking through the windscreen for goats, Peckover saw only the rocky slopes, patches of green, and high snow—the candidates were limited. He would have guessed Becker, but Becker was alive and well, so far, and away back to Zürich where bank accounts were numbered and the murder-rate was low.

Jean-Luc?

Peckover would have been ready to switch off Business Matters and rehearse aloud his telephone call to the Mordan bluebottles, rolling his French r's and snapping his consonants, were it not for the *Comment?* and *Hng?* which would have been all he would receive back along the air waves of his mind. Bleedin' frogs, they didn't even want to understand.

He was content to give up for the present on who might be bucketing about with the knife. He would have put a quid on Hector if Hector had been missing, but Hector not only was not missing, Hector was sobbing on his wife's lover's shoulder, had been, when he might as easily have put the knife in.

Another question exercising Peckover was where he was going to eat. He believed he might be about to swoon from hunger but with respect to Andorra he was not ravenous for Andorran paella, couscous or cassoulet. He knew what he wanted but it was another hour's drive to the border and La Belle.

'Darling Miriam, I might be about to deceive you,' Peckover roundly announced above dire news about cocoa futures. 'If there are chips in Andorra, I'm going to have them, too many of them, but if ever you ask I shall deny it until one is blue and black in the face. Give me an inch and I'll take a mile.'

Driving and announcing, Peckover noticed but did not recognize or become excited by a pale blue car parked among pines off the track, half a kilometre from the main road. A tax-dodger, he supposed. He would have become excited had he seen the occupant who lay full length across the front seats, not asleep, or in distress, or dead, but simply preferring not to be seen.

CHAPTER 11

'Brrrrp,' burped Peckover, and washed down with a mouthful of rusty plonk what he fervently hoped was the last chip in Andorra.

There had been a tureenful of them, dosed with salt. Extraneous elements were what had slowed him down: the potato-packed Spanish omelette especially, which had arrived with the chips, and more bread, and had followed a shoal of small but numerous grilled fish, which had followed a soup sporting three sorts of meat, a cabbage,

barrowloads of beans of different kinds, chopped vegetables, white lumps of garlic like the tips of drowned
men's fingers, and many doughy, golf-ball-sized balls not
unlike dumplings, though tasting of olive oil as had everything else. Superlative! He would write one day an ode to
the Last Chip in Andorra, though not now, having no
notebook.

The temperature not being broiling, and this side of
the street being out of the sun, everyone except himself
and one or two wholly liquid lunchers was inside the Café
Cataluña. Peckover sat smiling and burping at his pavement table for two, an unashamed tourist neither
expecting nor looking for company. He would have preferred a mountain view but he quite enjoyed watching the
traffic stopping and starting in a roughly Franceward
direction on his side of the street, a roughly Spainward
direction on the other side. He did not know what the
town was called or if it were a town. He was in Andorra
but still, he judged, a thirty-minute drive from France.
His map named towns, possibly they were villages, on this
sole road linking Spain and France but the reality was a
continuous duty-free paradise or hell of shops. Who knew
where a town began and where ended? The gimcrack
supermarkets creaked with identical competing booze,
butter, cassettes, car tyres, handbags. Behind the
cratered, dusty loading-bays and parking areas soared the
mountains. A charabanc of smugglers crawled past,
speeding up as the light ahead became green, in its wake
anonymous traffic, and a battered black Mercedes.

Peckover, inattentive, failed to notice who was at the
wheel, but in the back window he glimpsed a sticker: a
label as Becker had called it. Twice before he had seen
the car: at the Château de Mordan and a couple of hours
ago at the Villa Azul. The sticker was not receding either
but advancing as the Mercedes reversed. Honked and
shouted at, its nearside wheels considerably on the pave-

ment, giving an extra inch to the traffic trying to overtake from behind, the Mercedes backed tiltingly and halted at the Café Cataluña. Mercy McCluskey climbed out.

No two ways, she's a knockout, thought Peckover.

'I know it's not important but you left that,' she said, and put his notebook on the table between the wine bottle and bread-sponged plate. 'I was going to give it to Miriam for you but as you're here . . .'

'Been through it?'

'I haven't even opened it.'

'So how d'you know it's not important?'

'It's all up here.' She tapped her forehead with her finger. 'That's what you said first time we met. 'Bye then.'

'Siddown.'

She had been turning to go. He supposed he must have sounded severe. What he felt was rising panic. She did not sit down but she stayed put.

'Where'd you find it?' Peckover said.

'Heinz did. On that box doodad with the magazines.'

Peckover, flipping the notebook's pages, dimly recalled a box doodad with magazines. After the bookcase he had avoided the magazines. He had assumed they would have been too specialized for him. Tax and sex. Whoever had deposited the notebook, whether Mr Balderstone or a passing goatherd or the King of Siam, he had not forgotten it. You didn't forget a stolen copper's notebook. So what kind of signal was being sent out in the Andorran fastness?

None in the notebook that he could discover, nothing in a foreign hand. How many visitors had Becker had anyway?

He said, 'In Lourdes yesterday, when you ran, that bloke in the wheelchair . . .'

'Hector?'

Quite so. The notebook seemed to signal that Hector McCluskey no longer cared. No more wheelchair deceptions. He had flipped, as Americans might say, unless they had a more recent expression. Worse, he seemed to be shrilly signalling, 'Come and get me, copper!'

'Come on,' Peckover said, standing.

'C'mon where? I'm going back to Mordan.'

Bearing down was an Andorran policeman in a plum-coloured jacket and music-hall hat. His uniform was the worst-tailored Peckover had seen outside a Christmas pantomime. In one hand the man held a whistle, in the other a cigarette.

'You're badly parked,' Peckover told Mercy McCluskey. He put too much money on the table. 'Get in. We're going back to Becker's place.'

'Like hell we are. I've just given him my everlasting goodbye.'

Peckover feared she was closer to the truth than she knew. He took her arm. She was protesting and he was not listening. Steering her across the pavement, holding her as if otherwise she might run, not for the first time, he offered the approaching policeman a smile and placatory gesture. He insinuated Mercy McCluskey into the driver's seat, hopped round the front of the car, tried the handle of the passenger door, and rapped on the window.

Mercy was not clear why she leaned, reached, and unlocked the door. Because he was capable, she supposed, of hanging on to the handle and galloping along-side if she had driven off without doing so. Because above all his merry yellow needlecord he wore a worried look. She believed she had never seen anyone look so anxious.

'Take the first right, down there, and round and back,' he said.

Nothing further was said. Mercy drove back along the duty-free road along which they had both come. His silence left her increasingly tense, swelling her own anxiety and causing her to drive faster, then still faster.

He made no complaint. After they had turned off the road on to the track up to the Villa Azul he began peering past her towards the woods.

Peckover failed to spot the pale blue car which had been parked, perhaps still was parked, among the pines. He accepted that it might be there and he had missed it. Either way he had not expected to see it.

When he drew up in front of the house he told her, 'Wait there,' and climbed from the car. No one came to greet them. Mercy discovered she was shivering. The door into the house was ajar and she watched the policeman go straight in with no warning rattle of the ram's horn or jingle of the donkey-bell.

Having started towards Becker, Peckover halted by the six-seater sofa, there being no need to go further. No need for pulse-taking or holding a looking-glass to the lips. Becker lay among the ashes in the fireplace, the top of his slalom suit shredded, the trousers round his knees. He was bloody and memberless. Blood was everywhere.

Peckover penetrated deeper into the cabin, past a kitchen, a guest bedroom, a loo, a bedroom with an unmade double bed. In the bathroom he looked at the bath, sink, towels, floor. Nowhere was immaculate but nowhere did he see blood. That probably ruled out Mercy McCluskey, whose gear and hands and fine white teeth had shown no signs of blood either. Whoever had slaughtered Becker must have been soaked in the stuff. No one had tried unsoaking themselves here in the last couple of hours.

He had never suspected her. Not, he assured himself, because he fancied her but because women did not do such things. She had been the last but one to have seen this boy-friend alive, not the last. The last, Peckover supposed, had been her husband.

He did not suspect her, but standing in the bathroom, staring at pointless soap and porcelain which never again would be needed by Becker, he blamed her. She was responsible. Jerome, the pianist, he could only guess about. But for the others—shadowy Ziegler, Charlie Spence, Heinz 'Death Merchant' Becker—she had been pretty literally the kiss of death.

Slag. Slut. Drab. Whore.

Leaving the cabin, Peckover saw across the floor, on the door handle and splodging the paved area outside, bloody stains which he had failed to remark on entering. He climbed into the Mercedes. If she'd had a scrap of imagination, he thought, she would have driven off and left me rather than face me.

'Dead,' he told her. 'Like the others. So the second thing you do will be write out a list, as many as you can remember, every Tom, Dick and Harry. They ought to be warned, wouldn't you say? Given a chance to dig themselves in? First, you get us to the nearest telephone.'

She drove with less energy than before. Her shaking and sobbing was at first so soft that he was unaware of it. When her misery grew noisy and he became aware, sod her, he thought. He stared through his side window, away from her. When her shaking became convulsive and she put her head on the steering-wheel and the Mercedes swung from one side of the track to the other, Peckover grabbed the wheel and shouted at her to stop.

They changed places. Driving, trying to remember if he had driven a Mercedes before, and to dwell on Miriam, family, cocoa futures, anything in order to be ignorant of the miserable, collapsed, sobbing heap in the passenger seat, Peckover refused to accept that all he was conscious of was the heap.

Sod bloody everyone, everything, he thought.

From a glass booth in the foyer of a half-built hotel on the duty-free road Peckover dialled the police. He identified himself and in fractured French and nursery English revealed that one of their part-time tax-exiles, Heinz Becker, awaited them at his Villa Azul, murdered. He would phone again, he said, he would try to present himself, but for the moment everything was rush. He replaced the receiver. How much of what he had tried to say had been understood he did not know. He brought Mercy McCluskey into the booth. On the assumption that her French was more effective than his he told her she was about to call the Mordan Hôtel de Police.

They stood pressed unpleasurably against each other, sorting coins and disagreeing about dialling codes listed in the front of the directory. The world record for the highest number of people crammed into a telephone booth would have been ten or twenty, Peckover guessed. Something astounding. But none would have been the size of himself and Mrs McCluskey.

'You say who we are and where we are, and we're on our way back to Mordan,' he said. 'You say another friend of yours has been stabbed, Heinz Becker, and I'm urging that your 'usband be found, all the stops out, and held for questioning. You ask 'em to relay that back to the police here, Andorra, and if they've got a Spanish or Catalan speaker, *tant mieux*. You tell them Jean-Luc Fontanille could be in danger and should 'ave police protection until Hector McCluskey's in custody. Then I'd better 'ave a word—Arsenal Rules OK?—so they'll know it's on the up. Got it?'

She nodded. She had calmed somewhat but she still fumbled, dropping coins, then the directory, sniffing unappealingly and failing several times to elicit even a ringing tone before a voice answered, '*Police. Mordan.*'

The booth was airless and smelled of tobacco and fried sardines. Peckover turned his head, aiming his luncheon breath against the glass door; but he faced her, nodding and interpolating when she began narrating into the mouthpiece. He heard answering French. Mercy

McCluskey's French seemed to contain almost as much English as his own but he judged she was doing all right, considering the shape she was in. She was pale enough to faint. Not surprising, Peckover conceded, in view of what had been done to her lover and who had done it. Correction. Lovers. She was offering him the telephone.

'Somebody called Gouzou. He speaks English, he says.'

She left the booth and waited outside, blonde head tilted back against the glass. Peckover made no effort to detain her. Impossible she could have heard or would have wanted to but he turned his own back and lowered his voice just the same.

'*C'est moi*. Peckover. *Bonjour. Allo? Ne quittez pas.*' Bloody marvellous, fantastic French, so it sounded to him, even if there wasn't much response from the other end. '*Enquêteur Gouzou . . . ?*' What was crucial, *très important,* was protection for Monsieur Fontanille, Peckover affirmed, because the bloke was Mercy McCluskey's lover, *amant*, and possibly with the exception of the château pianist the connection between the victims was that they all had been her lovers, Ziegler, Spence, now Becker, each one stabbed to death— stabbed, knives, *les couteaux* — then chopped.

'*Comment?*'

'Chopped. Lopped.' Cropped, dropped. '*Couper*, right?'

'*Hng?*'

'*Avec un couteau.*' Jesus. 'Cut. Excised.'

'Customs and excised? *Les douanes?*'

'Who? Hold it. *Non. Pas les douanes—*'

'At *frontière, oui,* is French Customs *douanes, mais après, faîtes attention,* Monsieur Peckover. Is not finish. In France is flying *douanes.*'

Gawd. 'Cleaved, hacked, hewn, severed, sliced, snipped, sundered, scythed. Forget *douanes,* can we? We're talking about Becker. Wait—amputate.' *Eh voilà!*

That was the word. Clinical, unemotive. '*Vous avez raison*. Not excised—'

'Excised, *non*,' agreed the frog linguist, confident to the last. 'Circumcised? Is that you mean it?'

Is not that I mean it, though in a sense the bloke was on the right track. Peckover wiped his moist forehead, said *Merci, merci*,' and hung up. He gathered Mercy McCluskey, led her from the hotel, and inserted her behind the wheel of the Mercedes. He got in beside her, a little apprehensive, but driving, he believed, might help her take her mind off distracting trivia. Life and death. Husbands and lovers.

'Next stop that Café Cataluña,' he said. 'Think you can manage?'

'Why the hell not?'

'Want to eat?'

'Nuts.'

'Nuts?'

'Go . . . please, d'you mind?'

Good. He wasn't for eating either. What she had wanted to say was, 'Go screw yourself,' and quite right. Her tone had become fairly savage, which was promising. Better than the vapours. He did not know how many stages of shock a case like Mercy McCluskey had to go through but she seemed already less distrait, to have gone from bleak to pique, from flopping about to hopping about. Not literally hopping about but her knuckles were white on the steering-wheel and her foot trod the accelerator into the floor with more feeling than sense.

Neither had anything further to say. They reached the restaurant soon after six, whereupon Peckover said, 'Next right,' and after she had done so, 'Stop here, anywhere.'

His hired car stood like a relic from another epoch: pre-chips, notebook, and dead Becker. He transferred his case and bits and pieces to the Mercedes, locked up, and at Mercy's side fastened again his seat-belt. The hire car firm would think of a number, double it, charge it, and with a laugh on their lips the British taxpayer would pay.

'Onward,' Peckover said. 'I'll take over at the frontier or wherever you like. Try the left there, then back up to the road. If you run over that policeman, if that's what he is—that one, Sancho Panza, in the Ruritanian costume—I'll give you a quid. Why do they never stop smoking, if they're on duty? If they're not on duty, why do they dress like that?'

Mercy missed the Andorran policeman, recovered the main road, and after a mile or so, when the emporia had sufficiently thinned for green to be visible between gaps in the concrete, and she had settled into a somnolent cruising speed, she heard the policeman say, 'I take it you were not having it off, ma'am, with your late pianist?'

Peckover waited so long for an answer that even for the jackpot he could not have dreamed up the replies she was aching to let rip. She settled for a longish sigh, and 'No.'

Taking no to mean yes, she was not, he said, 'No. Right. Your 'ousekeeper though, Madame Costes?'

'Ask her, don't ask me.'

'Why was he killed?'

'Christ, how would I know?'

'Your 'usband killed 'im, why?'

'I've said I don't know.'

'I know that. But you've got an opinion.'

'I've got no opinion.'

'Try. Reach out. You've got no opinion but I've got you, ma'am, and it's what—five, six hours to Mordan? Coppers are so thick all they have is persistence, did you know? Bloody tedious for both of us, I'll tell you. I don't mind if your opinion's not interesting as long as it's honest. Why did Hector kill Jerome?'

'It was a mistake.'

'Go on.'

'Hell, go on how? I wasn't there.'

'Fortunately for you.'

'What's that supposed to mean?'

'You're not saying a mistake like the knife slipped, really he was trimming his beard?'

'I'm saying Hector never intended to kill Jerome. Who said he killed him anyway? Or anyone? It's all so sick. I don't believe any of it.'

'You've been trying not to believe it for some time.'

'Look, whatever, Hector didn't aim to or want to, not Jerome. Why, for Chrissake? But if Jerome saw him and he was supposed to be in Hong Kong and . . . Oh God.'

Hong Kong, Timbuctoo, or anywhere the action was not, such as Portland, Peckover agreed. Thank you, Mrs McCluskey. Not necessarily Hercule Poirot standard, more Henry Peckover standard, which roamed between D-minus and B-natural depending on his liver. All the same. Success in the detection factory resulted from plod-plod, expensive contacts, a comprehensible filing system, once a decade a lucky guess — referred to in the textbooks as the imaginative leap, or analytical deductive ratio-cination, as if you were either Einstein or a com-puter — and a healthy, functioning liver.

Hector McCluskey had aimed to kill someone that Saturday night but no sharp instrument had been found and none had been found missing, or not before the circus had departed for Lourdes and points south. So the maniac had brought his own and taken it away with him. Presumably he had hoped to expunge Jean-Luc and Mercy but he had blundered into the wrong room. Plausible, if he had been lurking outside the château, dripping with jealousy, avoiding Peckover among the begonias, and watching the light going on and off in the bedroom which should have been empty apart from day-time decorators. He was not to know that on the other side of the corridor the light was going off and on in the Over the Sea to Skye and Vive l'Alliance France-America

Room, though as boss he must have been aware his château was a medieval fornicatorium dragged throbbing and thrilling into the twentieth century. When he burst in—did he burst or sidle?—lucky Madame Costes was absent gathering more eiderdowns because of his Scots canniness with the central heating, or borrowing champagne, or why not changing her mind and deciding she preferred her own bed after all? But Jerome was there, in or around the bath, pomaded chevalier of the Château de Mordan in the buff, scenting and powdering himself in readiness for the joust, the tilt with his paramour under the eiderdown. '*Sacré parbleu, patron, mais vous êtes à Hong Kong*,' quoth Jerome, fatally, and on seeing the *patron*'s snickersnee hoisted high, he snatched the nearest defensive weapon, which was not his Right Guard roll-on or Bay Rum or Vaseline or even a safety razor, but the cerise undercoat, which sploshed everywhere, for a time, until the snickersnee went in and he screamed.

Peckover watched the grey-green mountains a little sorrowfully. In a moment they were going to be gone, obliterated by a fresh stretch of the glass and concrete duty-free. Not for the first time he tried to put himself in the paint-sodden shoes of Hector, standing by the bath and its bloody contents, the pot in his hands. He too might have tipped in what remained, though he might not. But if you could hack like a latter-day Macbeth at a guiltless pianist, you could tip paint over him afterwards. Who looked for reasons from someone who had lost his reason? What you did not do was cut his cock off, because why would you, this not being the cock that had offended? The cock which had to be removed was the lunging, plunging Jean-Luc cock which filled your wife. O Lady Mercy! *O belle dame sans merci!* O blessed damozel! You wrapped yourself in a dustcover to hide the cerise and yourself and off you bunked. Seen bunking, you had doubtless given birth to a legend of a Château de Mordan ghost which would entertain customers and add another ten per cent to the bill for as long as there were customers.

Customers or not, the château was going to have to find itself a new governor. A new châtelaine too, Peckover suspected, though that might depend on how passionate the present one was about Jean-Luc.

No problem for her, of course, if Hector reached Jean-Luc before the police did. No Jean-Luc—no problem.

One problem at a time, he thought. The Mordan gendarmerie had several hours' start on Hector. They should have had Jean-Luc cordoned off already. All should be well.

In his belly sooner than in his brains Peckover knew that all was not well. Hector was behaving too desperately, as if doomed and knowing it. Killing Becker merely added fresh confirmation of the link between the dead, chopped men. Hector knew that, he was not simple. But he seemed to have given up even trying to cover up. Caution flushed away, cunning flung to the wind.

Suicidal was the word. He was behaving like someone who resented Mitterand for having done away with the guillotine.

Peckover watched Andorra slide by: consumer goods and mountains. Hector McCluskey's damning of the consequences might not have bothered him quite so much if the life of Jean-Luc alone had been at risk, though heaven knew that was bothersome enough. But Hector intended killing his wife too. Again it was the belly talking; but Peckover believed that his brains would have told him the same, and still might, if they had been sharper.

Frightening, the kamikaze pilots. The nose-thumbing schoolboy who knows the wrath is to come and has nothing further to lose. The desperate Highland stag at bay.

CHAPTER 12

'What made you tell me that fib about not having seen Ziegler for two years?'

'You wouldn't understand.'

' 'Course I wouldn't, I know that. I'm making conversation. What made you?'

'It was automatic. Scarlet women get to be very automatic. As autumnal leaves in Vallombrosa, so fall the lies.'

How, Peckover asked himself, did you question someone in shock? Shocked, uncomprehending, and plainly bitter, probably asking herself how guilty she had to feel. He had experience, she was not the first, but he had never learned. Patience? Tranquillizers? A separate, distracting shock such as a smack across the face? If he smacked this one's face she'd likely drive the two of them into the wall of the nearest supermarket. Driving might be all that was keeping her from collapsing in a heap.

'I could be pompous and say you lied to a police officer in the performance of his duty.'

'The only performance you were interested in was on the drums. What you were most interested in was getting out and buying your truffles.'

'Asparagus. Can't afford truffles. Why did you lie about Ziegler?'

'You're a sensational conversationalist. I didn't want Hector to know, okay?'

'Scared?'

'I didn't want to hurt him. I said you wouldn't understand.'

'Why would he have known? You were telling me, not Hector.'

'Oh, come on. Everything becomes public. Somebody hears, everybody hears.'

'Wouldn't surprise me, place the size of Mordan. You should have had more sense. As well try to keep an affair quiet in Chipping Sodbury — Apple Creek in your case.'

'This wasn't Apple Creek and it wasn't Mordan, it was Paris. I met Rick for two lousy days, not even that, and one of Hector's buddies, I didn't know he was even a buddy, some shopkeeper who'd once sold him cut-price cutlery, he saw us in a nightclub, dancing. First time I'd danced since practically high school. How'd you like that? The news of the year got relayed back, natch. Your sins will find you out.' Smoothly she overtook a caravan, a Fina petrol tanker, and a chain of lorries. 'Can we talk about something else? I can't explain and I don't feel like trying. You won't have realized this but you just insinuated I was looking for an affair, so I got one on my own doorstep, in Mordan, and that was stupid but I wasn't aware I had much choice. Just to enlighten you, I wasn't looking and the word "affair" doesn't enchant me, though I guess it's only a word. I happen to have three kids, a husband, work at the château, my own selfish interests like the arty-crafty bit, simpleton that I am, and there aren't enough hours in the day. But if you fall in love, you fall in love.'

'You don't think you choose to fall in love?'

'What does that mean?'

Peckover, ignoramus, was not sure. He believed he meant that it did not necessarily have to be bigger than both of us, though then again it might be, in some cases. Who was to say?

He said, 'You love Hector?'

'Yes,' she said.

'And whassisname — Jean-Luc Fontanille?'

'Why the hell not? Don't start trying to tell me you can't love two people at the same time.'

'Blimey, no. Or three, why not? Or seventeen?'

'*Merde* to you.'

Peckover was not wholly sceptical. He accepted he was an innocent in these matters and fair game for her contempt. He was fortunate in loving his wife, most of the time anyway, and nobody else, not in the same everyday sort of way, or not so far at any rate. If his chauffeur in her red trousers and a silky, swanky white blouse had sounded a little too adamant about loving her husband, she was perhaps reassuring herself. She had loved him, doubtless. But did one go on loving a killer? She had not married a killer. You were not, say, a weaver until you weaved, and you were not a killer until you killed. People married, then changed. You fetched up married to someone different. You could read about it all the time in the Sunday supplements: articles on open marriages, second marriages, standards, separation, custody, division of the spoils. Helpful stuff to be found between the think-pieces on disarmament and the football and racing.

'If you fall in love, you fall in love,' she was saying, not contemptuous so much as plain insistent. Was she out to convert him? 'Simple,' she insisted. 'Fact of life. End of argument. You're better off not falling in love, obviously. I would have been. That's not what I'm saying. All I'm saying is it happens. Why are you trying to complicate something that's simple?'

Peckover put on his beret, which was still damp from immersion in the miraculous bath. He took it off and said, 'I'd have thought it possible to wake up and think, Today I could press on with my weaving—not you especially, ma'am, I mean generally, people—I could press on with my stamp collecting, or gardening, or I could fall in love. Must be a school of thought which says love's the word we give an elementary, animal urge so as to posh it up, lend it soul. Not that I'd subscribe to that. 'Orribly cynical. Mean, look at history—Dante and Beatrice,

Romeo and Juliet.' He refrained from offering Heloïse
and Abelard, who in the circumstances, considering what
became of Abelard, might have been apt but in rotten
taste. 'Adam and Eve, Elizabeth Taylor and Richard—'

'If you've got to make conversation, why not the
scenery?'

'Sex, falling in love, it's all smashing. Who needs
excuses? You've been lucky. You say if you fall in love,
you fall in love, and for all I know it's exactly that, purest
chance. Far as I can make out, you fell in love with four
geezers at the same time, roughly. That's apart from
loving your 'usband. If not at exactly the same time,
pretty smartly one after the other, with overlapping.'

Her mouth opened, then clicked shut, a closing of
white picket fences from the green fields of Vermont.
Withering silence wrapped Peckover as he tried to sort
out her recent love-life. Charlie Spence, first for the
knife, dead in January in the Paris Hilton: probably the
briefest and passion-wise the most tepid. Around the
same time she was cheek-to-cheek with Mr Ziegler, an old
friend, possibly flame, who had surfaced in Paris but who
was put to rest in the USA only last week. Why? Well, the
cut-price cutlery witness who saw them dancing might not
have passed on the news until last week. Ziegler might have
been only briefly in Paris and Hector too tied up with
business until last week to make his Hong Kong noises and
pursue him to Portland. Or Hector had decided to let
Ziegler off with nothing worse than curses but was goaded
beyond endurance by finding a lover on the Mordan
doorstep and perhaps another who was an arms salesman.
Thumbs down on all lovers, whoever and wherever, past
or present. After Ziegler, the bungled attempt on Jean-
Luc Fantanille, resulting in one cut forearm. Then the
fiasco with the pianist. Now Becker, on whom a com-
petent job had been done, thanks to the gift of Becker's
name and address in the notebook.

'How much did you tell Hector about Heinz Becker?'

'I haven't seen Hector for ten days.'

'Did you tell 'im Becker existed? You were seeing him?'

'I hardly was.'

'So you didn't. Expect you realize you'll not get away with non-answers when serious coppers question you. That's by the way. Same with Jean-Luc, was it? Kept it quiet? Tried to?'

'I did not. We discussed it.'

'He knew Jean-Luc's name, everything?'

'Certainly.'

'He accepted it?'

'Yes.'

'Civilized and tolerant?'

'What are you trying to say?'

What he was trying not to say was that she was in as much danger from her civilized, tolerant husband's knife as was Jean-Luc. Always had been. More so now. If she knew that, likely she'd drive into the nearest tree. Anyway, he could be wrong.

Peckover did not think he was. Hector's ideal was to interrupt his wife *in flagrante delicto*. She would watch him dispose of — she would be given no choice — the lover, whomsoever. Then, Peckover guessed, before she were disposed of, she would be required to listen to a sermon on virtue, fidelity, and the marriage bond. Alternatively, or after the lecture, particularly if Southern Comfort were to hand, he might hold her hand and weep a little. Then stab her.

Impossible to have realized this aim with Ziegler because before Hector knew what was going on his erstwhile pal was back home being a restaurateur, many thousand miles apart from his Mercy. Impossible with Charlie Spence because that affair probably was over before Hector knew about it. Disappointing, yet so far as avenging himself went, irrelevant. If they were not to be sacrificed while in each other's arms, lover and mistress, they would have to be sacrificed independently, and first the lovers: polluters, corrupters, whose flesh had defiled for evermore flesh that was his, and his hers, by holy sacrament at the altar.

What had nagged him from the start, his first ten minutes with the squalid business, meeting Madame Mercy in her bathrobe among the looms and drum kits, had been the hopscotching kids or the monkey—Hector anyway—trying to break into the bedroom. Why the bloody hell did anyone try to break in at nine o'clock in the bloody morning and the place occupied by loving lovers?

Same with Becker. Hector had wanted Becker and Mercy together between the sheets. He would have entered like God's avenging angel, ended the death-merchant's career before any chance of retaliation with defensive weapons or skis, then lectured, sobbed, and killed at leisure his Desdemona. But Hector had arrived too early, Mercy was not yet there, and talking about her he got pissed. He left, parked his blue car among the pines, and saw her arrive, drive past, if he were not too pissed. But when he returned to the villa in the small hours when they would be supremely awash with sweat and sperm and saliva the place was a fortress, a tougher proposition than even Mercy's Mordan flat. When the door finally opened the sun was shining and the visitor was the copper who had harried him through Lourdes. After the copper left, patient Hector gave the couple an hour to recover from coppers and get back between the sheets. Instead of getting back in, Mercy swept past in the Mercedes, possibly to do the shopping but from the face on her more likely a goodbye-for-ever-girl, done with lover-boy. Foiled again. So Hector had killed lover-boy anyway.

He recalled having read somewhere long ago that in

crimes passionelles a young cuckold killed the cuckolder. The old cuckold killed his wife. Or was it vice versa? As generalizations went, this one must have intrigued him or he would not have remembered it. Half remembered it anyway, forgetting only the point.

'How old is your 'usband?'

'Forty-three.'

Voilà! Living, breathing statistical evidence of the generalization's truth. In middle-age the cuckold killed both wife and lover.

'Tell me about 'im.'

'Tell you what?'

'Anything you like.'

'He's from Glasgow. He works hard and he's made it. He's a celebrity in a small way, if you're into cuisine. It's all been in the press, he's been written up a score of times.'

'What else?'

'His wife's a fallen woman, what about that? Nineteen unsullied years before she fell, but so what? You're not going to believe it anyway.'

'Unsullied but humdrum.'

'You could say that. In some ways.'

'In one particular way.'

'Gosh, golly, you're quick.'

'Where did you meet?'

'Here, France. He was fresh out of Glasgow's College of Catering, the ink wet on his diploma, washing the celery in a swanky restaurant in Nice. I was fresh out of Bennington. There were three of us, dewy Bennington girls on the grand tour, first time overseas, on this packed beach, all pebbles and flesh, you practically had to stand. If you stood you got rubbed against by these Algerians with baskets selling peanuts. Don't know what we were singing, probably the first Beatles hit ever, whatever that was. We were two guitars and Donna played the flute.

Hector was studying his recipes, trying to, ten inches away, and looking daggers. It was droll. There we were jamming it, softly, well-bred Bennington style, and no one caring or listening except this pallid character with the cookery books. He was the pallidest guy on the beach except he was going red and blistering. He's got this very fair skin and he'd sooner fry than pay out for sun oil. He didn't even have sunglasses. Coming from Glasgow he'd probably never seen sunglasses, though I didn't know where he was from, not then, he could have been from the North Pole.'

A little breathless, she clicked shut the picket fence. Her jaw jutted, her brows frowned. For a moment she had forgotten where she was and why, who, what and how.

'Who spoke first?' Peckover said.

'What does it matter who spoke first?'

'It doesn't. I was interested.'

'Probably Donna, she was the yakker, asking him either to quit staring or start singing. He was low. Black Dog with doubts. That was early Hector—doubts, all tensed up with soul-searching and ambition. He'd become unconvinced cooking and restaurants were his bag. Out of hotel school with a string of A-pluses and into peeling potatoes, which he stuck with anyway. He was older than me, not much, I was twenty-one when we met, but he'd gone into the Black Watch when he was eighteen, that's some Scots regiment. I guess you'd know. Three years a soldier before having his first career doubts, packing it in, and switching to *la bonne table*. If he'd stayed a soldier he'd have been a colonel or something now and I'd have been on the cocktail circuit with the wives. Except if he'd stayed a soldier he'd not have gone to Nice and we'd never have met.'

She dried. Her eyes stared through the midge-spotted windshield. That, concurred Peckover, would have been best.

He said, 'When did you marry?'

'Four months later. Only time ever he's acted without taking for ever weighing up every angle of fifteen hundred angles.'

'Until now.'

'What's that mean?'

'Careful, is he, as a rule? Cautious? Weighing up the angles?'

'It ought to be a fault, Jesus knows it sounds dreary, but it isn't, not with Hector. Sure he's careful. He's not mean but he's careful, like he'll never throw anything away, you wouldn't believe his recycling in the kitchen. If you didn't know him you'd say he was dour, maybe insufferable, but he can be very funny. He can laugh at himself. Okay, he's not bouncing with spontaneity, he's never told me, "Och, woman, pack a bag, we're off butterfly-hunting." But he's reliable and gifted, he applies himself. If he starts something he finishes it. Like he's a musician too. On the beach he was going on about how I should have modulated from C major to D major because my G had been serving D as the subdominant. Some such gibberish. How the flute generically included the fife and the flageolet.'

Sorry, ma'am, but he sounds pretty insufferable to me, thought Peckover.

'What you'd call a whirlwind romance,' Mercy McCluskey said. 'It blew me off course. I was never going to look at a man who wasn't taller than me, let alone marry one. Hector must have had to swallow a whole dollop of pride because he'd have preferred to tower, I guess. He always said he would, but who knows? People are too complicated for me. What musical instrument does he play?'

'Don't you know?'

' 'Course I know. I was wondering if you were listening.'

'Castanets?'

'Oh sure. Hector happens to be a professional Scot. He

gets more Scottish every year and he's hardly seen Scotland since he left the hotel school. That's twenty years. The real professional nationals are the expatriates.'

'Like you?'

'I don't know what I am any more. I tag along shepherding the children. I'd sooner be in the States, if that's what you're asking. When we get an American couple at the château I want to beg them for a spare seat in their car for a home-loving American girl if that's where they're going—home. *La foi* is faith and *le foie* is liver, or the other way round, but how the hell do you remember?' She fell silent, concentrating as she overtook grimy vans and lorries with Principat d'Andorre licence plates. 'So it goes, as they say.'

Peckover said, 'Has to be the bagpipes. Did 'e bring them to the beach? Can't be much written for two guitars, flute and bagpipes. Still play, does he?'

'He practises. God knows why. Only time he plays in public is Hogmanay, and Burns Night, when they bring the haggis in. He loves piping in the haggis. Black Watch bonnet, kilt, sporran, dirk down the stocking, tartan everywhere. He's dressed up like a Come to Scotland advertisement. He gives them *Westering Home* or *My Ain Folk*. Something achingly yearning. Is that France down there?'

The road swung left and the glimpse of France was gone, obscured by the mountainside. Then it reappeared beyond the ochre supermarkets and debris of Pas de la Case, looking exactly like Andorra. Peckover's heart lifted none the less. He had had enough of Andorra.

'Last time I saw him, Hector, about ten days ago, he asked me what I was like in bed.'

The change in her tone as much as what he thought she had said startled Peckover. He had to lean closer to hear.

'The staff were cleaning away, we were having coffee, and he asked with this terrific reasonableness, genuinely curious, or pretending to be. "Would you describe your-self mainly as jocular or placid or outrageous or inventive or what?" I told him he was disgusting. He said, "What's disgusting about words? All I've done is say words," and he apologized and walked away looking baffled. He wasn't baffled, he'd made his point. That was Hector's way of telling me I was disgusting. Okay, I'm a mess, I'm not original in that, but I'm not disgusting. I've done nothing disgusting. Why couldn't he have talked about it if he felt like that? How was I to know? Why didn't he tell me, we could have talked, we could have discussed separ-ating, divorce—why not?—instead of all his sick, silent, noble, puritan suffering? God . . .'

Peckover was uncertain whether she was still speaking, she had gone so quiet. Her lips seemed to be moving. He stayed leaning towards her, ready to snatch the wheel if need be, because she was shaking, the tears running down.

'I'm okay,' she said. 'Other people's affairs are always sordid, wouldn't you say, Mr Peckover? Sordid and enter-taining—right?'

The workforce had made no obvious progress towards rendering Pas de la Case the show frontier town of the western hemisphere since he had driven through on the previous evening. Shutters were going up outside the gim-crack supermarkets; the piled baskets, espadrilles, strings of garlic and cans of olive oil were being hauled inside. In the square, laden day-trippers from France were boarding coaches. The Mercedes avoided rubble and skirted the Hotel Refugi dels Isards.

'D'you want to eat?' Peckover asked.

'No.'

'Thirsty?'

'I don't care. I don't want to hang about. I want to get home.'

'Stop there by those cheeses. I'll get some cans of something. Then I'll take over.'

He supposed he should have asked her to accompany him or at least requested the keys. He knew no reason why she would drive off without him but he would not have been surprised were she to do so even without a reason. People were complicated. She had said so herself, unhelpfully.

The supermarket smelled sweet as if from rotting fruit or somewhere a leaking can of jam. The only cleaning it received, Peckover judged, would be a weekly sweep. He put a six-pack of beer into his trolley and added Coca-Cola, not for himself. Then several bottles of spirits and two sherries as an investment, unless he had mistranslated the price, which was more than likely. The trolley's contents still looked fairly miserly. He added a wheel of probably Pyrenean cheese for Miriam, who would find a use for it, perhaps force-feeding him with it for the next three months. Next, a five-litre drum of olive oil—Vierge Extra, which sounded tasty. Peckover was not sure how he, or preferably Miriam, was going to get this lot back to London.

He looked over a pyramid of tinned sardines and through the supermarket window. In the Mercedes, Mercy McCluskey had shifted from the driver's to the passenger's seat and was presenting her face to the driving mirror, applying lipstick. Not with ulterior motives, Peckover was as sure as he was sure of anything. Simply, there were moments when a woman needed to put on lipstick.

Jean-Luc was still a four-hour drive away and as well might have been four thousand, Peckover thought, for all the chance his affair with Mercy had of surviving recent developments. Unless of course recent developments drew the pair closer together. Peckover, no prophet, made no attempt to guess.

Not guessing, instead he dropped into the trolley a

bright red cannonball of Edam; a monster tin of what he believed, going by the picture, might be palm hearts, which would be a godsend if ever he and Miriam gave a dinner-party for forty; and a catering pack of Toblerone chocolate for Mrs McCluskey. If she were going to drink all that Coke she would need her solids as well. A shelf of miniature bottles labelled Extrait Pastis delayed him. He tried to make sense of the instructions on the label. Sort of essence of pastis, like concentrated Pernod juice or Ricard, it seemed to be, which you mixed or perhaps filtered — *filtré?* — through or with a half-litre of alcohol and a half-litre of warm water. The miniatures cost around two-pence a bottle. He fed the trolley with a dozen of them, adding for good measure a couple of dozen *extraits* of rum, brandy and whisky.

The soap powders were probably a bargain. He hefted in a jumbo Omo. At the check-out the whole trolleyful came to around a fiver.

Not that it would last but something almost approaching cheerfulness had crept in. Peckover supposed the proximity of France was one reason; another the cost-conscious Henry having stocked up with bargain goodies; and perhaps most of all the sight of M.M. lipsticking her-self, which suggested she intended soldiering on: she was not totally distraught: she had not, like her husband, turned suicidal. Apart from the beer and Coke, which he placed on the back seat, he unloaded the booty into the car's boot, announcing each item in turn to Mercy, thereby diverting her, taking her mind off more sombre matters, if she could hear. He took the wheel and entered the line of traffic advancing towards the frontier fifty yards ahead. Adios, Andorra.

'Marvellous, the essence of Pernod, could be,' he chat-tered, diverting her, making her cheerful. 'Never seen it before.'

'You'll never see it again if the Customs stop you. It's

like bringing in heroin.'

'Don't be daft. It's not even alcoholic.'

'I'm only saying what I've heard. Maybe it puts the Pernod workforce out of work. If I were you, I'd put my hand on the horn and my foot on the gas and go through like Burt Reynolds.'

Bloody 'ell! Even had he been inclined to do so he was wedged between an unpassable smugglers' charabanc in front and on his tail a queue of tourist cars.

'We'll go through the green channel. They stop one in every forty.' He had made the figure up but it sounded reasonable; varying according to peak hours, the season, staff enthusiasm. 'They're not going to stop us.'

'Nothing to worry about then.'

Customs and Immigration were undistinguished single-storey buildings on each side of the road. There was no green channel as far as Peckover could see. No red either. The absence of channels he interpreted as a good omen, though he noted French Customs officers in blue, not Andorrans in plum, and at the side of the road one poor tourist bugger parked with the lid of his boot lifted high, contraband strewn all about, explaining how it was a mystery, he had never seen any of it in his life, to two of the boys in blue who shortly would be applying the electrodes. But for the most part the traffic was streaming through unmolested. A blue uniform sauntered in front of the Mercedes, pointed with one arm at Peckover, between the eyes, and with the other arm beckoned him out of the stream.

'Somebody has to be the one in forty,' Mercy McCluskey said.

Peckover later acknowledged to himself that if anything had been capable of lifting her spirits, this was it. Germans, he understood, called it *Schadenfreude*: the biter bit, the copper copped. Uproarious when the boom was lowered on the Law itself. For the moment he was not too perturbed, apart from the extract of pastis, which was akin to bringing in heroin.

He pulled up beyond the Customs building and switched off. 'Stay there,' he told Mercy McCluskey, who had no intention of moving.

Peckover climbed out. The Customs officer who had summoned him from the line dawdled along, looked through the windows at beer, Coke, and Mercy, then ambled to the boot. Neutrally he looked from the boot to Peckover, and nodded, neither hostile nor agreeable but a non-smoking, impersonal pipsqueak trained in *la politesse*, probably a vegetarian, and meticulously preserving his textbook cold-bloodedness until such time as the contraband was spread out and the bastinado might be brought out. Coppers could become emotional, Peckover saw it all the time, he was that way inclined himself, but whether Customs pipsqueaks were ever other than smug and expressionless, never raising their voices or letting drop their air of disapproval and excruciating moral superiority, he doubted.

Thinking these thoughts, Peckover felt considerably better. He opened the boot. Why did the victim have to do all the opening, not to mention the putting away, as if to touch were for the Customs officer to risk infection? When they did probe the bag they did so with tip of thumb and forefinger which they liked you to believe they had first had to disinfect. At the end of the day they were cowards though. The cash prize awaiting the Customs officer honest enough to tie on a hospital mask before probing was still to be won.

The officer dipped into the boot, turning the spirit bottles to read the labels, transferring them to the concrete. Everything else from the supermarket he placed beside them. After counting the miniatures he regarded Peckover with what Peckover thought might be the merest trace of pity. He gestured towards the suitcases:

the jaded one his own, the decent one with straps and studs, Mercy's.

Enough was enough. Delving for his warrant card, Peckover said, '*Il n'y a pas rien dans la baggage. Vraiment. Je suis policier de Scotland Yard.*'

Policier sur la piste, he would have added had he been certain this meant 'on the trail'. He had a suspicion it might mean he was on a ski-slope. He handed the ratbag the blue card. All right, he should have checked what the allowances were, what this foul essence of pastis was. Just the same. What about the Common Market, the free and unfettered passage of goods and bods across frontiers?

'*La police en France et en Andorre aussi me connait—connaissent?*' Peckover plugged on with slow, round vowels and a cracking of consonants. Never since General de Gaulle had delivered that '*Français, Françaises—aidez-moi*' speech had French been so resonantly spoken. '*Demandez-vous à eux, monsieur.*'

'*Comment?*'

Peckover stepped towards the front of the Mercedes. He opened Mercy's door and said, 'Sorry. Come and translate.'

'You're kidding.'

'We've got a right whippersnapper. An attractive woman just might unsettle him.'

A second, older, equally impassive Customs officer had joined the first. Together they were perusing the warrant card. Mercy opened her suitcase and brought out a knitted jacket. The sun had gone down.

'*Bon, ça va, ça va, ça va,*' said the older Customs man, passing the card back to Peckover. He made a sweeping gesture which appeared to indicate everything might go back into the boot, though he personally was not about to lend a hand, and turned on his heel. The pipsqueak officer sneered and padded after him. Sod off then, Peckover thought. He had been all set to feel grateful, invite them to London for the Policeman's Ball.

He gathered up contraband. Mercy was having a problem intruding an arm into an inside out sleeve. He plucked and fiddled one-handed with the sleeve's cuff, trying to find her hand inside it. His other hand held to his breast Toblerone and an Edam.

'Thanks,' she said, then went rigid.

By the time Peckover saw why, the traffic was advancing again, and the pale blue car which he and Mercy could almost have reached out and touched was drawing away. Peckover and the driver, head turned through forty-five degrees, regarded each other. Though Peckover instantly recognized him, his immediate reaction was, Mr Balderstone. He found that he too had become a statue, his mouth open in surprise, his hand up Mercy's sleeve.

'Stop—McCluskey!' he called out, still not moving.

The traffic was moving though, and by the time Peckover was on the move, Hector McCluskey was going to be catchable only if someone ahead slowed the flow with a flat tyre. The traffic was accelerating as if determined to be home before dark, which would not be long now.

Peckover glanced round for support. No one, only Mercy, and accelerating motorists. The Customs pair were trekking ever more distantly. Peckover started to run after the blue car and lost the Edam, which bounced once, then bowled redly in the direction of the traffic. He ran a dozen purposeless yards before stopping, not with any great dismay. What would he have done had he caught up? Tapped on the window? Thrown himself across the bonnet? While fancying his chances against Hector McCluskey the chef, minor celebrity and bagpipe-blower, Peckover was less sure about kamikaze pilots. His chief beef was that he had failed to see the car's registration. Fore and aft this burst of traffic had been bumper to bumper, as the press described Bank Holiday traffic. A blueish, largish car was the best he could have said. The same, he supposed, he had glimpsed parked in the pines.

He saw it once again, going well, a hundred yards distant down the winding road from Pas de la Case. He ran back to the Mercedes.

Oh no. No Mercy McCluskey.

He looked through the windows. He ran round the car and looked beneath it. The bottles, oil, palm hearts, Omo, stood abandoned on the pavement by the open boot. He turned through a circle, searching. He could not believe it. Why, why? His fists clenched.

Here she came: the termagant, the sad, unfathomable, beanstick wife, mistress and mother of three, dodging through the traffic in her heavy-knit jacket, holding two-handed the Edam. She was flushed and unsmiling, yet he believed there was an air of accomplishment.

'Ta,' he said. 'Did you recognize the car—is it Hector's?'

'Never seen it before.'

The cheese had escaped car wheels but its Cellophane-wrapped skin had turned from red to black, or at any rate grey. Embedded gravel gave it a resemblance to the cheese smothered in grape pips which Miriam brought home from time to time, snitched from her archæologists. Peckover put it in the boot. He loaded the rest of the rubbish.

'Did you notice a police station?' he asked. 'Never mind. Customs will do. Come on.'

He took her arm and they stepped out across the concrete. He took her arm, Peckover told himself, to comfort her and to be on the safe side. He invented these reasons so as to avoid the real reason, which was to touch her, and failing to avoid contemplating this real reason, he decided he might as well keep hold of her arm. He was fairly flabbergasted by his urge to touch Mercy McCluskey, considering, and by the pleasure holding her arm gave him. He thought the pleasure did not arise primarily from the protective instinct. Not being old enough to be her father, he believed the feeling was not fatherly either. Or brotherly. He decided to let analysis be.

Approaching the Customs building, weary, far from satisfied with his part in the whole sorry business, Peckover none the less enjoyed a surge of relief, his first for some days. It was finished, as good as. If Hector were here, he was not in Mordan murdering Jean-Luc Fontanille.

Not getting the car's registration, that was a pest. Even so, the next hour should see Hector McCluskey collared. Two hours at most.

Sorry, Hector, your chopping days are over, Peckover thought, mistakenly.

CHAPTER 13

Mercy McCluskey lay curled in her knitted jacket and under the cop's canary jacket on the back seat of the cruising Mercedes. She no longer needed another jacket because the heater was blazing like a furnace. She needed them only when he wound down the window and let in a blast of night air, as he did frequently. On one occasion when he rolled the window down he stuck his head out and shouted into the darkness what sounded like, '*Chacun à son goût!*' And after a pause, '*Autres pays, autres moeurs!*' On another, he started singing at the top of his voice the Cole Porter song about loving Paris in the springtime, but he stopped in mid-phrase, wound up the window fast, and embarked on shushing noises. Did he imagine she was asleep?

She would not have said no to a bottle of sleeping pills.
The whole bottle. Fergus, she believed, would miss her
most. Angus least. Angus had always preferred his father.
He shared Hector's moral rectitude. He would reason that
her death, though unfortunate, even in some ways sad,
was fitting, and a warning. He would interpret it as the
inevitability of natural justice. Ishbael probably wouldn't
notice.

How did you keep going as the wife of a mass-
murderer? Even as the ex-wife, because whom God had
brought together lawyers were now going to have to put
apart.

Was 'mass-murderer' correct? Four murders were not
masses. How many before you qualified?

She was shivering again, and hot, and the policeman's
jacket had slid to the floor. God! Why her? Why, Chrissake, anyone? An affair, so what? Didn't everyone? Why
the fuss and nightmare—why? There were betrayed
wives, oh yes, one or two, she had heard of husbands who
played around, but did their wives go killing the girl-
friends?

Jesus, she hoped so!

No, she didn't. She hoped nothing because there was
no hope, nothing ever again. The whole sexual swindle
was kissed goodbye. If only he had told her, talked to her!
Outrage possessed Mercy. He had deceived her a thousand times more cruelly than she had him, pretending he
accepted, he understood. She had not even deceived him,
or not at first. Even later she had never deceived him; if
she had not told him her every coming and going it was
simply because he understood, and to save him the hurt
to his pride. But at first she had tried to explain and he
had been understanding.

What an actor! Twenty years and only now was it plain
she had never understood the man she had married.

If I reach out, Mercy thought, God will trickle sleeping

pills into my palm, a river of them, and I shall suck them like candy, like when I was little in another age and another country. One hand was flat against her stomach, the other was between her teeth trying to stifle noises. The cop would not want to hear.

What matter if he did? His lousy job, he'd be immune, there'd be people weeping all round him all the time. He was okay though, on her side, Mercy thought, though he had not committed himself. His job would be to be neutral. Over an hour, best part of two hours, they had spent with the *flics*, hanging on for word that Hector had been arrested. Every mobile cop in the south-west was apparently looking, including the *douanes volantes,* the Customs men in vans and on motor-cycles who might waylay you even a hundred miles past the border. There would be road blocks. Oh, Hector, give it up, it's all over!

The telephone had not stopped. The Limey had telephoned Scotland Yard, and Miriam, whose voice was managing a marvellously improved rustling sound, he had told her doubtfully. He had proposed that she, his Yankee burden and travelmate, telephone Jean-Luc, just to reassure each other, but she had not felt like it, and the last place she would telephone would be his home where the wife might answer. According to the Mordan police, Monsieur Fontanille was well and at home, the house patrolled by a plain car.

Odd she should have felt pleased, still did, to have been able to help the Scotland Yard man with his French. Certainly he had been less incomprehensible than the elderly bloodshot Frenchy who had had the wine, fancied his English, which hardly existed, and kept on about La Guerre de Centaine Ans, five centuries ago, and Magg-ee Tatch-air, and *les Anglais* being his *chers amis malgré tout,* and how in nineteen-fifty-nine he had spent two weeks in Bournemouth, which he pronounced Bun-mousse, like some kind of pudding. Guesswork and close attention to his gestures and face-twitchings had been needed both by herself and the lost, weirdo, Cockney copper to grasp what he had been trying to say. The sobs which filtered through Mercy's knuckles became gulped laughter. '*Comment?*' He had congratulated the French cop on his English, beaming, admiring, placing a hand on the blue shoulder—for a moment she had feared kisses—and assuring him; '*Mon vieux*, your English is execrable.'

They had returned to the Mercedes only after a blue Citröen had been found abandoned, or at any rate unattended, at Foix, an hour away, and identified as more than likely the car used by Hector. Stolen in Toulouse the day before, according to thirty seconds' cerebration by the police computer. Filled with possibly Barbudos butts, which she had confirmed was a cigar smoked by her husband; on the door, dashboard and driver's seat, smears which probably were going to turn out to be Heinz Becker's blood, in the Limey cop's opinion. Now it was up to Foix.

Unless he had found another car and was already approaching Mordan, if that was where he was going. The computer had no opinion.

'What time is it?' Mercy said, sitting up.

' 'Ello there. Midnight. 'Ad a good sleep?'

'Where are we?'

'Not lost, not yet. Trying to avoid Lourdes. Go back to sleep—unless you'd like a sing-song?'

'Do you get promotion for all this?'

'All what?'

'Hector.'

'Why, what've I done?' Apart, Peckover thought, from mileage. He had found two bodies but they did not promote you for that. He did not think they did. 'There was a link anyone would have seen, couldn't 'elp seeing. Not going to award me the Légion d'Honneur, are they?'

'What link?' Mercy said.

'What d'you mean? You. Isn't any other, is there? Don't tell me Mr Ziegler was a secret arms salesman.'

'What're you talking about?'

'Exactly. Well may you ask. Apart from your pianist, all the dead and mutilated were your boy-friends, or had been. I'm sorry. Still, Monsieur Fontanille is going to be the exception.'

'What's "mutilated" supposed to mean?'

'You know. Their thing cut off.'

'What thing?'

She was leaning forward, hands on top of the passenger seat, chin on her hands. The headlights' glare was two amber cones illuminating the road ahead and to either side a swathe of flat countryside. Peckover silently swore. Dammit, didn't she know? But why would she? The Ziegler and Spence choppings had not been publicized. She had not seen Becker dead.

'Doesn't matter,' he said.

'What thing?' she repeated. 'Whose?'

'Theirs, of course. Whose d'you think? His own?'

'Own what?'

Was she naïve, or frightened to hear stated what she only suspected, or mocking him? Peckover, mountingly angry, did not risk an answer. He was angry with her persistence and the entire wretched business: people, wandering husbands and wives, the whole boiling. Most of all he was angry with his mealy-mouthedness.

He took a breath. 'Male member.'

'Ah.'

'All right?'

'That the same as the virile member?'

Peckover wound the window half way down, inhaled, and wound the window up.

'You sure spell things out,' Mercy said.

Unmoving and unmoved, she watched the amber road. Cock, prick, dick, male member, they were words registering nothing. She felt nothing. She imagined she should have felt nauseated but it was too late. Must have been. She no longer felt sick, shocked, hot, cold, anything. She hoped she had passed beyond feeling for ever.

'So what did he do with them?' she said.

'What?'

'I said what did he do with them? He must have done something with them. Even if he did nothing, if he just left them there —'

'He didn't just leave them there.' Didn't he? Peckover had no idea. He had not thought about it. At the Villa Azul he had neither observed nor conducted a search. 'He's a chef, isn't he?'

'Sure.'

'Well then. You said he was careful. Not mean but careful is what you said. Never threw anything away.'

'For God's sake.'

'How the hell would I know what he does with them? He keeps them in a shoebox and brings them out at Hallowe'en.'

'Stop it!'

'Gladly.'

The Mercedes slowed for a village, though not much. St Joseph. Half the villages in France, Mercy guessed, were named St Joseph. Most of the rest were St Antoine or Villeneuve-sur-somewhere. Not a light showed. Not a cat. Already the village was behind them.

She heard herself saying, 'Good old Hector. Quite right, too.'

'Mind passing me a beer?'

'Wasn't he right, seriously? God knows they're pretty unappealing. Not what you'd call appetizing, æsthetically. If I were president of the world I'd abolish them, by decree, a quick operation, every last one. Away with them.'

'You might meet some resistance.'

'Not from women. It's not even they're ludicrous or they've caused more misery than anything since time began. They're just damn boring.'

'If you say so,' said Peckover, doubtful whether Mrs McCluskey of all women were the woman to say so. If they were so boring why did she keep on? He saw a signpost with a mention of Mordan. Fourteen kilometres.

He wondered whether her bitter, inconsequential chat were a sign she was surviving or was she already round the bend? She had fallen silent. In Mordan he drove the wrong way down a deserted one-way street, looking for the Rue du 17-Août. He parked on the pavement behind the boulangerie. Cartons of rubbish and blue half-sized dustbins had been put out on the corners of the street. Dogs from the alleys had upturned most of them. Peckover hauled both suitcases from the boot.

'I'm your guest,' he said. 'If you insist we can go to the château. I'll still be your guest.'

Mercy shrugged. Had she protested, he would have explained, but she did not. Did she suspect she herself was not safe until Hector was shut away or did she not care? In the flat he checked first the bedroom windows and shutters. Next every other means of access, as they called doors, windows and chimneys at the Factory. They were few. He took his toothbrush and pyjamas to the bathroom.

The divan bed he pulled into the middle of the sitting-room so that it was aligned with the door into the flat, the bedroom door, and the bedroom window.

'Leave your door open, would you mind?' he said.

'I'll give you clean sheets.'

'No need. Change them tomorrow. Go to bed.'

He placed a table lamp on the floor and switched it on. He switched off the main light, got into bed, and closed his eyes. He ought to have been telephoning, checking whether Hector McCluskey had been caught, because if he had all this palaver was wasted effort. But he preferred to sleep.

The telephone awoke him. Ten past eight. A blade of light pierced the vertical join in the sitting-room shutters. Peckover looked through the open bedroom door. Under the bedclothes Mrs McCluskey was stirring.

Enquêteur Gouzou of the trendy gear sounded excited and irritated in equal measure. He had been trying, he appeared to be saying, to telephone Monsieur Peckover at the Château de Mordan, he had not known he had spent the night with Madame McCluskey. Jean-Luc Fontanille arriving for an eight o'clock class had been stabbed in the staff parking behind the *lycée*.

'*Mort?*' Peckover said.

'*Non.* Is wounded at the neck. Is en route at *l'hôpital.*'

'*Bon—ni mort ni mutilé?*'

'Is okay maybe. Agent Blois is 'urt at the *genou*—knee.'

'Have you got Hector McCluskey?'

Presque. Almost. *L'assassin*, having fended off the policeman Blois, and failed to kill Jean-Luc Fontanille, had driven off in a grey Simca, *matriculation* 3061-HK-09.

'Since twenny minutes. Twenny-five maximum. Is only now time question. *Le commissaire arrive, et le préfèt.* In Mordan. Big action. Everybody demand Chief Inspector Peckover. You come 'ere *au lycée, ou à l'hôpital?*'

'*L'hôpital. Donnez-moi quinze minutes.*'

If everybody had been demanding Chief-Inspector Peckover, believed by Peckover to be the least likely event of the week, they were no longer. For a start, the commissaire, in steel-framed Gestapo glasses, far from demanding him, did not want to know and plainly resented his presence in France. After a peremptory handshake he turned his back to talk to a policeman wearing a képi.

The prefect wore an advertising executive's striped suit. From the shirt collar with sober silk tie emerged a thick, mottled neck and solidly above it a peasant's shorn head, big-featured and weatherbeaten. He was affable, doubtless brilliant — his English was excellent — and possessed of a roving eye which, having lighted on Mercy McCluskey, roved no further. He asked Peckover, while eyeing Mrs McCluskey, to convey his regards to his friend Commander Bray of A Division. He urged Peckover to sample the *tournedos Henri IV* at the Restaurant de la Gare, and looked forward to reading the account of his activities over the past day or two, when available, at Mr Peckover's convenience. But he could not have been called demanding. What he might demand of Mercy the moment he was alone with her was something else. Peckover doubted he would get far.

Not in demand, Peckover stayed close to Mercy. He would have done so anyway. His sole function was to remain at her side until her husband was found and locked away. At its first serious test this priority took a slap on the face because she strongly did not want to see Jean-Luc, and Peckover thought she should, if only for a moment.

Still, if she were not going to be safe with the prefect, the commissaire, and a dozen police in the corridor, none of them smoking, one or two of them built like mountain forts, they might as well all curl up and die. The man he had seen in the Loch Lomond Bar with *Le Monde* and the Bloodsucker cocktail, bussing Mrs McCluskey, now lay bandaged in a room where eddied white nurses and doctors, too many police, and a girl with a typewriter and tape-recorder who was not a journalist. He had had twenty-two stitches. You'll be able to invent and adapt a bit, Peckover thought sourly, and boast of it in years to come as a love-bite from an American woman with fine teeth. Regaining the corridor, he observed that the prefect had a rival. Inspector Pommard had homed in: two lechers bombarding impervious Mercy with smiles and sympathy.

Peckover led her away for coffee and croissants or whatever she might want. A sleep and a forgetting more than likely.

Then to the Hôtel de Police where she regarded the same page in the magazine, and from time to time her fingernails, without interest, while he telephoned silent Miriam, and Scotland Yard, and hunched for two hours over a typewriter, typing and muttering, asking at one point for the spelling of McCluskey, and cursing the French keyboard with its strewn accents and upside down question-mark.

Then to the château. Mercy did not appear to care whether she went or what she did. Her one murmured preference was for seeing none of her children: not just yet.

They stayed only briefly at the château. Madame Costes believed Fergus was here somewhere with two friends, which left Mercy visibly jumpy. Miriam, in the kitchen, looked up at her husband and cringed, as if he bore down on her with a smoking knife in each hand and blood dripping from his teeth. Peckover considered this an exaggerated reaction to what eventually he gathered was his beaten-gold needlecord. Fortunately her voice had not yet returned, and gent's suiting apart, she seemed happy to see him, as he was her.

Their eyebrows, Miriam's and Madame Costes's, had lifted for news. At the reception desk the woman with teeth like the Klondike asked right out if Monsieur McCluskey had been found. Peckover was evasive. Both within and without the château were plainclothes men failing to look like guests.

To Peckover their presence was gratifying. Here was a

small but unneglected corner of the big action which had excited Enquêteur Gouzou. Mordan itself had been hopping with police going through the motions. Trouble was, surmised Peckover, going through the motions was about all. From the brass at the hospital he had gained two impressions. One, that he personally was not in demand, an affront which had not stopped him in his tracks. Two, that wherever Hector McCluskey might be, in the opinion of both the prefect and the commissaire — and such opinions had a way of seeping down from the summit — he was not going to be in Mordan.

Peckover disagreed. From the reception desk he telephoned the Hôtel de Police.

'*Non, monsieur. Pas encore.*'

He drove back towards Mordan, Mercy at his side. The local force had no need of him. Other than keeping Mrs McCluskey close and his eyes alert there was nothing for him to do.

Nothing, only looking after Mercy and killing time. Every copper was expert in killing time. Here ought to have been the place to kill it. The sun shone. Pink and white blossom loaded the trees. By the river the fields were green, brown and sumptuous yellow. He saw an ancient couple hoeing or thinning or whatever, the grandpa wearing his blues, the grandma in black and a straw hat, as in an Impressionist painting. Even in the car he could smell the lilac, almost.

Mercy said, 'I appreciate all this. I'm sorry, honestly, about everything. You don't have to stay with me. Hector — okay, I know. But he loves me. I think so. He's not that much of a . . .' She failed to find the word. 'Drop me at my apartment. I'll be fine. Go back to Miriam.'

'I can arrange for a couple of policemen to keep you company.'

'Would you prefer that?'

'I thought you were suggesting you would.'

'What did I say?'

'I wasn't listening. I was looking at spring in downtown France. There—are those swifts? Everything's out and burgeoning, it's bloody marvellous. What's that yellow stuff?'

'Rape?'

'Not while I'm driving, ho-ho.'

'Rape-seed—colza.' Mercy smiled, surprising herself. Her first encounter with this Cockney ox, she remembered, through the peephole, she had wondered about rape. 'Take the next left if you like. It's the scenic *route touristique*.'

'Are you going to give me lunch?'

'Hadn't thought. Am I?'

'Very light. Something salady.'

They had grilled trout and a salad of broad beans and avocado at the sitting-room table. After cheese, Peckover telephoned the Hôtel de Police. Negative. He decided he should try to limit his query to no more than one every hour.

He asked her to weave and show him the magic of the loom, which she did. At first the deft, rhythmic *clunk* of the shuttle, if shuttle was what it was, riveted him. Eventually the monotony drove him to finish the claret. They washed the dishes, read, and found nothing to say.

At four o'clock Peckover stood up. 'Good. The *thé dansant*, okay? Lead the way. I've got claustrophobia.'

First he telephoned.

'*Non, monsieur . . .*'

She took him to the Café de la Paix on the boulevard. At a pavement table they watched the traffic and drank tepid tea made from a used teabag, or so it tasted to Peckover. He watched the customers and passers-by. As well as his beret and notebook he had brought a street map, believing they might walk, and in an alley walk into cowering Hector, succeeding where the massed police were so far failing, and thereby bringing to an end the tedium. Tedium, he considered, was not quite the word for this waiting for Hector to strike at his wife.

The beret had dried out with a mysterious rigidity, like pemmican. An ingredient from the miraculous baths, he supposed. Mercy flipped open the notebook.

'Is it private and secret?' she said.

'Yes.'

' "Two pounds neck lamb," ' she read aloud. 'Is that a clue?'

'It's a code name and its none of your business.'

'So what's it mean?'

'I'm not at liberty to say.'

' "Yeast extract. One small granary." ' She flipped pages, peering at the scratchy longhand. 'You've got a conference with someone called AC, Wednesday, nine o'clock.'

'Last week. Don't frighten me.'

'A poem. May I read it?'

'No. What poem? I suppose so. If you promise to like it.'

'You'll never know anyway. I'll pretend to like it.' She eased her shoes off under the table. 'I get straight As for pretending, always did. The yellow jersey.'

She read.

Marriages of Inconvenience, 2

Having cheated her past measure,
Perhaps nine hundred times since when
He said, 'I do, I will',
He startled her: 'Seek sexual pleasure.
Ours has long staled. Go out with men.
Be free, fulfilled. I love you still.
Deprivation sours. My life, my treasure.'

★

When she replied, 'I have, I do,'
He did again surprise her
With a looping left which loosened two
Bicuspids and the lower right incisor.
'Yes,' she said. 'Mm. I'll have to—'
'Look at me and try to smile,' Peckover told her
He was neither smiling nor looking at her. He was staring ahead to the far side of the boulevard where Hector stood, staring back.

Peckover put a hand on Mercy's hand, his other hand on her cheek, and kissed her on the mouth.

CHAPTER 14

The monstrous Common Market lorries bearing surplus wine, butter mountains, and overproduction of all manner of overpriced everything, pounded along the boulevard, north and south, spouting fumes, grinding to a stop at lights, and, as they moved roaring and vomiting on in bottom gear, causing the foundations of every building in Mordan, mediaeval and modern, to shudder. Private motorists kept patiently their distance, though here and there a thrusting young insurance salesman would show the world by swinging his company car out of the lane and overtaking.

Mercy McCluskey, who had been kissed before, began to wonder when this kiss would stop. More than anything she would have appreciated advance notice. Had she known kissing was going to figure in the afternoon tea-break she would have brushed her teeth vigorously before leaving the apartment and been extravagant with her Femme. There had been a time in Vermont, she reflected, when such a kiss in a public place would have brought the justices galloping up and prompted editorials in the *Clarion* on shamelessness, vile concupiscence, and the slide to Gehenna.

At least he was keeping his tongue to himself. Far as she recalled, he hadn't cleaned his teeth either, he had been too busy telephoning, but he smelled clean enough, she was unlikely to be about to catch anything. O he has herpes and she has his. Hang in there, Mercy, he is the boss man. As kisses went it was one of the least thrilling of her experience, considering its duration. On the other hand it was not obnoxious. It was a fence-sitting, middle-of-the-road kiss, lacking commitment, like a floating vote. Actors and actresses probably felt similarly detached, Mercy thought, or at any rate strove to do so, in order not to become inflamed and forget their lines.

She opened one eye. Simultaneously the policeman opened one eye. One-eyed they blinked at each other, seeing only a bright, beady smear of eyeball. Mercy thought: This really is where we came in, moons ago, eye-ball to eyeball through a peephole. Peckover thought, mystified: Fried egg. Abhorring mysteries, he traced the thought back through an association of useless ideas to eggs fried on one side only, in the States, which were 'sunny side up', or sometimes, he believed he had some-where heard, 'with one eye open'. He drew back and looked across the boulevard. Hector had gone.

Peckover pushed back his chair. His eyes searched the far pavement as it became visible, now one stretch, now another, through the traffic. He looked both ways along his own pavement and at the trickle of prams, mothers and old men on the zebra lower down the boulevard. Not a copper in sight, naturally. Like London. Though here they had good reason: they were all elsewhere looking for Hector McCluskey.

If they were not, time they bloody well started.

He stepped off the kerb for a better view of the far pavement though he knew he was not going to see him. Where Hector had watched from outside a corner window filled with guns and fishing tackle — *P. Bonnet — Pêche, Chasse* — there stood two boys dividing into each other's palms something out of a paper bag. An alley along which Peckover believed he would be wasting his time led away from the fishing tackle shop. He stepped back to avoid being squashed by a pantechnicon. Mercy, on one foot, leaned on him briefly as she pulled a shoe on.

She said, 'Hector?'

'He was there, where those lads are. There'll be a phone in the café. Or would it be quicker on foot — the police station?'

'Same. Simpler to go if we hurry. He saw us?'

'Yes.'

'Like he saw us at the Customs?'

'More or less.'

'Baiting the trap, is that what it's called? That what you're doing?'

'With any luck there's going to be no need for baiting traps. Maybe this lot will now get their finger out.'

After a spell at the Hôtel de Police listening to the reassurances of Inspector Pommard, Peckover and Mercy walked to the Mairie, where the prefect apparently was. Increasingly anxious, alert for a Glaswegian with an up-lifted knife, Peckover was of the opinion that the prefect should have come to him. He had the impression he was the only copper in southwest France taking the business seriously.

Well, no, he exaggerated. But the quiet confidence of this mob he believed to be misplaced. A minor point but had they even thought to ask themselves, for example, which of them would be Hector's priority — himself or Mercy?

The prefect offered Monsieur and Madame an *eau de noix* which he described as *exceptionelle*. His eyes roved over Mercy, up and down, side to side, finding her equally *exceptionelle*. If they were in doubt where to eat that evening, he said, might he recommend the Belle Epoque, which offered a very fair *cou farci à l'oseille*? He audibly sighed at Madame, indicating without hypocrisy or sniggers that Paradise would be precisely that: *cou farci à l'oseille* and Madame, in no particular order, perhaps both together.

As for Monsieur McCluskey . . . Temporarily the prefect forsook sighing and ogling to look with reluctance at Peckover. Everything that could be done was being done, monsieur. Photographs distributed. A watch on all roads in and out of Mordan, the rail station, the airport seventeen kilometres away. Surveillance at the Château de Mordan doubled. The prefect's lip-lifting betrayed his scepticism, as he intended. Every policeman in the department had been brought back to duty, day or evening off or not. Hector McCluskey would be found, monsieur, and soon.

Peckover shared the prefect's scepticism about the château, though probably not for the same reason. Hector would turn up at the château only if he and Mercy were there. The prefect's reassurances were intelligent, lucid, even reassuring.

Peckover was not in the least reassured. 'If you 'aven't got him by midnight, I'll be with Mrs McCluskey in her flat.' He held out his glass for a refill, more in desperation than because he enjoyed the sweet, sticky stuff. 'Might I suggest you keep it closely watched? I also suggest you don't keep it obviously watched, like a 'undred men with linked arms, because if that's what he sees he's going to bugger off and we're back where we started, right? I 'umbly suggest the discreet deployment of a half-dozen of your best. Armed.'

'You persist in this belief of a threat to Madame?'

'You could say that.'

Those of the local lot who had believed that wherever
he might be, Hector McCluskey would no longer be in
Mordan, probably now believed it a hundredfold.
Spotted on the boulevard by the interloper from Scotland
Yard, would not the butcher of Mordan have put a kilometre or two between himself and Mordan? Peckover
unfolded his beret. Those who had disagreed or had not
much thought about it no doubt agreed now that Hector
McCluskey, sighted, would be heading for the South Seas.

Walking with Mercy back to the Rue du 17-Août,
Peckover crossed to what appeared to be the better lit
north side of the boulevard. They had no small-talk. He
steered her into a pokey grocery and patrolled the shelves.
They left with three boxes of peanuts and a bottle of
Bell's.

'I'm depending on you to look after me,' he said. 'Me
and us. If you see the level reach around halfway, tip the
rest down the sink.'

In the flat he checked windows and shutters. He pulled
the divan bed from the wall and pushed it against the
locked, bolted door. He telephoned the number he knew
by heart.

'*Non, monsieur . . .*'

'Sorry,' Peckover told Mercy. He sat in the cushioned,
creaking, canework chair where he had sat on his first
visit four days ago. Only four? As long as that? More or
fewer than four days he would have accepted but four did
not seem right. 'It's a pest. Bugger everything. Does
Hector have a key?'

'Couldn't say. He never comes here. He organized the
spyhole and locks, so he might. He didn't use it last week
when he tried to break into the bedroom.'

'You think that was Hector?'

'I do now.'

'Why didn't he come in the door?'

'Maybe he doesn't have a key. Maybe he heard you

banging the drums.'

Maybe, Peckover conjectured, he preferred the drama of the bedroom window. God's Presbyterian angel exploding through windows to visit judgment on the coupling sinners.

'Scotch?' he offered.

'Yes, please.'

'Shall we have some music?'

Mercy put Verdi's *Requiem Mass* on the record player. After side three and the Sanctus she switched to Dolly Parton. *Daddy Won't be Home Anymore.* Peckover looked at his watch.

'Twenty to eight. *Cou farci* at the wherever-it-was?'

'Oh sure. Terrific. A night on the town.'

'Glad you agree.'

They ate bread and cheese in the kitchen and finished the peanuts.

'What's on at the flicks?' Peckover said.

'Flicks?'

'Flicks, right. I just had a whiff of nostalgia, a yen for whelks off a barrow and hearing someone say, "Full up, no standin' inside." I'm not interested in a movie or *un film* but a flick might pass the time.'

'All right.'

He telephoned the Hôtel de Police. Zero.

Watchful, Peckover stepped out with Mercy McCluskey through the empty market, past the Café du Centre, past the Priory, across the boulevard, and into the Palais. They sat in the balcony and saw Gérard Depardieu in a comedy set in a high-income milieu within whistling distance of the Eiffel Tower. There were comic adulteries, a comic gangster, and comic policemen speaking French far too fast for Peckover to grasp more than the occasional *Alors* and *Voilà*. He did not like to ask Mercy for explanations in case she was having difficulties too.

He suspected her chief difficulty might not be the film but holding on.

While Mercy McCluskey and Peckover sat in the balcony of the Palais, Hector McCluskey let himself into his wife's flat. He sauntered abstractedly, drank a glass of water, then entered the bedroom and closed the door behind him. He lifted the patchwork quilt and slid under the bed.

The film seemed to end happily with everybody with somebody in bed, having been to bed, or about to go to bed. From a telephone-box in the foyer, Peckover telephoned.

'*Non, monsieur . . .*'

'I know. Find your Monsieur le Préfèt and remind him about *la surveillance, s'il vous plaît. L'apartement de Madame McCluskey.* He's probably eating. Somewhere *exceptionel.*'

They walked back along the boulevard, Peckover needlessly vigilant, though he was not to have known. Apart from an occasional car, Mordan was dead. He hoped the occasional cars might at least be police cars. In the Rue du 17-Août a shadow, cat, some movement or other, was shiftingly there, then gone.

'Wait,' muttered Peckover, and he stepped into the alley down which had vanished the shadow.

In a doorway stood a man in a sensible hat and coat who nodded and said, '*Bonsoir, m'sieu*'.

Peckover thought he remembered him from the hospital corridor. Mainly he remembered the man's size. He was about seven feet tall, as if imported from Texas. Not a surveilleur who could be easily disguised as a cat but not one to come at with a knife.

'*Vous êtes seul?*' Peckover said.

'*Nous sommes cinq.*'

'*Bonne chance.*'

'*Bonne nuit, m'sieu',*' said the surveilleur: not Texas but Mordan and environs.

Supine beneath the bed, his nose inches from the wooden slats supporting the mattress, Hector McCluskey heard the door into the flat close. He turned his head and reached out to lift the patchwork quilt. Light shone beneath the bedroom door. The voices he heard were indistinct murmurings.

'Coffee?' Mercy said. 'Tea?'

'I don't think so.'

'Scotch?'

'Look, Mercy—ma'am—I'm sorry about all this. Do you believe me?'

'Yes.'

'If you can think of a better way, for heaven's sake say.'

'Don't worry about it.'

'I'm not sure you understand. We're going to bed together.'

'I understand. I said don't worry about it.'

Easy to say, Peckover thought. He brought the drum kit from beside the wall and arranged it piece by piece like a minefield in front of the door into the flat. He changed his mind and moved it back against the wall. Either he wanted Hector McCluskey to come right into the bedroom itself or he did not. From the fireplace he collected the brass poker. If Hector were going to be discovered before he killed again, Peckover believed, it was going to be by seeking out and discovering the pair of them as lovers.

If Hector did not discover them as lovers, would he ever hang around long enough, like a moment or two, for the wrestling which Peckover believed he, the strong arm of the law, ought to win? If this time Hector succeeded in coming through the shuttered window—God knew how, but no future in puzzling how if he achieved it—and he found his wife a chaste, solitary Sleeping Beauty, would he linger? Wasn't retribution what the poor bloke was after, vengeance delivered on his whoring wife and lover? Would he even think to harm his Mercy sleeping chastely alone?

Yes, he might. Who the hell knew? But again, if he came through the door and found the copper celibate in the divan bed, unloverly and blameless, he was pretty certainly going to light out at a sprint, slashing at anyone who stepped in his path, as he had slashed at Jean-Luc's *flic* in the *lycée* car park.

Was he? In spite of the kiss in the café?

The question was not going to arise if they were together in bed, lovers. That was what Hector expected to find, and finding it, testing his snickersnee on the pad of his thumb should delay him for the two seconds needed for the collar. Might be longer than two seconds. He might want to deliver a sermon first.

It's me who needs his head examining, Peckover thought. He wanted to take his jacket off but he was aware of dampening patched under the arms of his shirt. When he spoke his voice was quiet, listening being more to the point than talking; listening for a noise at a window, a key in a lock.

'Nothing's going to happen,' he said. 'Hector, I mean. But just supposing he turned up. He won't but he's out there somewhere. Supposing he did? Can't you be brilliant, think of something better?'

'No.'

'You and me, we're not going to touch each other, obviously. But it's better if, if there's any sense in this at all, if it's going to work, well, better if we seem to be, that's to say, attached. With what that implies. Pertaining to, for instance, dress. Let me explain.'

'You don't have to.'

'Yes, yes. I must.'

'Do you have a gun?'

'I can cope. Anyone arrives, I'll hear. You won't know anything, you'll be asleep.'

'You think he's going to come, don't you?'

'How? There are five coppers outside.' He could not have explained why he did not feel more confident. 'What 'appened to that drink?'

She brought the bottle, water, and two tumblers.

Later she said, 'I'm looking after you just like you asked, captain. I'm watching the level. It's not half way.' Her laugh was perilously close to a giggle. 'If you measure from the bottom up.'

'You're going to sleep like a top, ma'am.'

'Mercy. Who's this ma'am?'

'Mercy.'

'Beddy-byes now, is it? Timber Hill? One for Timber Hill then. Alcohol heightens non-performance, did you know? Might as well finish the bottle.'

'Leave it. You go first.'

Light bathed the bedroom, illuminating the patchwork walls of Hector's space. The bed's slats squeaked above his nose. A clunk of dropped shoes.

The wardrobe sighed open, then closed. Bare feet as soft as silence. Silence itself. Next, shower sounds, farther away. From the sitting-room a male grunt and mutter. A clatter of something heavy in the fireplace and a curse.

Another half-hour passed and a multitude of shameless, putrid, bed-going rustlings and patterings before the coloured walls of his space went black.

'Don't talk. Where's your hand?'

'Here, captain. Who's talking?'

'Now, go to sleep.'

'Sure thing, captain.'

They spoke in whispers. Peckover because he needed to listen, one ear for the window, the other for the door into the flat. Mercy because the cop whispered.

He held her hand in brotherly fashion, until he pressed it. To reassure her, she guessed. She pressed back. He withdrew his hand. She turned on her side, away from him.

Peckover lay on his back with his eyes open, listening, looking into blackness, and doing his best to ignore the woman beside him. The only sound was a ticking clock. The night was going to be a long one. He doubted his ability to stay awake. But that was the exercise. He saw himself finishing up by sitting up saying his thirteen and fourteen times tables and pinching his cheeks.

She turned on to her left side. 'What're you going to tell Miriam?'

'Ssh. Tell her what? Nothing to tell 'er.'

'She'll have had ten separate reports by now of that kiss this afternoon. Mordan isn't London.'

'I can believe it.'

'Two in every five French wives are unfaithful, can you believe that? One in every four thinks of some other guy while she's making love. The magazines here are stuffed with sex statistics. I love them. You don't have to believe them. What else? One in five has group sex and the same number dream about it. I'd sooner spend a year in a salt-mine. Half of all couples make love for up to half an hour once every three days, usually with the light on. Half the women have fantasies to keep going, like they're doing it with a bisexual Martian or on a motorway.'

'I'm glad for them. Can you sleep now?'

'It isn't easy.'

'Get off the bloody motorway. Think of Vermont.'

He found her forehead and started to stroke it, stroking her to sleep. His fingertips caressed the hairline above her ear. His knuckles brushed her ear, up and down, on and on.

Idiot, he told himself. Raving idiot lunatic.

She was already moving closer, as he was.

Hector McCluskey listened to the ticking silence. He tested the point and edge of the butcher's knife with the pad of his thumb, though they needed no testing.

How long did fornication take? His one hesitation was whether to allow them to or not. Perhaps they already had. They were whispering again. A slat creaked.

Now they were not whispering.

On elbows, back, backside, and rubber heels, he started to inch towards the patchwork wall.

Not, Mercy knew, that a happening was going to happen, not with her of all people, the woman in the case, Jezebel McCluskey-O'Toole, fallen, free-range wife and divorcee-to-be, maybe widow if Hector, as she believed possible, chose to kill himself, which could be the best for him.

Oh, some best! She could not think about it and she could think of nothing else. Almost. The cop's hand was on her, though motionless.

Not that she minded one way or another whether he made love to her, being numb and finished with the love-swindle for ever; though he might have been a gas, in another country, another time. So she was content to leave it to him, whatever he wanted or did not want, except if he did not want or wanted to put his honour first she would still have given plenty to have heard what for Pete's sake the soppy, hairy brute said, if he said anything, in his moments of passion, because it wouldn't be 'Oh, mein Schatz' or 'Oh, mon cœur.'

'Oh, gorblimey, knees up, Muvver Brown'?

Peckover thought: This is mad, I must recite the names of the wives of Henry VIII, I must think about England

and Nelson, and my expenses, and matters in hand.

Trying to concentrate on the precise position of the poker he had propped in snatching distance against the wall beside the bed, he found himself boring himself with thoughts of pokers as tiresome Freudian symbolism, as what was not? Under his hand was Mercy's breast, not only not tiresome but the softest, most stirring, inexcusable place in God's world for a Scotland Yard man's hand to be.

He was listening, though, wasn't he? Listening hard and dutifully for the door and window? Mercy's breathing was a soundless warm patch on his chest.

His arm was round her, her head was high on his chest. Her fingernails absently and slow-motionly scrunched in the hair on his chest, either not knowing what they were doing or knowing what they were doing. That was to say, they had been on his chest, scrunching and tracing, absently or otherwise, but now were tracing in the hip region somewhere. Mercy hoped the hand on her breast was glad. She assumed it was. Glad hand, backhand, hand to mouth, hand in glove, handsome is as handsome does . . . She liked the hand there. They turned their heads at the same time and found each other's mouths.

Oh yea, yea.

Catherine of Aragon. Anne Boleyn.

Slow, slow enough to go on, on, for ever, the warmth. Peckover believed for ever would do nicely. Anne Boleyn the one with six fingers each hand long ago m'dear what matter now? Where, wondered Mercy, had all the swindle numbness gone to flowers every one? The fingernails moved into stripey Marks and Sparks hundred per cent cotton or could be polywhatsit to fit male waist thirty-three thirty-five yes made in UK maybe Taiwan Catherine Anne Boleyn Seymour Jane Anne Somebody. This was no bloody good, Peckover decided, suddenly shifting.

He reached down to the stripey knickers because blokes on the silver screen might make love with their pants on but he for one had never fathomed how.

Hector preferred to come up on the policeman's side of the bed, if he had a side, if both were not dead centre. The whispering had ceased. The patchwork wall had a blitzed feel with here a gap, there a bunched, irregular fall which sometimes moved, dragging against his fingers. No hurry.

He preferred the policeman's side because any resistance would come from there, where he would strike first. Not that there had ever been resistance yet.

Soundlessly, holding the knife against the seam of his trouser-leg, he edged from under the bed, through patchwork in disarray which now moved, now was still. He inched backwards towards the wall, then started to lever himself up. His crooked elbow behind him touched something which made a scratching sound as it slid to the floor with a thud.

CHAPTER 15

The poker's fall was no shattering cacophony but it was distinct enough. Its thud penetrated Chief Inspector Peckover's preoccupied state, and Mercy's, with the celerity of a long drip of syrup.

Had he been sitting up, working on his thirteen times table, the thud must have alerted him three, four seconds sooner. Time to have girded himself and acted, which he would have admitted had been the point of his presence in Mercy's bed. The poker itself, his only weapon, now was undiscoverable in the dark; not that he had seen himself swinging it except as a last resort. Such as now.

Unarmed, ungirded for anything other than love, Peckover was aware through several senses of the shape above him: almost above him, still a little to his left, but rushing closer. There came a whirring sound as of dead leaves in argument with the wind and a whiff of fear and tobacco which may have been Barbudos. In the next instant there would be more than a touch of steel, haphazardly stabbing. The steel would stab him at random, anywhere. Peckover flung Mercy bodily from him and himself after her.

But they were still on the bed. Not too far from his back, perhaps a centimetre, he felt and heard a thump and tearing. Then another, and probably more, though now there were too many rival noises to be sure: Mercy falling to floor as he thrust at her again, his first effort having achieved no great distance; a man's sobbing in unison with the thump and rending of the knife; and the breeze of his own flailing fists as he tried to rise, wobbling as his foot buckled on squirming Mercy, but trying again, and flailing windmill arms to keep away the berserk shape, the crazed, cuckolded McCluskey of Inverbrae. Mercy was screaming. On the bed her husband competed with incoherent foghorn hootings. Peckover's fist landed high on possibly Hector's head: on some part of him for the blow elicited a howl. But the knife was slashing again, its gleam all that was visible in the dark.

Peckover swayed back, stumbling over Mercy. The gleam vanished, the animal hooting ceased.

Whatever the new tactic might be, Peckover decided, best give him no time for it. Groping forward, he grabbed two fistfuls of patchwork quilt, He hoisted the quilt in front of him and sprang to where the knife had last gleamed: the bare-arsed bloke with the net and trident ensnaring the gladiator. Except he was bare-arsed without a trident. He ensnared something but not enough.

It was a leg, ferociously kicking, as was a second leg. Peckover let go of the patchwork and punched and flailed. The gleam passed in front of his eyes. Something cracked against his shoulder. He caught hold of what he believed to be an arm, twisted it, heard Mercy distantly and irrelevantly scream, felt pain, and found himself grappling and falling, though not far. Fighting to keep hold of Hector's arm, he lost it. He wanted to shout to Mercy to go, get out of it, but he had no breath. When he punched, his knuckles hit the wall. The gleam came at him from the left and in ducking he butted the side of Hector's head. Either his head or the wall again. The gleam hovered. Peckover snatched, aiming behind the gleam, and found the wrist.

Two-handed he twisted the wrist until Hector cried out. The gleam planed through the dark, vanished, and clattered. A knee, fist, foot, something from crying Hector, put Peckover on his back, where he awaited the battery of kicks and punches which at least would not be the knife.

Nothing. No pain. Had he somehow lost and was dying, already dead? A second knife perhaps, or one of the blows had been the knife, not the wall.

Sound of sobs and choking. Bumps, scrabblings. The bedroom door opening.

Get after him, Peckover wanted to say. But he needed to say it to Sergeant Sutton and a bevy of the lads, not to Mercy. He heard the door to the flat open but not close. Departure not arrival. There fell what would have been sweet silence but for himself and Mercy: weeping, sighing, puffing, swearing.

He was able to stand.

'You all right?' This was himself asking, was it? 'Can you find the light?'

He opened the window, the shutters, and shouted into the subfusc courtyard, 'McCluskey! Police!'

Christ, wake yourselves, effing Mordan!

'Police!' Peckover bawled.

Perhaps he imagined an answering, unidentifiable something. A shout or a wail. Cats on the rooftops. The bedroom light came on.

She's pretty old: well, anyway, not a teenager, Peckover unchivalrously considered, looking at leaning, naked Mercy, her hand on the light switch, mouth open and drooped, showing too prominent teeth, her terrified eyes staring back at him through sticky hair. There were reddening blotches on her from where he had fallen and trampled, or from where her husband had fallen and trampled. Sod your husband, I love you, he thought.

Others before him had said exactly the same and mostly they were dead. He had forgotten. Sod the others too.

'Oh my God,' Mercy was saying, staring at him through her matted hair. 'Oh my God.'

Peckover glanced down at his own pathetic nakedness. He saw a fair amount of blood, Smeared though, not flowing, didn't seem to be. Not necessarily his own, even.

He believed he might be cut a little. Perhaps his back. Out of view on his bum was a wound from a holy water bottle, but that was old and trivial. New was a good deal of ache, both general and particular. He delved in the turmoil of patchwork and sheets for his pants, finding first her nightie, then the Marks and Sparks, and seeing on the floor beyond the bed, where he would leave it for those who came to mop up, Hector's knife. Twelve inches of Sheffield steel, or maybe the Ruhr, with an admirably stout black handle. Through the open window sounded a police whistle. Not near, not far. Then either an answering whistle or the same whistle repeating, enjoying itself. A distress signal in the night.

He had blown it because of her. Because of himself. The old sodding Adam. Why couldn't everyone become bloody monks! He would be the first in line for registration.

She said, 'You've got to get to hospital.'

'What about you? Anything broken?'

'No.'

'Get dressed.'

He was going to no hospital. Jean-Luc territory. Perhaps now she was ready to leap into her prof's arms.

Lord, was he jealous? Already? It was a contagion.

'Hector's out there,' she said.

He had never heard a tone so plaintive. She loves him, he thought. Hector. Oh Christ! Hopeless, hopeless.

He said, 'Not for long. Daybreak, ma'am, you gather up your children and go to Vermont. A reviving holiday until everything's, you know, all right again.' Well, it was a thought. He had had worse. 'Look, he's your 'usband, ma'am—'

'Mercy,' she corrected him, blotched and sobbing, propping up the wall by the light-switch, not looking at him.

'Darling Mercy.' He wanted to go over to her. Instead he climbed into his pants. 'You know 'im, your 'usband. What does he do now?'

'If he gets away again?'

'If. Right.'

'He goes home.' How, Mercy wondered, would he do it? How end it for himself?

'Glasgow?'

'The château.'

'Never. What makes you say that? The château's crawling with police.'

'He said it. He didn't say it in words. I don't know—he sounded it, as if it was finished. I've never heard him like that. Those noises.' She was pushing back her hair, wiping her face with both hands. 'How long does he go on and on? His gear's at the château. The letters we used to write, oh, ages ago, when he was away cooking.'

'You'd better get into the bathroom.' He brought the nightie and a blanket. 'There's company.'

First, two plainclothes men, failed surveilleurs. Then the uniform branch. None was amiable. Peckover had the impression he was being held responsible for this latest flit of Hector's. He understood about one word in fifty and no longer cared. The alleys of Mordan were a labyrinth, he believed he was being told, something to that effect. His informant was a fleshy plainclothes *flic* with red lips and what he, the *flic*, plainly believed to be a penetrating look. A brigade, the *flic* might have been saying, would not have been sufficient. But it would be minutes only. At most a half-hour possibly. He was on foot, *l'assassin*. He had been sighted, almost certainly, running south, across the Pont Neuf.

Something like that.

South was not the château. South was Lourdes, Andorra. Africa. Sympathy surged through Peckover. He hoped Hector would make it to Mozambique. Zimbabwe. Grow a beard, change his name. Quietly prosper as chef to the Zimbabwe-Scotland Association. Find a quiet wife. Live out his days.

'Our Monsieur McCluskey, he's taken—' Peckover queried—'French leave?'

'*Comment?*'

At five o'clock there remained still an hour until dawn and the raiding and darting of a thousand swifts round the walls and turrets of the Château de Mordan.

Mercy and Peckover sat at a furrowed, oak worktable in the château's kitchen, between them a pot of tea. If any guests or staff had stayed up later than they might normally have done, hoping to be in on a resolution, if not action, they had gone long ago disappointed to bed. The only visible presence was scattered but substantial police, some drowsy on sofas in the public rooms, others in doorways, or wandering, checking. Miriam was in bed. He had peeked in. Madame Costes too, presumably, though he had not peeked. Pedro the barman, and the bullfighter-waiter. His dancing partner, if she were still here, what was her name? Martha and Arthur someone.

Mercy said, 'Hector used to walk here from Mordan. Through the woods.' She was remembering, not pretending this was what he might now be doing or planned to do. 'It took him an hour, thereabouts. Unless there were blackberries or stuff. In November he'd come in with great bags of mushrooms.'

Peckover, made melancholy by the past tense, nodded.

'He was an outdoor man,' she explained. 'Bet that surprises you. He could find *cèpes* like he'd been born here.'

'Those the big slimy ones?'

'Listen.'

He was already listening. Somewhere a child had started crying. But though distant, the wailing, keening, throbbing was too powerful to be a child. Listening, heads angled, they watched each other across the cold teapot.

'Wait here,' he told her, though she was on her feet with no intention of waiting. 'Is it from the private wing — Hector's bit? Can you tell?'

She was neither telling nor pausing to chat. She ran from the kitchen and along the corridor. Past the Loch Lomond Bar and up the stairs. Another corridor, dingy and uncarpeted, with walls in need of paint. As they crossed a landing at the head of more stairs a young policeman with tenderly cultivated tufts of hair on his cheeks joined them.

'It'll be one of his records, he has all these Black Watch records,' Mercy said, panting and weeping, turning down a side corridor.

Peckover had never seen this part of the château, which

was dilapidated, as had been the staff wing. The doleful skirling was now stereophonic. Round the next corner two policemen were in the initial stages of trying to open a locked door. One was pointlessly knocking, his rat-a-tat inaudible through the din of the pipes. The other was trying pass keys. Peckover's sole thought was to keep Mercy from entering, finding her husband hanging, bleeding, whatever.

Should he though? By what right? Husband and wife . . .

'*J'ai gagné!*' cried the policeman with the keys, triumphant, turning the lock. He beamed, licking his lips and looking round for applause. He opened the door.

Peckover grasped Mercy by the arm but she was thrusting her way into the room, pushing aside the policeman with the keys. Peckover was hauled in her wake.

The room was a spacious, untidy living-room with armchairs, bookcases, and framed family photographs on a baby grand piano. Neither the shutters nor curtains had been closed. Above a gilt mirror over the fireplace hung a flag, the blue cross of St Andrew, such as was waved at Ibrox Park and Murrayfield when the Scots scored against the Sassenachs, or come to that against the Welsh, Irish, and French, and waved whether they scored or not. Now the din deafened. How, Peckover pondered, did pipers keep from permanently deafening themselves?

Neither hanged nor bleeding, not at any rate bleeding from anything more recent than an affray earlier in the night in his wife's bedroom, Hector McCluskey was slow-marching round the perimeter of the living-room playing his bagpipes. He might have been piping in the haggis. He wore full dress regalia: kilt with a pin in it, sporran, lacy shirt, jacket with silver buttons, and a magnificent slouchy black bonnet with curling feathers of a deep-greenish sheen. He was marching with funereal tread away from the door, his back to Mercy and the policemen. He did not turn when they came in, though whether because he did not hear or because he was indifferent, Peckover could not have said. The tune, so far as there was a tune, was not a golden oldie, not *Auld Lang Syne*, or *I Belong to Glasgow*. Peckover guessed it to be an authentic, ethnic lament, a pibroch for the long-dead of Inverbrae, for the mists and ghosts of home, for ancestors, the yet-to-be-born, and the piteous everywhere.

As Hector left-turned at the far end of the living-room, the policeman with tufts of hair on his cheekbones reached him and with a punch to the head knocked him down. The feathered bonnet fell off, the bagpipes dropped with a rattle of spokes and a whimper. The *flic* bent over him, lifting his fist.

'No!' Mercy cried. 'Please.'

The young policeman looked at her, startled. Peckover wondered if this were the worst of all worlds: Hector in some French dungeon or asylum for the rest of his years, a living reproof to Mercy. The hairy-cheeked *flic* and the one with the keys were dragging him to his feet. They hauled and pushed him through the living-room. The punched, delicate face, running with tears, was turned to Mercy. His red eyes implored—who knew what?—but he said nothing. In the next moment he had been dragged through the door.

Mercy stood with her arms by her side and her head back, weeping aloud.